PRAISE FOR THE WORK OF PAGAN KENNEDY

BLACK LIVINGSTONE

A New York Times Notable Book of 2002
Winner of a Massachusetts Book Award Honor in Nonfiction

"A deeply felt and moving book.
—*New York Times Book Review*

"Kennedy resists the temptation to inflict a politically correct paradigm on her story and simply lets it tell itself—which it does, compellingly. The result is a page-turner that illuminates while it breaks the heart."
—*Philadelphia Enquirer*

"Kennedy offers a smoothly written tale and is to be commended for bringing this extraordinary story to greater prominence."
—*The Washington Post*

THE EXES

"Pagan Kennedy, Queen of the 'Zines, writes with a sweet, trenchant wit and the delicacy of a modern-day Chekhov."
—*San Francisco Chronicle*

"Pagan Kennedy is my new literary god. Not only can she write . . . but she also knows how to tell a great story. Kennedy's take on the indie music scene is both hilarious and real."
— *Mademoiselle*

"What Nick Hornby did for the insufferable record geek in *High Fidelity*, Kennedy does for the touring rock musician: makes him (and her) real and layered. [*The Exes*] offers a basic 4/4 beat, something you can groove to, but underneath is a lovely swirl of countermelodies and sounds that are unfamiliar but engaging."
—*Salon.com*

"You can't help falling for [Kennedy's] characters. Like rock and roll itself, they are both sloppy and eloquent, vulgar and earnest, dopey and poetic."
—*New York Times Book Review*

PLATFORMS: A MICRO-WAVED CULTURAL CHRONICLE OF THE 1970'S

"In this hilarious, highly personalized popular history of what may be the goofiest of modern decades, pop culture critic and fiction writer Kennedy (Stripping and Other Stories) offers her insightful version of "guerrilla nostalgia."
—Publishers Weekly

"Once considered a 10-year exercise in bad taste, the 1970s are now being rediscovered . . . Including sections on television, ecology, sex, and the cult of nostalgia, the book is an excellent starting-place for reexamining a decade many Americans seem to love and others, to hate. Equally valuable as a serious read or a coffee-table book, it's an item no popular culture collection should be without. (The section on P-Funk alone is well worth the purchase price.)"
—Booklist

ZINE: HOW I SPENT SIX YEARS OF MY LIFE IN THE UNDERGROUND AND FINALLY . . . FOUND MYSELF . . . I THINK

"Delightful comic strips, fumati, and prose from the zine into the narrative, and a look at the slacker generation sans the usual belittling and reproof, Zine is reminiscent of Kominski-Crumb and her husband R. Crumb's autobiographical comics—for many, that constitutes a strong recommendation all by itself."
—Booklist

Also by Pagan Kennedy

Black Livingstone: A True Tale of Adventure in the 19th Century Congo

The Exes

Pagan Kennedy's Living

Spinsters

Zine: How I Spent Six Years of My Life in the Underground and Finally Found Myself ... I Think

Platforms: A Microwaved Cultural Chronicle of the 1970s

Stripping

Confessions
of a
Memory Eater

A novel by

Pagan Kennedy

Leapfrog Press
Wellfleet, Massachusetts

Published in 2006 in the United States by
The Leapfrog Press
P.O. Box 1495
95 Commercial Street
Wellfleet, MA 02667-1495, USA
www.leapfrogpress.com

Printed in the United States of America

Distributed in the United States by
Consortium Book Sales and Distribution
St. Paul, Minnesota 55114
www.cbsd.com

First Edition

Library of Congress Cataloging-in-Publication Data

Kennedy, Pagan
  Confessions of a memory eater : a novel / by Pagan Kennedy.-- 1st ed.
    p. cm.
  ISBN 13: 978-0-9728984-8-5
  ISBN 10: 0-9728984-8-4
  1. College teachers--Fiction. I. Title.
PS3561.E4269C66 2006
813'.54--dc22
                                                                2006001912

10 9 8 7 6 5 4 3 2 1

Confessions of a Memory Eater

Chapter
1

The phone was ringing. I stared at it, wishing I didn't have to answer. The black cord was tangled in knots and nooses; the receiver was smudged with shadows of my own fingers. This morning I'd skipped another meeting. I expected this would be the dean, summoning me to his office. I picked up.

"Duncan?" a strange voice boomed at me from the earpiece.

"Yeah?" I said.

"So you are alive."

"Who is this?"

"Phil Litminov."

It took me a moment to remember. "Litminov?" I said. And then I found myself laughing. "No shit? Really?" I hadn't seen him in more than ten years—not since graduate school. An image came to me now: Litminov dismounting his motorbike, yanking a white crash helmet from his head. I remembered, too, that pale scar on his lip that gave him an unvarying expression of sarcasm. I tried to ask him how he'd found me, why he'd called, but he never gave me a chance.

He was talking again, rapid-fire. "So, my friend, you ended up in New Hampshire. And you once swore to me that you'd never leave the City. Remember how you used to lurk around that Cuban diner. What was it called? That place you used to hang out?"

"I forget."

"La Taza De Oro," he supplied.

"Yeah, that's right," I heard myself say. His words had triggered a wave of nostalgia so intense I had to hold on to my desk, letting the sharp edges of it bite into my hand to keep me anchored in the present. La Taza De Oro—just the name brought back my younger self, hunched over a legal pad at 3 AM scrawling notes, a neon sign reflected in a parabola of a spoon, ideas fizzing in my brain. I'd been happy then.

"So how'd you end up teaching at some Catholic college?" he wanted to know. "That can't be fun."

"Yeah, it's not."

"What happened, Duncan? You were supposed to be a genius."

I sighed. "I'm here partly because of Edie. You remember her, right?"

"Your girlfriend?"

"Wife. It was the only place where we could both get jobs."

"So you moved up there because *your wife* wanted to?" Litminov made a puffing sound of disgust.

"Yeah, that's about the size of it." It was a relief, I realized, to discuss my situation with someone who had not witnessed my slow ossification, who still remembered me as I used to be, burning like the neon in the diner window. In fact, I was glad Litminov could not see my surroundings now, this cubbyhole office with a view of a trash-strewn ravine and factory buildings in the distance. Above the bookshelf on the wall opposite me hung a crucifix; Jesus's outstretched arms had turned furry with dust. Years ago, when the college assigned me to this room, I'd tried to pry the crucifix off the wall with a screwdriver. All I'd succeeded in doing was digging scratch marks into the paint. Jesus wasn't going anywhere. And, it appeared, neither was I.

"Duncan," he said. "You don't sound good."

"I'm not," I said.

"Luckily, I'm here to help."

"Luckily," I said.

"You know I own a pharmaceutical company now."

"You do? How'd you get your hands on that?"

"The usual way. I bought it."

"You just went out and bought the whole thing?" This, actually, I could imagine. Even back in graduate school, Litminov had been freakishly wealthy.

"Sure," he said. "Couple years ago. And ever since, I've been working my ass off."

"Hmm," I said. The fact was, I'd never seen Litminov do work of any sort at all; his parents had died a few years before I met him, leaving behind a trust fund. I don't know whether it was being orphaned or inheriting all that money that did it to him, but for some reason, Litminov had developed a voracious appetite for trouble. Back when we were in graduate school, he'd call me at 2 AM to propose that we go for drinks at a whorehouse or to try out the Glocks at an underground shooting range; he preferred exploits that were just this side of legal. For some reason, I always agreed to his invitations.

"So, listen, my friend, this company is the best investment I ever made," Litminov was saying now. He spewed some numbers that meant nothing to me—stock prices and such. "And we're going to make a killing soon. We've developed this product—a drug we'll bring to market soon, if we can get it through the legal pipeline. That's why I want to get you involved. I need your brains, Duncan."

"Mine?"

"Sure, yours. Why not yours? You're an expert in drug policy," he declared.

"Not really. I've written some papers about laudanum in the nineteenth century."

"Good enough," he interrupted. "I want to get you in on this."

Now, *that* sounded like the Litminov I knew. Back in the old days, he had always wanted to bring me in. He dragged me to his apartment so he could show off shelves full of rare jazz albums, a bottle of absinthe that he'd smuggled out of Spain, a pearl-handled Smith & Wesson from the 1920s. One day I realized that I was just another piece of his collection, less a friend than a bit of loot he had acquired. He thought me worthy because I had won the Whitman Prize for Humanities Research, which had seemed like a big deal back then when we were in our twenties. "Do you know," he said once, swinging his feet as he sat on the railing of a balcony, balancing himself precariously over three stories of air, "that pretty much every guy who ever won that prize became famous within ten years? Don't forget me when you're famous, Duncan."

But I hadn't turned out to be famous after all, far from it. So why did he want to collect me now? "Are you offering me a job?" I asked.

"Yes. Maybe. What I want is for you to come down to the City and meet with me. Pronto."

"I don't know," I said. I glanced up at the wall opposite me, and my eyes rested on the scratches I'd made there, the punctuation marks of my desperation. Litminov's invitation tempted me, just as his invitations always had. "So what's this drug you're making?" I asked.

"The drug," he said slowly, relishing the word, as if he could taste it. "The drug, my friend, restores memory. I don't mean it helps you remember where you put your glasses or anything as inane as that. No, this drug restores you to your very self."

"Oh now come on, Litminov!" I said, and I must have been laughing, because he began to laugh too, joylessly.

"Really," he went on. "Like, say you wanted to remember what happened in the apartment you used to rent on 114th Street. You take this pill, you go back there, you can see every title of every book on the shelf or that weird stain on the wall. You could re-play anything that ever happened there, any girl you took home, any conversation you had."

"That's ridiculous," I snapped.

"Oh yeah?" he said. "Speaking of your old apartment, there was a photo of your mother over the stove. She was leaning against a light-blue car, holding a dog on a leash. A Schnauzer, I believe."

For a moment, I couldn't find words. That photo now hung in the living room of the house that I shared with my wife Edie. He was absolutely right about it. "Is this a joke?" I finally said.

"Ask me any question you want about your old apartment. Test me. I can describe the whole place to you, just as it was." I could hear him breathing into the phone, waiting.

"OK," I said, and then "OK" again. But I was too disoriented to come up with anything.

"How about this? You used to wear a shirt with the name 'T. Miller' on the pocket. Army surplus. Blue."

I reached across the desk and a picked up a pen, and made a note on a scrap of paper. "T. Miller." I could only vaguely remember that name, those stenciled letters and the faded denim. The shirt, of course, was long gone.

"Well," he said, "am I right?"

"Maybe." I stared at what I'd scribbled. "This is so strange," I said. "How can *you* know that?"

"Because I saw you wearing it just a few days ago. I was planning to use the drug to remember something else, but damned if I didn't get sidetracked and end up shot back into your old place on 114th. You had these scraps of paper spread out all over the floor, covered with notes. You were working on some grand theory about the history of American history."

"I was?" It appeared that he knew more about my twenty-eight-year -old self than I did. A younger Win Duncan lived on inside Litminov's head, wearing a blue shirt with someone else's name stamped across it, and arranging his ideas into a grand pattern across the carpet. All of a sudden, I wanted to *be* that young man. Or, if that was impossible, at least I wanted that young Win Duncan to live inside my head too. By all rights, that memory belonged to me, not Litminov. How did my past end up in his mind? It didn't seem fair at all. "So what else happened? What else was I doing?"

"Duncan," Litminov sighed, and I could imagine him shaking his head, "it's a long story. So anyway, you interested in coming down here?"

I tried to say yes, but my voice wouldn't work.

On his end of the phone, someone hooted in the background. "Look," Litminov said, "I've got to go. You still stay up late like you used to? Two, three in the morning?" It wasn't exactly a question. The Win Duncan he knew stayed up for days on Cuban coffee, chasing down ideas on a yellow pad.

"Sure," I lied. I couldn't bear to tell him that most nights I went to bed at eleven now, that I nodded off woozily over my own papers, that a certain light in me had gone out. "You know how I am," I heard myself say, "I don't sleep." And I gave him my home number, so he could call me as late as he wanted.

"Excellent," he said, and hung up without a goodbye.

• • • • •

Edie ate dinner in the kitchen that night, while I sat in the living room with the TV blaring, picking at a sandwich. For the last year, she and I had been like this—pursuing our own agendas in separate rooms. We didn't even eat the same foods anymore, now that she'd given up white bread.

Here on the couch, I'd planted the phone next to me, so I could grab it as soon as it rang. Edie must not answer it. I hadn't told her about Litminov. Not yet, anyway. For now, the strange events of this afternoon were still my secret. At first, I was afraid that she might wander into the living room, notice that I'd moved the phone and start asking questions.

But no, Edie stayed in the kitchen, hunched over the table, grading papers, a bottle of wine beside her. She drank when she graded; she would go through a bottle of wine by herself, to dull the blows of insipid thought and bad grammar. Crazy as this method might seem, Edie had made it her own: She could plow through weeks worth of student papers in an evening, and then return to what she cared about, her reading and her research, her own candlelit interior.

Two hours went by. I continued my vigil on the couch. I was pretending to follow a Knicks game on cable, but actually monitoring the VCR's clock, those numbers constructed out of dashes of light. 9:58. Still no call from Litminov. 10:14. No call. The numbers under the black plastic of the VCR changed soundlessly, dashes rearranging themselves, an 8 melting into a 9. This bothered me. Seconds should tick. Minutes should click. Clocks should pant, huff with the effort of their work.

10:32. Across the street, the Clark's living room light snapped out, along with the trapezoid of snow it had illuminated. The plastic reindeer on their lawn became gray wolf-ish creatures. I was beginning to suspect I would never hear from Litminov again. Or maybe, days from now, he'd send me an e-mail message, proving this had all been a gag: GOT YOU!

11:15. 11:28.

"OK, I give up," Edie announced as she padded through the living room and clutched the banister to haul herself up the stairs. Drunk and burned-out on freshman essays about *Jane Eyre*.

"I'll be up soon," I called.

I could have told her then. At this point, I assumed Litminov had played me, and I could have spun the events of the afternoon into a bitter, comedic tale. In fact, I almost called out, "Hey, Eeds, wait a second. I forgot to tell you something." But I didn't.

Why not? Because she didn't want to be told. She liked her privacy. Edie had grown up in Montana, wandering back roads with an entourage of invisible friends, disappearing into an imaginary city she'd constructed out of bits of pieces she'd read in books. When she was ten or eleven, she named her city Eglantine and gave it topiary ramparts so high that no one else could enter; she stocked its larders with quince pies and elderberry wine, all the foods she'd read about but never tasted. This was what had charmed me about her in the beginning—the way she could have been one of those women in the Victorian novels she studied, as happily self-sufficient as a Brontë sister, lying in some fire-lit parlor playing with paper dolls. But in the past few years, what had once seemed most endearing about her began to strike me as stagy and artificial.

I hardly saw her these days. She holed up in her office with Angela Carter, the Brontës, that woman who wrote *The Yellow Wallpaper*—what the hell was her name?—and a coven of French philosophers. And now she had her mad women too. The whole lot of them plotted together like a clique of high-school girls. Edie and I would be pushing a shopping cart through the supermarket, and she would suddenly stop in the cereal aisle, whip out her notebook, and begin scribbling. She wrote theory in the bathtub. A show-off, I thought. And was I envious? Damn straight, I was. I'd stopped writing. I'd stopped burning. Ideas refused to come to me. My mojo had left me; my winning streak was over. And meanwhile my wife was on fire; she had so many thoughts they spilled out on notepads and stray pieces of paper all over the house.

A few months ago, Donna Perkins—yes, *that* Donna Perkins—had called my wife and asked her to co-edit a collection of writings by nineteenth century mad women. Any woman who was certifiable would do—schizophrenic, hysteric, baby killer. Edie gorged herself on this "autobiography of transgression," manuscripts piled all around the bed, dusty books taking up the entire backseat of her Ford Escort. "Check this out, Win," she said to me one night, and read me the letter of a Mrs. Dearie who in 1843 had fantasized about murdering her husband with a handkerchief soaked in ether.

"Did she actually kill him?" I asked.

"Of course she did. I can't believe this is my job. This is so fucking cool."

A few days ago, she'd sent an e-mail out to the English department, which she C.C.'ed to me. "My friend and co-editor, Donna Perkins will appear on NPR this morning. As you know, Donna has become one of the foremost public intellectuals to raise questions about—" blah, blah, blah. I listened to the show in my car, alone, staring out at the chewed-up football field and the sleet spitting down, patiently, dot by dot, covering the hood of my old orange Saab. A year from now, Edie might be the one on the radio, talking about her mad women. And how would I stand that?

· · · · ·

At 12:30, the phone squatted in its corner of the bedside table, stubbornly silent. I climbed under the sheets, and leaned over to touch Edie on the arm.

"You awake?" I said. If she'd answered, everything might have gone differently. The glare of a streetlight filled our bedroom with a kind of pink moonlight, and Edie's face blended with the pillow. She'd drunk too much wine. I could not wake her. And soon, I too, drifted off to sleep.

I woke up at three in the morning—according to the angry red numbers on the digital clock—and it took me a moment to realize what was wrong and what I must do. The phone was ringing—not its usual demure purr, but a kind of obscene shriek. I grabbed it off the table, and hurried into the bathroom, shutting the door behind me.

"Duncan," he said, "It's me. Listen, we'll have to make this fast. I'm on the West Side Highway, and I think I'm going to lose you when I go through the tunnel."

"We could talk tomorrow morning," I suggested. I was sitting on the toilet, watching a slice of moonlight shiver on the tiles, still half asleep.

"Oh, for God's sake, Duncan." Litminov's voice had changed since this afternoon—it had sped up, was curled at the edges with impatience. "Listen. You're going to come down and hang out with me in the City."

"How about this weekend?"

The line crackled, and I lost Litminov, except for a few mutilated words. But he came back again. "—meet my associates," he was saying. "You could see my place here."

"So how about this Saturday?"

"Yes. Goddamn it, yes, Duncan."

"In the morning?"

"Yes. Fine."

I wanted to ask about the job. But I knew better than to push him.

"OK, fine, Saturday," I said.

"I'll have my assistant, Andrea Lu, e-mail the directions to you tomorrow. OK, here's the bridge. I'm going under it." And then the line broke into particles of sound, little stabs of static in my ear. He was gone.

I padded down the hall and settled under the covers. Curling myself against the bow of Edie's back, I knew I would not tell her. "You're doing business with a guy like Litminov?" I could hear her saying. And then she'd catch herself—Edie is not a mean person—and add, "Well, that could be cool." Still, she would have already made it sound so small.

And besides, I liked having a secret.

• • • • •

But I decided I would tell Bernie. He was my closest friend at Mercy College, and what's more, he was likely to remember Litminov, since he had also been in New York back when everyone, everyone in the world was getting a Ph.D. at Columbia.

The next day, I tapped on his door and let myself in to his office, a junkyard of old documents and academic journals. He had piled books on his windowsill, leaving only some chinks through which the light from outside could gleam, so that I had come to think of the room as a kind of ant farm, a series of tunnels through the dirt of his research. He looked up now, and there was something ant-like about him, the bug eyes of his eyeglasses and his air of unflappable determination. "Have a seat," he said, gesturing to the armchair in the corner, its split seams repaired with duct tape.

But I couldn't sit. I paced around, in the little paths through his piles of documents. "You remember Phil Litminov? From grad school?"

"Kind of," Bernie said, fingers steepled together, as he rocked in his desk chair, watching me. "That crazy guy. The one with the motorcycle."

"Motorbike," I corrected.

"Right," he said. "What about him?"

"He might want to hire me." I poured out a story about a company that had just produced a new drug to restore memory, making no mention of the bizarre abilities that Litminov had displayed the day before.

"So what would this drug be used for, exactly?" Bernie wanted to know.

"Oh, they're not sure yet," I ad-libbed. "But you can imagine the applications."

He listened, threading fingers through his scraggly beard. "Hmm. But why you? You're an academic. You don't know anything about business."

I felt wounded. "I could work for a pharmaceutical. I've done a lot of research in that direction."

"I suppose," Bernie said, poking at his glasses, so that his hand hid his face for a moment. "But here's the thing, Win. You've already got a job. And right now you have to finish De Quincey."

For years I'd been laboring on a book about the birth of pharmacology as a discipline in the early 1800s. Specifically, I had set out to prove that Thomas De Quincey, the author of *Confessions of an English Opium Eater,* had helped to usher in a new branch of science, one that linked chemicals and cognition. You might say that he became the first great publicist for the new field of neurochemistry.

Lately, though, my book about De Quincey had gotten stuck. Every time I jotted down a sentence, it withered and died. And so I had not finished. If I didn't have a book contract in hand soon, Mercy College would deny me tenure, and I'd lose my job.

"The thing is," I said slowly, feeling some truth hovering just ahead of me, "I never really meant to end up mired in De Quincey. It all seems like a mistake now."

"That's how everyone feels," Bernie said. "You've just got to finish it anyway."

I had turned toward the window now, was staring out through a crack between the books at some dirty snow outside. It was heaped near the building's entrance, and the students used it as an ashtray. Butts stuck out of it from every angle. I could feel Bernie behind me, cogitating. "How are things with Edie?" he finally asked. "Are you guys still having trouble?"

"Yeah." I turned now, and leaned against the books. Bernie was rubbing his glasses on the edge of his flannel shirt, and his naked eyes struck me as wrong somehow—unprotected.

"She doesn't seem to have much use for me," I said.

"Well, at least you're still married." Years before, Bernie's wife had left him, moving with their daughter to New Mexico. Somewhere in the desert, his girl grew up without him.

"Yesterday," I said, "when I was talking to Litminov, it was the first time I felt *good* in a long time. I felt like my old self again. I want more of that. I'd do anything for more."

Bernie shoved the glasses back into place and his eyes disappeared behind circles of white. "Then maybe you should go meet with Litminov. Maybe I was wrong."

• • • • •

I called my father at noon, because I knew he'd be at a lunch somewhere. I didn't want to reach him; I wanted his voicemail. "I'm going to be down in Manhattan this weekend. Is it OK if I crash with you?" I asked the machine. "I'll just let myself in with those keys you gave me. Appreciate it, Dad."

My father, aged seventy, ran one of the largest advertising firms in the country, and showed no signs of slowing down. Whenever I visited him in Manhattan, he took me out to three-star restaurants, ordered in French, shoveled steak *au pouvre* into his mouth without getting a drop in the snowy folds of his linen shirts, and extemporized about the stock market.

Last time I saw him, a few months ago, had been something of a debacle. He'd taken me out to one of those restaurants of his, starched tablecloth stretching between us. He'd ripped off a morsel of bread and scooped some herb-speckled butter with it.

"Win," he'd said to me, "You're smart, you've got the looks, the charm. The thing is, you undersell yourself."

"Dad," I had said, a warning note in my voice.

"Hear me out. Your old man knows a thing or two." He leaned

back, savoring a mouthful of wine. "You're no academic, Win. You know why? Because you have a taste for the finer things. Power being the finest. You've got a hell of an imagination, a way with words. You'd shoot right to the top."

"Dad," I barked, but it did no good.

"Think about it, Win. The world is your oyster."

I pictured a pocked, vomit-colored oyster shell, swaying on the ocean floor. Inside of it, a grain of sand has lodged itself in the flesh of the poor mollusk. That sand, that tiny grain, acts like such an asshole that the oyster has to cushion itself with its own spit.

"I don't like oysters, remember?" I said, turning down the world he'd ordered for me like an appetizer. But the truth was, he'd hit a nerve; I regretted the choices I'd made.

Seven years ago, Stanford University offered me a gig as an assistant professor, my dream job; but the university had nothing for Edie, no work at all, and she would have ended up as just another faculty wife. I couldn't do that to her. So instead, we said yes to Mercy College, where we would both work as temporary professors. New Hampshire was supposed to have been a prelude to our real lives. Years later, we imagined, we'd regale our friends with stories about this place. Can you believe it? We once worked at a Catholic college with the Virgin Mary on the school flag! Yes, *us.*

But here was the trouble with that plan: we never found any other jobs. So we stayed on at Mercy College, and slowly became a part of it. Or Edie did, anyway. She'd grown to see the place as home.

Not me. I woke in a cloud of dread every morning now, suffering from the persistent feeling that this wasn't really my life. My license plate read "New Hampshire - The Granite State" and I understood that's what I'd chosen, a granite state, years stretching ahead like so many stones. I didn't know how I'd endure it.

Lately, I had taken to hunting through my old notebooks from years ago, studying the handwriting for clues. Who had he been, that young Win Duncan? And why had everything come too easily to him? What had been the source of his frenzy of ideas and enthusiasms? Where had I lost the trick of being happy?

• • • • •

I was sitting in my office at school, studying a diagram, when Edie knocked on my door with the end of her car key and let herself in.

"Quitting time," she said. And then, seeing me engrossed in a book, she paused. "Oh. You're on with Thomas De Quincey again. Well in that case, don't let me interrupt."

I stared at the page before me, willing this conversation away.

But she kept right on. "If you need to stay, you could take the car." She dangled the keys, as if to tantalize me.

I lifted up the book so that she could see the cover: *The Complete Manual of Saab Repair*. Her face fell for a split second, and then she laughed. "Oh," she said. "My mistake."

"I'll work on De Quincey tonight, at home. I promise," I told her.

"Whatever you want, Win." She drifted out into the hallway. I could hear her motorcycle boots echoing as she paced around, waiting for me to gather my papers.

When I came out and locked the door, she watched me, raking her fingers through that wild hair, and then twisting it into a knot in back. In a few minutes, the hair would fall down again, and she'd begin all over, twisting and kneading and pretending to get it under control. "I have so much to do," she said, as we hurried down the stairs. "Let's not cook anything real tonight. Let's just scrounge in the freezer. I call dibs on the Tater Tots." She was trying to pick up the faint tune of one of our old jokes. It was the only thing that worked these days—those moments when we could impersonate the couple that we used to be.

"OK," I said, without trying to keep the banter going; I was preoccupied; I needed to find a way to tell her I'd be leaving in two days.

I finally got around to it when we were in her car, stopped at a light, the wipers thwacking away bits of snow. "Listen, Sweetie, I've decided to go to New York on Friday. To stay with Dad. I've been wanting to spend some time with him."

She shot me a bewildered look, eyebrows angled down. She knew I was avoiding my father. Clearly, my explanation didn't add up. But the expression lasted only a moment, and then she pasted a smile over it. "Oh, great," she said. She was an easy person to lie to. She helped you. With a little prompting, you could get her to come up with the entire lie by herself, and hers would be better than yours.

"You want to come?" I said, because I was sure she wouldn't.

"Can't," she said. "I have to be here on Sunday. There's that thing."

"What thing?" I said.

"The secret meeting."

Thwack, thwack said the wipers, giving our conversation a tempo. I tried to answer perfectly on the beat. "Oh, are you plotting something?"

"Yes. Remember? Mary and Alice and I are pretending to form a Women's Studies Department."

"So you're just pretending?" I said. "You don't need me there?"

"Yes. Just pretending. No big deal. You should go to New York and have fun."

I glanced over toward the passenger seat. She was kneading her hair. I could only see a sliver of her face, pale in the winter twilight. I was pissed off at her for her distracted air—at the way she let me get away with this.

• • • • •

Thursday, midnight, I padded to the bathroom and tried to pee, read a journal article, then came back to bed and flopped on my side with my arms and legs curled toward my stomach. This has always been my best position for defeating insomnia.

I lay like that and thought about how I'd tell Edie everything in the morning. I wound up tight as a spring, wanting to hurl myself four hours into the future, to breakfast, when I would fix the situation. It had to be at the breakfast table. I had to have a cup of coffee in my hand, with just the right amount of cream. Edie would have to be reading a book as she shoveled cereal into her mouth, her toes curled around the feet of the chair. When I started to speak to her, she'd stare up at me myopically, and then gradually begin nodding. Actually, the more I mulled it over, the more I began to think Edie might approve. "I'm so jealous you're going to have some unwholesome adventure with Litminov, and I have to stay here," she might say. And she would fire questions at me about the drug. Maybe it would help to bring us together again, give us an enthusiasm we could share. In four hours, when she woke up, I would put everything right—not just the lie about why I was going to Manhattan, but so many other misunderstandings between us. Four hours and it would all be OK.

I woke to the sound of Edie's voice. She was hurrying down the hall, the phone digging into her cheek, having an intense conversation.

When I found her in the kitchen, she was still on the phone, measuring out coffee as she gossiped.

I glanced up at the clock. I had a class in a half hour, so I began stuffing papers into my leather bag with a doomed feeling. I'd had a window of opportunity and it had snapped shut.

"Hold on a minute," Edie said to whoever was on the other end of the phone. And then, to me, "Win, you're going to be late." She grabbed my bag, leading me to the door. "Listen, you sure you don't want me to take you to the train station this afternoon? I'm not neglecting you am I?"

"No, no," I said, as she ushered me out onto the porch. "No," I said, as she locked the front door behind me and I walked out to the car under its new pillow of snow.

• • • • •

In 1959, an obscure Tennessee company readied a new soda for the market, a sticky, fizz water that was as red as transmission fluid. King Foods hired my father to name the drink, come up with a slogan, packaging, etc. It was Dad's first big job, and he threw everything he had into it. After weeks of market research, he finally found a name that he knew would be a hit: Win Cola.

"Your dad loved that name," my mother would say, years later, in her honey-thick Georgia accent. "He reckoned you could sell raw sewage, and as long as you called it Win Cola, people would buy it. But the man who owned King Foods thought different. He named it Atomic Soda, the fool. It tore your father up, to have that good name and no way to use it. So that's how you got it, Winnie. That's why he gave it to you."

Indeed. When I was born in 1963, my father bestowed a name on me that might have otherwise gone to a ruby soda in a fluted bottle. People always ask if it's short for Winthrop or Winslow. No, it's just Win.

"With a name like that how can this kid fail? Thousands of dollars of market research went into packaging him," Dad liked to joke when he introduced me to clients. I would stand beside him in my striped t-shirt and Wrangler jeans, offering my orange hair for tousling, with a smile pasted between my freckled cheeks, trying to live up to my name. Win, the all-American boy, star of his Little League team. I actually sat out most games on the bench, but Dad had taught me that didn't matter. The important thing was to act like a winner, keep your chin up, never let them see you blink.

I had my own slogan too: "Cool down with the red hot." That, of course, had originally been intended for the soda. But Dad thought it would do just fine for a boy.

Chapter 2

I unlocked the door to his apartment with as little rattle and fanfare as possible; I hoped that my father had already gone to bed. But no, he was sitting up in the living room, poring over one of his financial magazines, pen in hand, alert as ever.

"Well," he said, drawing out the word in a way that invited me to sit in the plump chair across from him. "Why don't you pour yourself some of that bourbon?" He pointed at the impromptu bar he'd set up on top of the TV.

I lifted an ice cube with the silver tongs and dropped it into a crystal glass, so the ice ricocheted around, like an animal struggling to get out. Then I tipped the decanter and gave myself a splash of bourbon.

As I lifted it to my lips, he scolded, "Just breathe it in first."

The bourbon filled my mouth like a tongue of flame, a new kind of fire with warmth but no bite.

"It's thirty years old." He crossed his legs, leaned back comfortably. "You don't want to know how much I paid for it."

It occurred to me that my father enjoyed his aged bourbons and his choice filets not so much because of the way they tasted but because of what they cost. Sipping from an ancient bottle was the closest he could get to consuming money itself. We were lapsed Catholics—very lapsed. But the idea of a sacred host lingered in our minds, the conviction that what you took into your body might mingle with your blood and produce a holy alchemy.

I sipped the bourbon again, and now I tasted the money in it. It made the inside of my mouth feel like velvet.

"Did I tell you? We're going to go to St. Bart's in May. For a whole month," he said. My father, who called Caribbean islands by their nicknames, my father who jetted around the globe with a girlfriend nearly half his age. "The light," he said, letting his Southern twang stretch the word. "The lie-it on that island does me good."

An image came into my mind—though God knows I tried to keep it from floating to the surface—of my father thrusting on top of Gloria in a patch of sunlight on the thick carpet of a rented bungalow. I could see his bare ass, with the smile-shaped wrinkles that divided it from the legs, jiggling over her young and firm skin.

"I'm all tuckered out, Dad," I said. "I'm afraid I'm going to have to turn in."

"You haven't finished your drink," he said.

I caught then, just a flash of disappointment on his face.

"I'll take it with me. A night cap." And I shuffled off to his guest room.

• • • • •

The next morning, I had a few hours to spare before Litminov, so I took the Number 2 train up to 102nd, and hurried up Broadway toward La Taza de Oro coffee shop. My nervousness about Litminov had turned into something else, the old excitement boiling in my stomach—as if I were still a graduate student with a notebook tucked under my arm and a new theory that would soon spill all over its sheets.

But La Taza de Oro was no more. Instead of a window with a neon teacup burning behind the glass, I found the lobby of a luxury apartment building, a doorman lurking on the steps. As I passed under the building's awning, my reflection slid over the surface of the door, and I caught a whiff of what was inside—warmth and newspapers and perfumed women. The building gave off the sacrilegious air of having existed for a hundred years. La Taza De Oro had been extinguished, along with my youth.

So I hurried ten more blocks uptown, toward Columbia University. That, at least, I could count on to remain intact. Campuses resist change. They are in the business of pleasing alumni, of bringing tears to the eyes of some codger in the Class of '47 who finds the exact spot under the oak tree where he lost his virginity—and *it looks just the same*—which inspires him to make a very generous donation. The job of a university is not so much to educate the young as to enshrine the youth of its alumni. The university exists to mothball, to preserve, to museum.

Years ago, I wrote a paper on this subject ("How Columbia University Decided To Stop Time") in which I highlighted a crucial meeting in 1921, when the administrators ruled that the campus must exist as a "pool of memories that the hoary graduate may bathe in whenever he pleases, refreshing himself in the echoing laughter of years gone by." Back then, as I typed up the paper, I never imagined that I too would someday graduate and return to my campus, seeking some echoing laughter, or indeed any trace of my old self.

But here I was, dodging traffic to hurry across the street toward the front gates of Columbia, those two statues I remembered so well: One robed woman held an open book; her twin, on the other side of the gate, held out what seemed to be a small bowling ball. I passed between the two guardians of my youth and sauntered down the brick pathways, relieved to be back in landscape I recognized. I craned my neck, counting off windows on the side of Lowe Library, until I found mine—the place where I used to perch as I read Jonathan Edwards, Locke, Du Bois, Hume, Jefferson. It had been a kind of ecstasy—though I can't say why—to catch up a lot of words in my mind and then glance from the page and out the window. I would watch students flow along paths below, and at the same time I would let the meaning of the words saturate me. I had the sense of my mind touching the authors' minds, miraculously, over a span of centuries. It was a high better than any drug. It was the reason I went into history.

Now—standing on the path below the library, with students rushing around me, the smell of dead rhododendron rising off the melting earth—I squinted up at the window, *my* window, and I thought I caught sight of a pale figure who flickered by. I could imagine myself at twenty-eight, still sitting up there, a chair against the radiator, the book smelling of vanilla and mildew. He—that young Win—would be staring down through glass that made everything below look wobbly and warped. The students would be hurrying along, blackening the paths, streaming up the steps. And his eyes would fix on a professor standing, as if lost, amidst the crowd.

•　•　•　•　•

I don't know what to call the place where Litminov lived. I want to say "apartment" but that's not nearly a grand enough word. Loft? Penthouse? Atelier?

Plate-glass windows stretched across three walls, so that the couches and lamps and small tables around the edge of the room seemed to lean against nothing but blue. Clouds floated by like slow-moving traffic. A plane patiently let out a white thread from its tail. Somewhere below, the streets sent up a dull roar, but didn't trouble us. We floated above the grime.

"Christ," I said.

Litminov laughed. "Yeah, that's a common reaction. Well, come on in."

One should not see such wealth. One should not know it exists. How I craved, after my long exile in New Hampshire, to belong to Manhattan again. Not to the Manhattan I'd known during my penurious grad school years, when I slept in sublets with cracked lead paint, filled with the sinister hissing of radiators. No, I had wanted *this*. Up here, you seemed to command the city, to stand at its control panels, as if it were a dirigible and you could steer it with enormous levers.

Litminov led me past three electric guitars displayed on special brackets so that they defied gravity, floated a few inches above the floor. He led me past a flat-screen TV that also levitated. The saliva in my mouth tasted of acid. I could feel envy, sharp as heartburn, corroding the vital and soft pipes inside my body.

"How'd you do it?" I asked.

He faced me now, across the corner of a mahogany table, and for the first time, I bothered to notice Litminov himself, as a man apart from his real estate. He looked uncannily the same as he had back in grad school. The scar on the end of his lip had not faded; it was still white and the size of a fingernail. It gave him an expression that I had come to think of as characteristic of Litminov, that joyless, lopsided grin. He never would talk about how he got that scar, but I thought I knew.

"I made some good investments," he sighed, already tired of talking about his money. He swiveled away from me and called out to the back of the apartment, "Andrea, do we have anything to eat?"

It was only then that I noticed the woman. She stood up, disentangling herself from the outline of a table, and glided toward us. Her hair had been buzzed so close to the scalp that it was nothing but blue-black stubble. This should have made her ugly, but it only emphasized liquid black eyes, the bruise of her mouth.

"Huh?" she said.

"Do we have any of that tempura left?" He waved his hand toward the gleaming metal appliances of the kitchen.

"You ate it all," she said. "But there are some blood oranges."

"All right, fine, bring us some." He rolled his eyes at me, conspiratorially.

We sat, and Andrea Lu carved them up for us, letting the juice stain her fingers with fuchsia. I was transfixed by the ballet of her hands, the knife, orange globes. A tart smell filled the air. She placed a few slices, just so, on a green plate and brought it to me, her heels clicking on the wood floor.

"So," Litminov said, "You're still with Edie." He twisted an orange slice so it bled all over his plate. "I always thought you'd outgrow her. No offense. But she was the quiet type and you, you," he described a swirling pattern in the air with one of his chubby hands. "You were the golden boy."

I thought it time to change the subject. "I still can't believe all this," I said. "What you've got here."

"I've done a few things I'm proud of," he purred.

"Like the drug."

"The drug," he said, suddenly serious. "I'm going to make my mark with that one. It was my idea, you know. Bunch of years ago, when I was still in the software business, I was reading about ethnobotany late one night, and I had this incredible freaking insight. So I wrote it up." He cupped his hands over his belly, swung back and forth in his chair like a boy. "Then I turned around and bought a pharmaceutical company. I hired some hot shots, told them what I wanted. And they found a way to manufacture it. Mem."

"Mem?" I was leaning forward now, as if his story were coming out on a spool and I could pull it along faster.

"Yeah," he said, "You like the name? It's a word I made up." Now he was out of his chair, pacing. "Don't think of it as an acronym. Think of it as 'mem,' like memory but so much more precise, pointillistic, sharp as glass, wrenching, heart-breaking in its absolute etched perfection. Once you experience this thing, Duncan, the ordinary functioning of your brain seems unacceptable." Litminov halted next to a coffee table, blinking in a patch of sun, his toes gripping the floor. When had he taken off his shoes? I hadn't noticed.

"Unacceptable?" I said.

He narrowed his eyes. He jingled something in his pocket. "Don't tell me that you're one of *those* people," he said. "Oh," he mimed in a girlish voice, clutching his heart with one pudgy hand, "have you thought about the ethics of this? What about the long-term health effects?" He pivoted on his bare feet and skewered me with his gaze for one long moment. "This thing is going to save lives, Duncan. So why the hell is everyone throwing up obstacles in front of me? It's going to take us years to get it into human trials. Until then, we're doing our own tests." His eyes landed on a pile of papers on a coffee table—what I supposed was his mail. He dropped into a chair far from me, and picked up the papers, began sorting through them, hurling whatever he didn't like on the floor, as if he'd forgotten all about me.

"So you're testing it," I said, to revive the conversation. "You mean on animals?"

He made me wait a long moment, as he flipped through the rest of the mail. Finally he said, "No, that's not what I mean."

Across the room, Andrea Lu leaned over a desk equipped with a light table, examining what appeared to be slides. Her short skirt skimmed her upper thighs, and as she leaned further, I had to yank my gaze away.

"I need human subjects," Litminov said. "And not just any humans, either. I need articulate people like you, who can describe exactly what they've experienced, help me make sense of it."

My heart thumped. "Oh," I said, struggling to keep my voice even, "is that the plan? I'm going to be your guinea pig?" I rubbed my cheek for its smoothness—I'd just shaved this morning, in preparation for what I thought would be a job interview. Now, it appeared he had other plans for me. And I didn't entirely mind. In fact, I felt oddly elated.

"Don't say 'guinea pig,'" Litminov snapped. "I hate that. Say 'beta tester.' And yes, you're going to be one. Why else would you have dragged yourself down here on four days' notice?" he said. "You want it very badly don't you? Maybe there's some girl you fucked a long time ago, and you can't wait to do it all over again in Technicolor. Is that it, Duncan?"

And now he was up—he'd thrown the mail on a cushion—and he crept toward me, closer and closer on his bare feet. "Do you know how lucky you are? You have a chance to experience a state of consciousness that's entirely new. It's as if there's a continent stretched out before us, unexplored, uncolonized. We will be the ones who make the maps." Then, with a flourish, he took out his wallet and pulled from it a white envelope. "Here are some of the little suckers." He threw the envelope down on the table.

"You want to do it right now?"

"No," he laughed. "Not today. I don't have time, and besides these aren't optimal conditions. We'd have to do it in the lab."

I stared down at that small rectangle of paper, creased as fine linen on the mahogany table. "So how do I know that I would live through the experience?"

He let out a huge, exasperated sigh. "I've taken it a zillion times. Andrea's tried it. And a few other trusted comrades have, too. We're all fine. Don't be a baby, Duncan."

"But I'm still confused. . . ," I began, and my voice seemed to fail me. "Look," I finally said, "this is what I don't get. Why me?"

"Because. How do I check the accuracy of what I remember on the drug? I need someone who was there with me, back in the day."

"None of this sounds very scientific."

"It's not." He had been pacing around the room, but now he found himself at the other end of the table from me, picked up a blood orange, and held it over his eye, pretending to look through it as if it were a telescope. "Believe me, Duncan, you take Mem and you'll be utterly convinced you're seeing the real-deal flash in front of your eyes. But what if it's an illusion? What if the drug lies? Maybe all those detailed memories are just hallucinations."

I nodded my head, as if this had already occurred to me. In fact it hadn't.

"Before I pour any more money in, I have to know if the drug's accurate. I'm bankrupting myself on this thing, Duncan."

"So why me?" I asked again.

He pointed at me, his hand like a pistol, three fingers bent and the thumb cocked. "Inside your head is a record of a certain night when we had a certain adventure together." Now he pointed his hand at his own temple. "Inside my head, I also have a memory of that night."

"Which night?"

"Never mind that. Listen, Duncan, bottom line is, we'd have a hell of a fucking good time. It's an incredible high when you take it alone, but it's twice as good when you do it with someone else. Of course, it has to be someone you knew in the past, otherwise, what's the point? And you and me, Duncan, we share a hell of a lot of memories. Good ones. We could get very fucked up."

"Oh," I said, drawing out the sound. "Oh, oh I see. All right then, let me make just one request. I'd have to be allowed to talk about the experience, to write and publish. No gag orders."

He grunted. "So that's your angle. This is a *career move* for you."

Somewhere at the other end of the apartment, a phone rang insistently. We ignored it.

"Fine." he said. "I wanted you to write about it anyway. Free advertisement. Just keep my name out of it."

Far away, Andrea stood up, a phone receiver in her hand. "It's upstate," she called.

"I have to take this. Can you let yourself out?" he said.

"So when. . . ?" I said.

Litminov laughed. "Now that's the spirit. You are eager, aren't you? We'll do it in a few weeks. I'll have you come down to the lab. Can you take off some time from work? A couple of days? Good."

He thrust his hand toward mine, so that before I registered what had happened we were shaking like two businessmen closing a deal. "I'll have Andrea e-mail you all the details. Goodbye, Duncan."

And then he turned, one hand brushing the table, fingers closing on that envelope, which I assumed he would whisk back into his pocket. Instead, he flicked it an inch in my direction. Was this some kind of signal? It seemed as if he meant to give me the pills without acknowledging he was doing so.

I found myself taking a step toward that white rectangle, which rested on top of its own ghostly reflection in the dark wood of the table. On the other side of the loft, Litminov was curling his huge body ear-first around a tiny phone. His back was turned to me. Andrea was watching him with her arms crossed.

My heart beat so hard that it seemed to clog my throat. I felt like I might choke as I slipped my hand on top of the packet, and it crinkled into my grip. I sauntered with forced nonchalance toward the door, slipping the pills into my shirt pocket. I wasn't sure whether I'd just stolen the pills or obeyed Litminov's subtle command, but either way, I couldn't get out of the apartment fast enough.

And then I found myself inside his golden elevator pushing the L button, staring at the smear of the reflection in brass, my face an oval, my hair a horseshoe of brown, my shirt a white blur. It was then that I realized I'd left my wool coat draped over a chair upstairs. I would not go back for it. I studied myself reflected in the bronze door, squinting, as if that would make the hazy image come into focus. But it would not.

Chapter
3

Coatless, my shirt billowing around my back in the gritty wind that blew up Broadway, I caught a cab. I gave the driver my father's address. Then I sunk into the vinyl, ripped-up seat as if I were sinking into a hot tub. Only now did I realize just how nervous I'd been around Litminov, what a relief it was to be free of him.

And then, there was the second but even greater relief of having the pills in my pocket. It had been excruciating to know that Mem existed but to not have access to it, to think that the drug might slip away from me, like so many other things.

But what if he was just playing with me? What if he'd left an empty envelope on that table?

The cab jerked forward in traffic and then slammed to a stop so quickly that I reached out to steady myself against the front seat. I shouldn't open it here.

Nonetheless, I found myself pulling the envelope from my pants pocket, carefully teasing the flap up, and ever so gently jiggling the tiny package over my open palm. Two tiny pills rolled into a crease of my skin. They were brown with black speckles, like the finest English tweed. I picked one of them up, sniffed it (a faint sweetness), studied its minute pocks and bumps.

The cab slammed to a halt and I closed my fist.

"This is it," the driver said.

A few minutes later, I was letting myself into Dad's apartment, the

pills still clenched in my left fist. A note on the coffee table waited
for me:

> Win—
> I'm helping Gloria hang her show—will probably take
> all day. If you'd like to meet us for dinner, we'll be at
> Jacques, 8:00.

I opened my hand. Ever so carefully, I placed my palm beside Dad's
note, tipping it so that the pills rolled onto the paper. Then I sat back
into an armchair, breathing in the aristocratic smell of leather.

Had Litminov wanted me take the pills or not? I tried to reason
that out, but my brain only ran around and around the questions like
a dog in a fenced yard. If I was a thief, then I should take a cab back to
his building and have the doorman send the envelope up to him with
a scrawled apology, because in the long run it would be a bad idea to
anger a man like Litminov.

All logic pointed to one conclusion: I should not take a pill right
now. And yet, I found myself pinching one of the little things between my thumb and forefinger, and rolling it flirtatiously across my
lip; if I swallowed this, I could meet my lost self, that long-ago Win
Duncan who had known how to be happy. Perhaps I could even steal
that secret from him. Then, before I even really registered my decision, I placed the pill on my tongue. It caromed off my teeth and was
gone. Only as I tasted the last chemical trace of it did I think, "I really
shouldn't."

With extreme care, I put the remaining pill into its wrapper, and
folded it into my pocket. My heart was ricocheting around my chest.
And yet, at the same time, I felt the kind of relief one does after making a decision. There was nothing I could do but slide back into the
leather arms of the chair and wait.

I picked up a heavy picture frame from the table and studied the
photo: My brother Bruce and I balanced on a tree limb, peering down
through the leaves. I was maybe twelve. My hair had not darkened
yet—it glowed in the sun, the reddish-blonde color of Irish Setters.
We must have been at Williamsburg because Bruce wore a tri-cor-
nered hat. I could imagine Mom standing below. She died when I was
seventeen, and that's when all the family photo albums stop, because
she was the one with the camera. No one had the heart to pick it up
after she was gone. "Sit closer together you two," she would have
called up. "But for Christ's sake, be careful."

It seemed as good a moment as any to go back to. I tried to stare at the picture, tried to leap through the glass frame. Nothing happened.

I had a new worry now. What if Litminov had tempted me with fake pills? What if he never had any Mem, and this whole production had been some kind of practical joke? He'd left sugar pills on the table, with the intention of proving that I would steal them. To distract myself from this idea, I picked up one of Dad's magazines, and tried to absorb myself in an article about tax-free investing.

Maybe a half an hour went by. I looked up from the magazine. Something was different. The traffic noises had faded as if my ears had been stuffed with cotton. I wiped my hand across my face. The skin felt rubbery, as if I'd gone a little numb. I swiveled my head and took in everything in the apartment—beige curtains, leather sofa, cut-glass advertising trophies on the bookshelves—and noted that my vision worked fine. But still, something was different about the way the room looked. It seemed not to *matter*, if that makes any sense. The part of me that clenched on the present moment had let go, and this was enormously pleasant.

The sun fell on one of crystal trophies, a glitter of reflected light spraying the wall. It reminded me of the surface of a lake, water heaving with the weight of its own gold. And then I found myself thinking of a specific lake from long ago, with cattails bearding its shore. I felt pressure on my side, a familiar sensation that I couldn't place. The skin on my legs seemed to glow with the heat of summer sun. Suddenly, the name of the lake came to me, like a revelation, Corey Lake.

I shut my eyes. I seemed to be able to look through the lids, as if they were made of glass instead of flesh. And, on the other side of my eyelids, as if it had always been there, the lake flared up in all its magnificence. I was trailing my hand in the water. The gunwale of the canoe dug into my side. My arm was tiny and hairless, and I might not have recognized it as mine except for the familiar mole at the wrist. My mother kneeled in the front, restored to life in a gingham skirt and a polo top, the back of her neck burned pink under the tendrils of hair that fell from her hat. "Watch out for that rock. Go right," she called, and I knew the person she was calling to was my father, though I couldn't seem to control my body to glance around behind me and check.

How could Mom be so concerned about hitting a rock? Didn't she know she'd come to harm, not here, but many years later? She clutched the side of the canoe and peered down into the water, and as we passed the rock, her head turned to follow it, and I caught her profile, the upturned nose, the Jackie O sunglasses, the pursed lips. It was so very much *her*, that I wanted to call out. But my mouth seemed to be glued shut. I couldn't control this boy's body, only feel what he felt, look through his eyes. But that was enough. More than enough. How can I describe the relief of being freed from the prison of the present moment, that cave where most of us are condemned to spend our lives? My own past had turned into a vast country, and I could go anywhere.

But for now, I was the boy in the canoe, six years old. And at the same time, I was not that boy. The arm lifted out of the water. The pink fingers dribbled drops. The eyes watched those drops blacken the wood of the canoe seat, and then slowly grow larger and larger, like spots of oil. I—Win Duncan, age forty—would have loved to wrench that boy's head upward from the drops of water and stare at my mother, collecting every heart-breaking detail of her vanished existence. But I could not lift the head, its head, the boy's head.

And here, a general note about Mem—what it does and how to speak about what it does. When you're on the drug, you do not so much "remember" as perch inside your former self. You ride silently in your own, long-ago body. You are two people at once. That makes describing the experience difficult. English language does not allow for the double being that Mem creates, a person straddling two times. The words "me" "I" "my" don't suffice. If I say "my hand" do I mean the soft pink starfish of flesh, each of its fingers tipped with silver drop of water hanging pendulously over the seat of a canoe? Or do I mean the hand that, three decades later, lay on the armrest of a leather chair, the fingers much larger now and dusted with blondish-reddish hair?

When I say, "I had to pee very badly," am I referring to the grown-up Win Duncan in his father's apartment or do I refer to the boy in the canoe?

That is why I have developed my own system of notation, which I believe will be helpful to anyone seeking to document the unique state of consciousness that Mem conjures up. You simply parse the self into a series of sub-selves, identifiable by age. For instance, when I write "Win-6," I mean the boy in the canoe. "Win-40" refers to the man in his father's apartment. And "Win-41" is the fellow hunched before his laptop now, turning his notes into a book. I am Win-41. Hello.

So anyway, I had to pee. Win-6 had to pee. Viciously. But he didn't dare speak up. Instead, he reached down, crawling his hand across the fabric of his shorts, and pinched his penis in between his thighs. The boy had mastered the art of "holding it in" during the hot, endless bus rides to school, and now school was out for summer, he'd use his talent—it seemed to be the only talent he did have—to keep his parents calm. For if he were to announce, even in his most polite little-gentleman voice, "I have to go to the bathroom," the boat would begin tossing with their efforts to get it to the shore. And then Mommy would say, "You should have made him go before we left, Rich," and Daddy would say, "That's not my department," and they'd be off, that cruel tennis game, where the ball flew over the boy's head, back and forth, thwack, thwack, thwack.

And so Win-6 held it in. The need to pee throbbed somewhere below his tummy and in the tip of his penis. Beside his mother's head, pine trees waved in slow motion. In back of him, the oar hit the side of the canoe with reverberating thuds, proof of his father's ineptness as a paddler, and in between the thuds, his father said nothing but radiated contentment and cigar smoke. His parents' amiable silence was as beautiful as the lake itself, suffused with sunlight, miraculous. Win-6 seemed to control his parents with the clamped muscle at the base of his penis. He held in the pee and he held his parents in their peace. He kept—with that the one small muscle—all chaos at bay.

And then he could hold it no more. The pee flowed out, delicious and awful, warm on his legs, seeping into the fabric of his shorts. The pee dripped inexorably the length of his thigh, and now it formed a pool on the bottom of the canoe that shivered with the movements of the boat, and in a minute his mother would turn around and see, and the world would rip apart.

And I, the man, watched his distress, felt the heart thumping in the little chest. I felt a soulful tenderness for that boy, as if he were my son. But I wanted to escape him, the cramped cage of his body.

Other, happier memories clamored for my attention. I could feel them pressing all around me—it was as if they had tucked themselves behind the fringe of pine trees or underneath the golden skin of the lake. I could go anywhere in my life, anywhere! It was this ability to edit and choose that is the most exhilarating sensation of Mem. Your past stretches around you like some turbo-charged Disneyland where you invent the rides as you go along. And what about the bad memories? Ah, friend, you can avoid them. You can leap away from anything that's painful. Which is what I planned to do now.

I could sense tantalizing memories hovering around me, and I itched to get to them. Somewhere above the lake, a crow squawked. I

associated that caw-caw-caw with sunlight and sports pages, with the
lackadaisical bliss of weekend mornings. I sensed something wonderful hovering at the end of that sound, and so I followed it, pushing
through it, as if it were steam or vapor, a wall made out of nothing.

And now, a room resolved itself, hazy at first through the screen of
my eyelids, and then suddenly vivid. A woman stood at the window,
sun blazing down on her gold cap of hair. She was trying to open the
window. It was stuck, and then it suddenly flew upward, with a squeal
of wood on wood, exactly the sound that the crow had made.

Could that woman really be Edie? Instead of an anarchy of curls
spilling around her shoulders, she wore her hair clipped short, like a
boy's. She turned to me now. Yes, it was Edie, but some tweaked version of Edie, an Edie from another universe. Her face was thin and
glittered with wire-frame glasses. She was nothing at all like my wife.
And yet, I knew her. I remembered those U-shaped shadows under
her cheekbones; I remembered the way she used to hesitate before she
spoke; I remembered that Columbia sweatshirt she was wearing now,
with the frayed cuffs. It stabbed my heart, this lost Edie suddenly
revived before me.

"I can't handle it," she said. "Too many good things are happening
to us. It makes me nervous."

She was talking to me—but who was "me"? I floated inside a body
that lay on the sofa. The seams of the old slipcover dug into his, this
younger man's, back. His cheeks itched a bit when he smiled at her.
He must have a beard. I recognized the apartment as the one that
Mercy College had lent us when we were temporary faculty. It was
November, I suddenly knew, a freakishly warm morning. And then
the rest of it came back to me too. I was thirty-two, no, thirty-three.

A few days before, Father Sullivan had called Edie and Win into his
office, had popped the cork on a bottle of champagne, and offered
them jobs as assistant professors. Yesterday, he and Edie had thrown
a party (a beer bottle still sat on the windowsill, the beautiful murky
brown color of pond water). Only this morning had the enormity of
the thing begun to sink in.

"We'll finally have money," a male voice said now. And though I
was floating in Win-33's body, looking out through his eyes, it took
me a moment to realize that he was the one who had spoken. Have
you ever plugged up your ears and talked at the same time? It makes
your voice sound echo-y and strange, not at all like something that
belongs to you. It was like that when Win-33 talked. Had I really
sounded like that? I used to speak so quickly.

"How weird. Money," he said, and now he laughed.

Edie came over to the sofa, threw some of the newspapers off the cushion, and sat down. "I think they're giving us too much money actually." She picked up one of Win-33's feet and placed it on her lap. Oh Christ! How long had it been since she'd done that, how long since this kind of easy intimacy existed between us? "If we get tenure, our whole lives will be taken care of, right straight through to death. That's kind of . . . creepy, don't you think?" Her voice was different back then, too—scratchy and hesitant. "We're not the kind of people who have money."

"Why not us?" he said. The sunlight pulsed on a wall behind her. The whole day seemed to be suffused with champagne-colored light. It had seeped in through his skin. He felt drunk.

"Good question. Why not us?" she said, and her hand paused in its caress of his foot, as she mulled it over. I felt a rush of longing for this woman, for that old Edie who loved me fiercely, with her frayed sweatshirt and her chewed nails and her bad haircut. And what had happened to her? She had been blotted out by her successor, a woman with a gold curtain of hair and contact lenses, with a published book, a tattoo on her shoulder and three pairs of black boots in the closet. But here was the *real* Edie come back to life. How would I ever get along without her, now that I had seen her again?

Win-33 let his head fall back against the arm of the sofa. His eyes came to rest on the ceiling. He studied the stucco up there; it reminded him of meringue on top of lemon pie, the white plaster forming nipples that you almost wanted to break off and eat. Harvard, he thought. Yale. MIT. He and Edie had Mercy College as their jumping-off place; they could end up anywhere. The next fifty years stretched out before him like a long delicious meal - the Victorian houses, the precocious children who would go to Ivies, the dogs, lazy Sundays, weathered gray wood of beach walkways, books, Swedish cars. He'd always disdained those people, the comfortable professors with houses on the Cape, but now that he knew he could be one of them he found that he quite approved. He would have *that* kind of life.

On the table beside him, sunlight formed knife-blades of glare inside a glass of water. Win-33 felt his joy like that. Sharp and beautiful and almost too much to bear.

"Tenure track," he heard Edie say. "Makes me think of train tracks. You know what I mean?" The words vibrated from her lap and up through his legs.

"Yes, I do," he said, because he did. He knew exactly what she meant. He could picture two strips of steel running side by side, gleaming in the forest, traveling through tunnels, and finally swooping down a hill into the heart of a city. Two beams of steel that run together but never touch.

"It scares me," he heard her say.

The most frustrating part of Mem is that you cannot turn the head; you cannot speak. You can only watch and listen. Now, I threw all my effort into taking control of Win-33's body, to force him to sit up and look at her. I concentrated on prying his mouth open. I wanted him to say these words: "Edie, everything's about to go wrong. We're about to lose each other. We've got to stop it from happening, right now."

Win-33 opened his mouth. He took a breath to speak. And for a minute, I imagined I'd gotten control of him. But then his own words rumbled up from his chest. "Don't be so neurotic, Edie. This is what we wanted." He stood up, not bothering to look at her, and the room tilted dizzyingly, and the ceiling spun and turned into floor, and he said, "Is it OK if I finish the coffee?"

And now he was in the kitchen, pouring the last dregs from the pot into his mug. He leaned on the counter, and stared out the window, surveying the campus that swept below him, the gothic buildings scattered across the lawn: Tyler, Holmes House, Merchison, McNulty. He'd have his own office in James Hall over there, with the tall spires. It surprised him how much satisfaction that gave him.

And while he sized up the buildings, as if they all belonged to him, I noticed - out of the side of his eye—the iron clock on top of the chapel tower. It was just at the fringe of his vision. He paid it no mind. But I saw. The clock was frozen at three minutes to noon. It was broken even back then, even all those years ago. The stopped clock reared up like a symbol of all that was to come. That was the future waiting for him.

How had he failed to take its meaning? How had he not seen? Win-33's head wobbled stupidly on his neck, as he turned back to the living room. The clues had been there, plain to read. But he hadn't wanted to. And why should he? Better to think you are blessed, that you have discovered the secret of happiness, and now you will always have it.

Christ, how I wanted to stay in that younger man's body, wanted to linger there and relive that whole glorious day. Soon, he and his young wife would make love underneath a mirror that cupped a lost world inside its solid square frame—branches that would have fallen off and turned to dirt by now, clouds that had long ago dissolved, a curtain that had been thrown in the trash and disintegrated. I wanted to stay there with the young Edie who loved me, and to hover forever just like this.

But I couldn't. The drug was wearing off. I blinked. Win-40 blinked. As my eyes fluttered open, I returned for a second to Dad's apartment, beige rugs, beige curtains, a world diminished in color, so pale next to the lurid memories. I squeezed my eyes shut, tried to return to the porch in the old apartment with its creaky wicker chairs. Instead, the flotsam and jetsam of other times floated up: the sound of crackling paper on a doctor's examining table, the wood stick stained red after the Popsicle is eaten, the vibrations in my hand from a lawn mower.

It was no use. I opened my eyes again. The Mem had worn off and I was stuck here, in the backwash of the present moment. The sunlight on the carpet had a gray cast to it. The air seemed dusty, a little bit filthy. I knew this to be a trick of the drug, but that didn't help any. I was in despair, stranded here with a bum knee, sour spit, the beginnings of a headache. The six-year-old boy, where was he? Dead. The thirty-three-year-old? Dead. And my beloved Edie, that woman who hid nothing from me, who trusted me with all her thoughts? She was dead too. I would have to get along without them all now.

I could not bear to sit down an instant longer. I jumped out of the chair and paced around the apartment, but every place I stood annoyed me. Gray light pounded from the windows, and I could feel the gray tumbling over my skin and turning me gray, too, the color of smeared newspapers. I twitched. I brushed bugs off my face that weren't there. I tried to find a comfortable position.

Imagine someone slipped you ten No-Doze pills and shot you up with speed for good measure; you're skittering around like a drop of water on a hot engine; you're thinking that if you race to the other end of the room, you'll feel better. But moving doesn't help. It's your own body you want to climb out of. You no longer can stand the weight of your own legs, the suck and draw of your lungs—and worst, worst of all, you can't bear the press of time. Time lies on you heavy as the lead suit the nurse drapes over you before she zaps you with X-rays. As long as you're high on Mem, you can fly anywhere in your life. It is a hard thing, then, to return to the plodding march of chronological time, conveying you to the inevitable and dark conclusion.

Of course, these days, no one would even consider taking Mem without popping a Xanax after. But I didn't know that then. Even

Litminov didn't know it then. We were learning, through painful trial and error.

So I was suffering a full-on twitch attack. I had to move. I had to travel. I glanced at Dad's VCR: 4:12. The numbers made no sense, seemed laughable to me. A clock on the mantle broadcast the same time with its two hands. And in the kitchenette, the tiny numbers glowing on the coffee machine concurred. They were all around me, this conspiracy of clocks. On my wrist, the second hand skimmed across the face of the watch, with a speed that struck me as cruel. Clocks everywhere, time everywhere, me trapped in it.

I hurried into the guest room, stuffed clothes into my suitcase, zipped it up, folded the bed back into a sofa with one desperate shove. Then, in the kitchenette, I scrawled a note to Dad, balled it up, threw it away. Scrawled another one. And another. Until finally my hand-writing would pass for normal.

I grabbed my suitcase and flew to the door in my rolled-up shirt-sleeves and good wool pants. I was struggling with the deadbolt when I remembered the matter of the coat—I didn't have one. What to do? What to do?

I swung open the door to Dad's closet, eyeballs jiggling in my head as I tried to focus on the rows of coats and jackets neat on their hangers. I clawed my way into the back of the closet and fished out a heavy knee-length number. Dad would never miss this one, I thought, a gaudy herringbone in orange and tan. I slipped it on. It fit perfectly.

• • • • •

By the time I'd boarded the train—I'd take that to Boston, and then the commuter rail the rest of the way—the panic had eased off some. It felt good enough to drop into the plush seat and dump my bag beside me. But still, my thoughts revved. I peered through the scarred window of the train, half-expecting to see Litminov rushing along the platform, searching for me. "I'm an asshole," I repeated to myself, knees bouncing. "Christ, what an asshole." I couldn't stop touching my face, scratching at my arms. This was an awful state of affairs, be-cause I had no idea when the tic-y, itchy torture would let up—if ever. In Bridgeport, people flooded onto the train, swiveling their heads this way and that as they chose their seats. Women with cigarette skin and bleached hair, men in stone-washed jeans, sized me up and then kept on waddling down the aisle. The seat beside me stayed empty.

Hours went by; the train clacking over its tracks began to soothe me. Outside, rivers and fields rolled past. The people around me in pod-like chairs had settled into their own trances. As we trundled through Mystic, the train seemed to toss off the scenery like shedding skin. I sat with my father's coat slung over my lap, and the smell of him—cigars and spice—wafted up. The drug's grip loosened.

I began to come back to the regular state of affairs that I called "myself." I hoisted a monograph out of my bag and pretended to read it. At least outwardly, I was able to resume the role that I usually played in public—the professor on his way to somewhere important, poring over an abstruse book about the introduction of aspirin in the nineteenth century, no time for chit-chat, please don't bother me. I'll be completely back to normal tonight, I told myself.

But even if that was true, I found it hardly consoled me. When the drug wore off, I would return to my familiar unhappiness. In the past year, I had begun to suspect that I did not belong in my own life. Now I knew it. Mem had opened my eyes. The train was hurling me back to—what? A wife who ignored me, a job that bored me, a landscape of winter highways where snow spit down on the gray domes of cars, in two words: New Hampshire.

At thirty-three, I'd been happy. Now I was not. What had changed in the intervening years? How had I lost myself and everything else that mattered? I spent a few minutes trying to figure it out, then gave up, exhausted. My memory—unaided by chemicals—seemed as useless as a cheap flashlight with dying batteries. I could rummage around in the vast basement all I wanted to, but I'd never find anything with that weak light.

Compulsively, I reached into my pocket and checked for the envelope with the remaining pill in it. For one panicky moment, my hand rooted around and couldn't find it. And then, there it was, the paper of the envelope gone soft as silk. One pill. That's all I had. I would need a lot more.

· · · · ·

At my station in New Hampshire, I followed the other passengers up the stairs. Edie and I shared one cell phone; yesterday morning, I'd left it on the hallway table for her, to remind her to throw it into her purse; she always needed it on Thursdays. Now, I hurried to the row of pay phones against one wall to call her on our cell. One ring. Two rings. While I waited I stooped over to examine a bit of my own reflection on the shiny metal around the coin slot. My face was warped by the curves of the metal, nose dimpled and mouth puckered like a scar. After four rings, I got the cell phone's recorded message: "You have reached Professor Duncan and Professor Nicola. . . ." I figured she must be out at a movie, with the phone turned off; it was Saturday night, after all.

So instead of going home, I drove straight to the Humanities building and climbed the stone stairs, opened the heavy door, and flicked on the light switch. For a moment, I lingered in that hall with the linoleum floor and light blue walls, color of Virgin Mary's veil gone grimy, then hurried past the classroom where I taught my Methodology seminar—how would I bear it Monday morning when my grad students filed in and listened to me drone about progressive historians from Turner to Beard, all of us under the florescent light?

But never mind that. Upward, upward I went to my office. I had work to do. Lexus-nexus, Altavista, Google, Worldcat, Medline. I consulted all the gurus inside my computer, typing in the words I hoped would lead me to some kind of understanding of what had happened today.

I clicked through medical articles for a while, but the internet moved too slowly for me. I was still speedy from the drug. Or maybe I was just inspired. Ideas kept popping in my head, and I reached for a legal pad, to catch this evanescence of thought before it disappeared.

• • • • •

Maybe an hour later, I stepped through the door of the Humanities building, the legal pad tucked under my arm. I could see my breath streaming out of my mouth, like a pale smoke against the black sky. My Saab was the only car in the lot. I settled into the cracked leather of its seat and gunned the engine, trying to coax some heat out of the vents.

It was past midnight and I should have been exhausted, but I was still quivering with nervous energy, jamming the clutch between second and third so the little car leapt over a speed bump and bounced on its haunches. Edie must be home by now, I figured, and I wanted to catch her before she fell asleep.

I wouldn't tell her about the drug, not yet. Instead, I would broach the difficult subject of our marriage. As I drove along under a moon like a great pill in the sky, I prepared some phrases in my head. "Grown distant," I whispered to her, imaginary in the seat beside me, and "don't know each other anymore." How long had it been—a year? two years?—that I'd thought about having this conversation? I had put it off so many times, reasoning that if anything were really wrong, Edie would come to me.

But now, fixing a marriage seemed like an easy matter. Edie and I would simply jump backward into the people we had been, into that happiness that we'd had. I imagined how she would look in a few minutes, as I fumbled through the dark bedroom toward her; the swirl of her body under a pile of blankets, one arm flung out to the empty sheet where I usually lay. Though she'd be sulky when I first snapped on the light, after a minute, she'd hoist herself into a sitting position.

"Did you have a good time with your Dad?" she'd croak, oddly formal, as if we'd just met at a party and she was making conversation.

I'd perch on the edge of the mattress and reach under her t-shirt to rest my hand in the crook of her waist.

"Eeds," I'd say, "We've taken a wrong turn somewhere. How the hell did we end up here? We don't belong here, Edie."

She'd sit straighter. She'd listen, her face growing serious. And then we'd talk. We'd stay up all night, the way we used to in grad school, our words like cigarettes that we smoked down to the nub, as we fomented revolutions, planned utopias, invented sexual positions from as-yet-unwritten Kama Sutras. We'd lie with the sheet tenting over us, blinking at each other in the bluish gloom of cotton-filtered light. "We're twins," she'd say. "We're in the womb, floating around." Or she'd come up with something else just as loopy. We were closest, Edie and I, when we were furthest from everyone and everything else.

Now I turned the car onto our street and eased past kids' sleds and mounds of snow. My headlights slid over our neighbors' yard, the Christmas display of deer wearing their plastic red harnesses. The harsh light made them look even more garish than usual—like prostitutes caught in the sudden flash of a camera. Yes, exactly. This was wrong. We had to get away from here, Edie and I.

I palmed the steering wheel and headed toward our driveway, bumping over the packed snow. My headlights lit up the garage. The door should have been closed, but it yawned open. One o'clock in the morning and Edie's car was gone.

Did I say that emphatically enough? Edie was not where she should be. My wife had not come home.

Chapter
4

I found the bed in a chaotic state of emptiness, a mess of blankets, sheets, books and papers. On her pillow, she'd left a manuscript, open to the middle, covered with scrawls. "Horror of fertility?" the notes asked. "Research connection to 18th c. birth-control methods."

I shoved the pile of papers away and wrapped the mess of blankets around myself, suddenly aware of how exhausted I was. I conked out for a while and then woke with a start, still alone. I couldn't get back to sleep, what with straining to hear the sound of Edie's car coming up the street, the particular double-thunk of it hitting the beginning of our driveway. I called her cell phone and got the voice mail, agonized about whether to call the police, and just when I'd decided to, I must have fallen asleep again. All I remember is one troubled dream: Edie in a canoe, rowing diligently away from me, the hourglass of her back retreating into a fog.

In the morning, I dragged myself out of bed and crept down the stairs. The house had been transformed by her absence. My footsteps rasped across the carpet, as if special microphones had been installed in the floor, to amplify my every move. Her black silk jacket lay slung across the back of a chair, its arms bulged out, still retaining some trace of her shape.

I checked the table in the front hall. The cell phone lay on its back, just where I'd left it yesterday morning. I sucked in a breath. Edie frequently forgot to stick the cell phone in her purse; so ordinarily,

I might not be alarmed. But now the phone seemed like an ominous sign, a piece of evidence. Why had she left it there? What had happened? The phone's message light was blinking. I punched in some buttons and listened. There was only one, terrifying message. Heavy breathing. A low growl. And then the click of a hang-up. Had some creep noticed she was in the house alone, had some creep. . . ? But then I realized that the breather was myself—the Win Duncan of yesterday, mildly stoned on Mem, his tall frame hunched over the pay phone. It was merely a message from one of my previous selves.

● ● ● ● ●

At 1:30 that afternoon, the car finally bumped up our driveway and then the hollow roar of its engine inside the garage and then the scratching of her key against the kitchen-door lock. She burst in, kicking snow off her boots. She hadn't seen me yet. I skulked in the hallway, watching as she unwound the scarf from her neck and gave her hair a shake, her fingers were pale and precise; for some reason, those fingers reminded me of tallow candles, the kind that might burn with a steady and secret flame in a monastery. It is eerie to watch your wife when she doesn't know you're there—that private smile on her face. You are seeing her as she might look after you are gone, either from death or divorce. It turns out that she does well without you.

"Oh shit," she said, hand on her chest. "You scared me."

"Sorry."

"Why are you lurking like that?"

"I'm not lurking."

"Actually, according to my definition, you were lurking." She shrugged off her coat, draped it across a chair. "You didn't say hi."

"Sorry."

She sighed. "I didn't expect you to be back in town until tonight," she was already losing interest in the whole matter. She sat down and began unlacing one of her combat boots.

I shoved my hands further in my pocket. "Where were you?" I hated the peevish tone in my voice.

"Donna Perkin's place. I crashed on her sofa last night."

"You drove all the way down to Cambridge?"

"It was a last-minute thing," she said, reaching for her other boot.

I said—with unaccustomed softness—"I worried about you."

She looked up sharply, and studied me while she coaxed the boot off her foot. "You did?" She stood up. "Are you okay?" she said, walking over and touching my shoulder with the flat of her hand, as if feeling there for a fever.

"I didn't sleep much," I said.

"Well, take a nap."

"Take one with me."

"Can't. I've got to go to my secret meeting, remember? About the Women's Studies department. It could be cool, if we actually convinced the dean to do it. But we'll see." Now she was talking more to herself than me, "probably nothing's going to happen." She ambled off into the front hall. I followed, watching as she headed up the stairs, one hand tapping at the purple roses that burst like bruises all over the wallpaper. She was halfway up the stairs before I noticed a secret design to her movements; she was slapping every third or fourth rose as she ascended.

"Are you doing that for good luck?" I called.

"What?" she said, half-turning, her face curtained with hair, her eyes two slashes in the dark stairwell.

"The roses."

"Oh that," she laughed nervously. "Yes, actually. It is good luck. You should try it."

"What do you need luck for?"

She turned away, finished the staircase, touching the last flower for my benefit. "Nothing special," she said at the top, and disappeared into the bathroom.

I couldn't seem to keep away from her; I couldn't stop myself from trailing behind. I stood in the bathroom doorway as she pulled back the shower curtain to test the spray with her hand.

"Do you want me to come with you?" I asked.

"Where?" she said, stepping over the side of the tub and ducking into the water. Behind the steamed-up plastic curtain, she turned into a shifting blur, pink and brown and cream, more squiggle than human being.

"To the meeting," I said, raising my voice over the roar of the water. "Wouldn't it look good to have your faculty husband along for support?"

"I suppose," she said, her voice reverberating against the tile. "Whatever you want to do is fine."

I retreated to the bedroom, and found myself at the window, swaying back and forth in front of it. The tall pine trees in our backyard blotted out the view of Mercy College, its gothic spires like children's birthday-party hats. But if I found just the right position in front of the window—ah, here it was—I could see some of the campus between the branches. There was the stone tower with its iron clock face—the same clock that had reared up like symbol when I was on Mem yesterday. I leaned in closer to the window, and a cloud—my breath—bloomed on the glass. I squinted, trying to make out the hands of that clock. It was just as I thought, they were still stuck at three minutes to noon. Why hadn't this crucial bit of evidence ever struck me as important before? Why hadn't I noticed the omens all around me?

Edie padded into the room, head in the blue turban of a towel, skin bright pink. She hurried toward the bureau, wiped her hand on her towcled head, leaned over and began to scribble on her notepad.

"Edie?"

"Yeah?" she said, reluctantly jotting a last word.

Across the room from me, inside the top drawer of the bureau, on a throne of old pennies, sat a small white envelope. A brown pill nestled inside that envelope. I had to tell her about it, if I wanted to set things right between us.

But instead, I found myself saying, "I deserve to hear the whole truth." I sniffed diffidently. It was one of those mannerisms that had crept into my body after years of being a professor. "You left town for a reason. Something you haven't told me yet," I added, with another sniff.

"Yes," she said. We fell silent for a moment. She slid onto the bed, pulling a blanket to her waist, her white arms like long elegant gloves.

I stared out the window with my jaw set. "You're having an affair."

She was studying me, her eyebrows hunched together. "I'm what?"

"An affair. With Donna Perkins. Or someone else."

"No," she said. "No, I'm not." She held my gaze. It was the first time in weeks that my wife had really looked at me. Edie was shaking her head slowly. "I'm not having an affair, Win."

"Then what?"

"I'm distracted. Work. I think I've made a discovery." She sighed. She pulled the towel off her head and threw it across the room, so that it landed on the lip of the hamper. Hairs snaked down her neck. "I didn't want to tell you because you get so upset about these things."

"I do not."

"You do, Win." She sighed. "Actually, you do."

"So what's the discovery?" I snapped off each word at the end.

Edie flicked her eyes away. "Remember I told you about the diary that came from some nuthouse in Maine?"

"Vaguely."

"It was written by an inmate who mutilated her face." Here Edie raised her hand to her cheeks and poked imaginary holes with her fingertips. "She did it with a hot knitting needle. The manuscript is so. . . ." She shook her head, played with one of the loose threads on the bedspread. Then she looked up, met my gaze. "It's brilliant, is what it is. Seventy years before *The Awakening*, and it's so modern. It could blow apart American literature. Anyway, that's what I told Donna. She said, 'Don't even Fedex it. I want to see it now.' So I drove down."

"And she liked it?" I said, though I didn't want to hear the next part.

"She said it's a major find. She's going to help me publish it as a book. She thinks I should hire a publicist. Can you believe that? A publicist?"

"This could be huge." I said, dully.

"I know." All the joy had dropped out of her voice. She pulled the blanket tighter. "I know," she said again. "So why do I feel so shitty right now—as if I've *done* something to you."

I couldn't see the freckles from where I stood, but up close, I knew, the tiny dots would be everywhere on her skin, splattered across her shoulders, creeping up to the aureole of her breast. My wife was speckled all over like that pill in the drawer near her. Edie was so very much like the drug Mem. She stored my past inside her. She contained pieces of me. I planned to tell her this, soon, when I introduced the two of them, the pill and my wife. But not yet. This was most certainly not the time for it.

"I'm not envious, if that's what you mean," I said. "But if I've been less than supportive, then I'm sorry."

"That's a beginning. Now, could you be happy for me?"

And we held each others' gaze. Years ago, this would have been my cue. I would have hurried to the bed, tugging off my shoes, and when I got there, she would yank my t-shirt over my head, and we would push our faces together in a frantic overture, and lose our balance, and laugh, and all the rest.

But instead, I held myself stiffly, and made a little grimace that was supposed to be a smile. "I *am* happy for you."

"You are?" she said hopefully.

"Of course, I am, Edie."

"Oh," she said. "Good."

Silence stretched between us.

"So, listen, I was heading to the office," I said. "You want me to pick up anything on the way home?"

"No, that's OK," she said, distractedly, and reached for the note-pad again. She was already retreating from me, tunneling back into the 1830s, into the fragile curls of a mad woman's handwriting. She would live in her manuscript now, in the labyrinth of sepia-colored sentences, far from me.

"OK, bye," I said, and pecked her on the forehead.

So that's how we were. That was our marriage.

• • • • •

A few nights later, I had sequestered myself in my office at Mercy, with the pill on the desk before me. I'd tucked it into my wallet that morning, comforting myself with the thought that I could take it later, could escape the pile of student papers and the dishwater gray of another New Hampshire winter night, the wind howling outside like a TV laugh track.

And now here it was, 8:00 at night, the humanities building gone quiet, and I still hadn't taken the pill out of its envelope. The square of white sat on my desk like a tiny door I could open into anywhere. I wanted it so badly that my mouth watered a little. And at the same time, I didn't want it at all. I was scared of the part after the good part, the awful twitchy agony that would hit as the drug wore off.

So I was smoothing out the envelope, staring at the bluish shadows in its creases, in a panic of ambivalence. What if I went nuts the way I had last time, and I skittered down the hall and ended up curled in fetal position in a corner somewhere, and one of the faculty found me? What I needed was someone to watch over me. Someone to make sure that I didn't hurt myself or act too foolish. A drug buddy.

I leaned back in my chair, put one boot up on the radiator and then the other, and gazed at my own blurry reflection in the window. Litminov had said that the drug could be more intense when you took it with someone else. He had tracked me down, I realized, because I housed a library of young Litminovs—twenty-seven and twenty-eight-year-old versions of himself—inside my own brain, and he wanted to get at my memories, to use them to amp up his own. Frankly, I really didn't see how having someone else in the room when you were high would make a difference—Mem was such a private experience. And yet, the idea had wormed itself into my thoughts, and I found myself wondering about who I would pick, if I could, to take the drug with me.

"Bernie," I whispered to myself.

Then I found myself on my feet, scooping the envelope off of the table and stuffing it into my pocket, gathering my student papers.

Bernie's office was two floors below mine. All of a sudden, I knew what I had to do. I just couldn't bear doing it alone again—and more than that, I wanted somebody else to *understand* what it was like to travel backwards in time. I couldn't be alone with something this tremendous. As I descended the stairs, the plan became clear. Bernie and I would split the pill; it would be enough of a dose, I thought, to unlock the cage, to let him see what it was like to fly up above his life and then dive down anywhere he wanted. I hoped the dose might be weak enough that neither of us would suffer too much at the end.

"Yeah," he called when I knocked on his door.

I expected to find him hunched over a journal, refusing to look up at me until he finished his paragraph. Instead, when I opened the door, he was leaning across his desk, eyes boring into me.

"What?" I said. "You're staring at me."

"I am. Because of *that*." He pointed at my chest. "Did you steal that off a wino?"

I glanced down and realized that I was wearing the coat I'd taken from Dad's closet. "Oh," I said. "Well, I lost mine. Actually, I left it somewhere." I took a deep breath. "Actually, I left it at Litminov's apartment."

"So you did see Litminov." He stared down at the papers near his feet for a long moment. Then he reached into his desk and took out a stick of gum, began unwrapping it with a precise dance of fingers. I smelled, faintly from across the room, mint. He stuck the gum into his mouth and chewed in the unhappy way of an ex-smoker trying to forget the bliss of cigarettes. "So did he sell you any used cars? Maybe a time-share in Fiji?"

"Bernie," I said, stepping over to the chair beside his desk, removing a pile of papers from the seat, and settling into it cautiously. "What do you have against Litminov?"

Bernie chewed. "What do you have for him?"

"He gave me this," I said. And then, with a little flourish like a magician, I reached into my pocket and produced the wad of paper. I smoothed it out, opened a flap and carefully tapped the pill out onto my palm. It rolled down a crease in my skin and stopped purposefully, just short of my thumb.

"No," Bernie said. "You've got to be kidding. You got some? For real?"

"For real."

Bernie bent over my hand and studied it.

"May I?" he said. He pinched the pill between his thumb and first finger, wedged his glasses up onto his forehead and stared at it. I studied his eyes—I'd rarely seen them naked. They were the color of brass, much lighter than you'd expect, which had the effect of making him seem both blind and all-seeing.

"You've tried it," he said, dropping the pill back into my palm.

"Yes."

"And?" He replaced his glasses and leaned back in his chair.

"Amazing." I placed the diminutive pill on the edge of his desk, next to an unruly stack of journals. "But unfortunately this is the only dose I've got right now."

"You sound as if you expect to have more."

"I'm going down to Litminov's lab next Thursday. He wants to do some tests." In fact, an e-mail from Andrea Lu had arrived that morning, and when it popped up on my computer screen, my palms had begun to sweat. I was afraid it might contain an accusation—"You stole our pills"—but instead it was just driving directions to the lab. Either Litminov hadn't noticed his pills were gone or he didn't care.

"Thursday?" Bernie said now.

"Yeah."

He was hunching toward me, a worried look pinching his face. "Don't you teach then? You can't just take off whenever you please."

"Sure I can. You're going to guest-teach my Methodology class next Friday. And I'm going to cancel all my Intro sections."

"Win." He rubbed at his cheek and under his glasses with one hand, as if I were exhausting him. "Don't give Sheehan an excuse to fire you."

I could not seem to summon up any dread of Sheehan. None of that mattered anymore. What scared me was how much I needed Bernie, how much I wanted him to cooperate with my plan. "We could split it, Bernie," I said. "My only pill." Was I whispering? My voice seemed to have weakened on me, turned to nothing but sculpted breath. "I want you to have half."

"Are you out of your mind?"

"No. Not at all." Now my voice turned almost flirtatious. "It's just that I was thinking of that day we climbed Mount Monadnock. It was the hottest goddamned day of August, and we got to the top, watched the sunset, drank some beers and then climbed down in the dark. That was fantastic, wasn't it?"

"Yeah," he said, his voice softer now. "That was pretty great."

"Bernie, look at it this way: Even with a whole pill, the effects don't last that long. Two hours max. We could rocket to the peak of Mount

Monadnock. And then before you know it, we'd be right back here in your office again. Just a quick thrill."

He pressed his lips together as if to hold back a stream of words. Finally he said, "Don't you have something more important to do with that pill? Take it with Edie."

"You don't get it, Bernie. That was one of the best days of my life."

And then a strange and utterly unprecedented thing happened: Bernie blushed. First the skin framed by the V of his collar turned pink, and the flush spread to his cheeks and forehead, until he could have passed for sunburned. He took off his glasses and wiped them on his shirt. Put them back on. "Well, I'm flattered," he said.

"Excellent. So we just have to figure out how to split the little sucker in two."

He shook his head.

"No? Are you kidding?"

"I don't have the slightest desire to try it," he said.

"Why not? What have you got to lose?"

"A lot," he said, curling deeper into the chair. In the harsh light of the desk lamp, his skin appeared very pale, almost bluish.

"You're not afraid, are you?" I heard a Litminov-like tone creeping into my voice, that particular combination of wheedling and threat, and yet I couldn't seem to stop myself. "I hope you're not just turning this down because you want to be fresh for your nine o'clock class. That would be sad, Bernie, very sad."

He held up one hand to stop the flow of my words. "Yes," he said, "I am afraid. But not in the way you think. When you brought up that day we went hiking, all those years ago, you know what my first thoughts were? Jess and Becky. They were still living with me back then. Every night, no matter how late I got in, I'd go upstairs to Becky's room, open the door a crack and watch her sleeping, curled up with her thumb in her mouth. And now where is she? Living in some subdivision in fucking Phoenix. You know Jesse's getting remarried? I told you, right? So now Becky's going to have a new father." He shook his head, sucked in a breath. "Do you know what it feels like to see your kid maybe three times a year? I fucked up, Win. I fucked up and I lost them. I don't need to take that drug of yours. I'm in the past all the time. Every day, I'm back there figuring out what I did wrong." He blinked to ward off tears. "No, I don't want that pill. Put it back in your pocket."

I sighed and did as I was told.

"Let's just forget the whole conversation," he said, turning his head away to regain his composure. A minute later, he had transformed into the Bernie I knew again, the cheerful man who rarely talked about his past. "So tell me more about Litminov's lab," he said, leaning so far back in his chair that he made it squeal. "What are going to do there?"

"I don't know yet," I said.

"Well, how long are you staying?"

"Don't know that either." And now I was standing up heading for the door. I knew he was warming up to lecture me about my career again. "Listen, Bernie, I'm sorry I tried to push this on you," I told him.

He waved his hands at me, as if to say, "Forget about it."

"You don't mind taking over my Methodology class, do you?"

He shrugged. "Fine. I'll do it. As long as you understand my objections."

"I do," I said. And then I was out the door and wandering down the hallway, dim fluorescent lights crackling overhead, posters for cheerleading tryouts and theater groups bristling with punctuation marks, the smell of incipient Catholicism everywhere. I was alone with my pill now. It was a new kind of loneliness that I'd discovered this week. The students in my classes, my colleagues who congregated by the Xerox machine, Edie, Bernie, my brother who called from California—they all plodded through their lives one stolid moment after the next, always forward, forward, forward like little clocks. They did not go backwards. But I did. And already that had made me a different kind of creature. I needed, now, to be among my kind. In six days I would drive to upstate New York, and I would meet people who had taken Mem, who knew the drug, who studied it. Until then, I was just doing time.

Chapter
5

Somewhere in Connecticut, I reached through my car's window to hand three dollars to the woman in the tollbooth. A gate lifted, and I burst out onto the highway. The pavement was bright gray in the sun. Trees whooshed by. Some of the branches had budded out with green fuzz. Everything dazzled.

On any other Thursday, you would have found me hunched in a corner of the faculty dining hall, leafing through *Candide*, a last-minute cram before my Intro to Modern European History lecture at one o'clock, a class I had taught sixteen times before. The odor of meatloaf would permeate the room. Jesus would droop on his crucifix above the salad bar, too bored even to suffer.

But today was not an ordinary Thursday. I pulled into the fast lane. My wheels fizzed against the road. The breeze that leaked in through a window ruffled my hair. The air smelled earthy as wet bark. I felt loose and free—except when I happened to glance at the passenger seat. The cell phone—the one I shared with Edie—lay there, its cord stretching out to the cigarette lighter, sucking the juice out of my Saab. It blinked as it charged, and I could swear that flashing red light was tsk-tsking me. Every time I caught sight of that cell phone, I remembered that I had lied to Edie.

Yesterday, I had made all the arrangements to leave town, except one: I hadn't told my wife. Last night, as I drove home, I had practiced my speech in the car. "Sweetie," I tried, "You remember Phil

Litminov from graduate school? Yes, I know you didn't like him much, but I need to go spend four days with him. Yes, I am going to cut my classes." And like that. Every way I tried to say it sounded unhinged, call in the shrinks, get the butterfly net. When I pulled into our driveway, the light was on the kitchen, making the shadows of trees stretch across the side yard. Sleet spit at me as I crossed the lawn to the house. My satchel hung heavy on my shoulder. I still had no idea what to say to her, but I'd have to say something.

And then I opened the door, and the warm moist air hit my face.

"Hey, Win," Edie said, stirring something on the stove. "Did you eat?"

"Kind of." I was leaning against the refrigerator, grappling with how to begin.

She turned, a spoon half-lifted in one hand, its wooden head splashed with red flecks. "Well, do you want some?"

"No thanks," I said. I swallowed and my Adam's apple seemed to get stuck in my throat. "Listen, Edie, I'm going on a little trip."

"Oh," she said, her eyebrows knitting together. "It's not your Dad again, is it?"

"Actually, it is," I said, crossing my arms across my chest. The lie, which I'd been struggling with in the car, came so easily now. It seemed to leap out of my mouth. "Remember I told you he wasn't feeling so well?"

"You did?" she said.

"Yeah, that's why I went down there last time."

"Oh," she said, puzzled but still willing to believe.

"Well, it turns out he's had a minor stroke."

"God," she said.

"Very minor."

She dropped the spoon on the counter, hurried over to me. I opened up my arms to let her in. "I'm sorry," she said.

"It's going to be fine. They just want to give him some more tests."

"Why didn't you tell me this before?"

"You had enough to worry about."

"Well, from now on tell me, OK?" She craned her neck to gaze up at me. It seemed a long time since her face had been so close, those freckled eyelids and her half-open mouth with the pink sheen of tongue inside. I ran my fingers through her curls and they got caught in the warm tangles, and then I kissed her, seeming to dive with my whole self into the soft and secret places of her mouth. She kissed back and then rested her head on my chest.

"I thought I'd go down there and keep him company, just for a few days. Take him around to the doctors."

"Yes," she said, "you should. I'm sure that would mean a lot to him." With her cheek resting just under my shoulder, I felt her words vibrating through my chest, spreading through me like a shot of whiskey. "You're a good son, Win."

"Anyone would do it," I said. I felt myself growing into the role. I liked being the kind of man who was willing to travel six hours just to sit in the waiting room beside his father, doling out small talk, glossy magazines, peppermints.

Edie seemed to like this man too. She leaned back, blinking up at me, and I knew she was seeing, just for a moment, the man I used to be, the one she loved.

I slid my hand under her shirt, tucking it into the crease of her waist, the moist skin. Edie touched my neck, examining something there.

"You want to, um," I paused, and brushed my lips across her hair. In truth, I was too nervous to ask for it by name—she'd turned me down so many times in the few months that she'd developed a whole repertoire of refusals: the half-asleep mumble, the curt "can't," the squirm away from my touch.

But now she nodded and flicked off the burner switch. It had been weeks—months?—since we'd had sex, and I'm embarrassed to admit how eagerly I stumbled behind her and up those dark stairs. In the bedroom, she peeled her shirt off and wriggled out of her bra. I don't remember how I got my clothes off. It all came so easily, me reared up, resting on my palms, and she twisted around underneath so that I could hit her sweet spot. I'd lost myself in a fog of pleasure when I looked down and caught a flash of her face. I expected to see her mouth open and her eyes turned to gleaming slits, that look of concentrated joy that I knew so well. Instead, I caught her staring up at me, studying me; she turned her head to one side, but it was too late, I'd already read her expression. She had been enduring this, because she wanted to comfort me, because my father had a stroke, which of course, he had not.

When I came, there was little in it except for a sneeze-like relief of a spasm. I rolled off and she wiped herself with some article of our discarded clothing. "That was good," she said, her back to me, not meaning a word of it.

"Yeah," I said, biting down on the word. And then, still naked, I felt my way along through the dim room to the closet and snapped on the light. Blindly, because my eyes were still adjusting, I began to grope around on the top shelf.

"What are you doing?" I heard her say from behind me.

"Looking for my suitcase."

"Why?"

"Because I'm leaving tomorrow morning. Remember?" Now, my fingers had encountered the canvas and the scratch of a zipper. I pulled down the suitcase.

"I thought you meant this weekend. You're going tomorrow? What about your classes?" she said, sliding over to make way for the suitcase on the bed. She'd put on a dress, something she must have found lying on the floor, and it gathered in wrinkles around her breasts and under her arms.

"Bernie will take my seminar," I told her. "I'll cancel the others."

She sighed. "God, Win, you're really going to piss them off."

"Look, Hon," I said, "I have to do this." And at that moment, I meant it; I was in the grip of some compulsion that I could not seem to shake, and I just needed her to turn her attention elsewhere for a few days. I hadn't wanted to lie to her, and I felt, now, ashamed and all the more eager to stuff some pants into the suitcase and be gone. The lie, I told myself, was only temporary. As soon as I'd been to Litminov's lab, as soon as I'd satisfied my curiosity, I would come clean to her.

"All right," she said. "You've got to do what you've got to do."

"Yeah," I said, and sat down on the bed beside her.

"I'm going to call you," she said, impulsively. "Tomorrow. Right after my last class. To find out how the tests went. When's your Dad going to be finished?"

I struggled to keep my voice even. "You don't have to do that." My tongue felt thick in my mouth. It was hard to push the words out. "They won't have the results until Friday anyway."

I felt her stiffen beside me. "But still," she said softly, doubt curling at the edge of her voice.

"The thing is, I'm not sure when we'll be at his apartment." I paused. She must not call Dad's phone. That must not happen. For a moment I considered admitting everything to Edie—the drug and Litminov and the lie I'd constructed just now to cover it all up. I opened my mouth, ready to come clean. But instead of telling her the truth, I found myself saying, "Too bad you'll need the cell phone. Otherwise I would take it."

And that's when Edie came to my rescue; that's when she gave me the equipment I needed to cover my own lie. "I'll be OK. You can have it," she said. "Take it with you. Go ahead."

"But you won't be able to function without it. Remember? You've got to have it on Thursdays."

"I'll manage," she said. "Really. You take it. I want to know where you are."

And that's how the cell phone came to be nestled into the passenger seat of my Saab now, plugged into the cigarette lighter, its cord swinging as I accelerated into the fast lane. She'd promised to call me tomorrow, after her last class. We'd made a date of it: Friday at 4:00. So tomorrow this phone would ring and I'd have to come up with another lie. I'd tell her that Dad's tests had been inconclusive. Or I would tell her the doctors had decided there'd been no stroke after all. Or I would tell her the truth. But for now, I narrowed my eyes against the metal door of the truck ahead, which burned with reflected sunlight. My hands rested on the steering wheel, loose. The hairs on my fingers glowed like filaments of gold. I was heading in the direction of Mem, which felt, right then, like going home.

• • • • •

Was I lost? I'd caught the exit, curled along an off-ramp, and gone straight for five lights, just as Andrea Lu had instructed in the e-mail she sent me. And now I bumped along past Victorian houses that wore the red and yellow-striped awnings of summer, though scraps of snow still clung to their lawns. This wasn't at all what I expected. Shouldn't there be office parks around me? Maybe some corporate logos? Ugly buildings with mirrored windows? I pulled into a driveway and checked the directions again. Yes, I'd followed them perfectly.

"Take a right turn on Sparhawk Street," she'd written, and so I did. It was a country road that wound past meadows and woods, a golf course, a few mansions, a field dotted with steeplechase jumps. Finally, the road turned to gravel and ended with high wooden gate. This, apparently, was it.

I let the car idle with its nose to the gate for a few moments, trying to figure out what to do next. A sudden despair gripped me. The green paint on the fence was peeling off the wood in long fangs. The skeleton of a vine clung to one of the fence posts. For a moment, I was sure Litminov had sent me here as a practical joke. This was someone else's house, maybe, or an abandoned place.

And then I noticed the intercom. It was half-hidden under the branch of a tree, a metal gizmo with a speaker and a half-dozen buttons on its face. I untangled myself from the seatbelt and got out, pushed aside the pine branch and punched a button. "Hello," I said, "I'm here for Phil Litminov."

The speaker crackled, and that was all. I tried again. Finally, a weary female voice issued from the speaker. "Darryl?" she said.

"It's Win Duncan. I'm looking for some kind of lab. I think I must have the wrong –"

While I was still explaining, the gates began to swing open in a slow-motion arc. I saw, first, more gravel road, then trees, then the glitter of water off to the left side. I coiled my long legs back into the car and drove more slowly than necessary, because something about the solemn movement of that gate had put me into a trance. A lake, or maybe it was a pond, lay behind a lace of tree branches and I stole glances at it as I negotiated the bends in the road. I smelled pine. Gravel pinged on the undercarriage of the car. The bittersweet atmosphere of bygone vacations hung in the air.

The house spread out along a hill, shingled and proper, with high turreted roofs and a prince-nez of narrow windows. It was a spinsterish presence, surrounded by bare trees and a skirt of shivering grass. I parked—the only car in the grand, circular driveway—and walked past a porch so old that the wire in the screen had turned greenish.

No one answered the doorbell. I thought of looking through the window, but the windows were lost behind overgrown boxwoods. Finally, I pushed on the door.

"Hello?" I called and entered a gloomy living room. As my eyes adjusted, I could just make out a stairway curling upstairs, a piano, overstuffed chairs in faded fabrics, paintings of ships— it looked as if a high-society family had lived here in the 1970s and then fled, the whole place mothballed in outdated tastefulness.

Just then, a woman bustled into the room. She carried a plate. When she saw me, she halted. "Oh," she said, as if she'd just remembered something.

She didn't seem to be afraid of me, but I held up my hands anyway, palms facing her, to prove my harmlessness. "I think I have the wrong place. I'm lost."

"Lost? Oh I doubt it," she said, in a clipped accent. "I'm Sue Fontaine." She stuck out her hand.

"You're Australian?" I asked.

Her hand was so cold and knobby that it didn't feel like a hand at all, more like some complicated machine. Her blonde hair had been clipped close so that it stood up in spikes, and she was unusually tall for a woman—she could look almost straight into my eyes. "I'm as

American as you," she said, and there was that accent again—Ah-meer-ee-kin. "Sit down," she commanded.

I stood. "Listen, do you know this area?" I said, trying to stick to my role of lost motorist. "Is there an office building nearby? Some kind of laboratory?"

She shook her head, set her plate onto a coffee table and dropped onto a sofa beside it. Dust rose up and a faint smell of mildew filled the room. She batted the air around her with one hand and leaned over the coffee table to cut up the bagel on her plate. "I wish to hell he'd get these cushions cleaned. No, there are no office buildings. But there is a rather nice pond."

I tried again. "I'm looking for Phillip Litminov."

"Well, aren't we all?" Sue Fontaine said, without glancing up from her bagel.

"So you do know him?" I felt my forehead wrinkling. None of this fit together, and the thought of trying to make sense of it exhausted me.

"Of course I know him. Sit down," she said.

And because I didn't know what else to do, I pulled a chair nearer to the sofa and settled into its bumpy cushion. "Is he here?" I said, and I was ashamed of how the question came out—I sounded desperate.

"Not yet." She took a careful bite of the bagel, then dabbed at her mouth with a napkin.

"When?"

She flicked her eyes up at me. They were an icy shade of blue. "Don't be pathetic," she said. "There are enough pathetic men around here. Don't be like the others."

"Where are they—the others?"

"They'll be here soon enough," Sue said. "I always come early. Just because I'm a woman, they expect me to stock the house with food. Put clean sheets on the beds. It's very annoying."

I combed my fingers through my hair, and the scrape of my nails against my skull felt good—one thing, at least, that I could under-stand. "He told me he wanted me here by mid-afternoon. He said it was a *lab* where there would be *testing*."

She laughed, threw one arm up on the back of the sofa, taking pos-session of it. "Oh, he'll test you all right. And you just better hope you pass. Because if you fail, you'll never get through those gates again. And from the looks of it, you'd be pretty sorry about that."

"But when will Litminov get here?"

"'Where's Litminov?' 'When will Litminov get here?'" she mim-icked. Leetmeenov. That's how she said his name. "If you have any sense, you'll stop worrying about that and enjoy the surroundings. Think of it as a holiday."

My jaw was so tight I had to squeeze out each word. "I'm. Not. On. Holiday. Or vacation. Whatever."

"I see that." She touched the spikes of her hair with one hand as if to brush my words off of her. "I was just trying to give you the benefit of my experience." She took another bite of her bagel.

I sighed, feeling my shoulders deflate. "I cancelled two days of classes. I could lose my job because of this."

She folded her legs underneath her, regarded me. "And you did other things too, didn't you, to get here? Worse things."

"As a matter of fact I did. I lied to my wife."

She nodded slowly. She wasn't looking at me now—instead she gazed across the room, as if she were transfixed by the portrait that hung over the fireplace, a businessman with wire-frame glasses and a blue handkerchief in his pocket. When she spoke, she seemed to speak to him. "I hate men who lie to their wives."

"Me too." I leaned forward, wishing I could get her to look at me. "But you have to understand, it's only temporary. After this, I'll go home and tell her everything. By then, you see, I'll know the full story. So it will be easier to explain."

Sue Fontaine stared down at the bagel, silent for a long moment. Finally, she said, "White bread. I don't know what I was thinking." She picked up the plate and padded across the room. By the cant of her shoulders, she broadcast that she did not want to be followed. She'd had enough of me.

• • • • •

I wandered through the house, flipped through old *National Geographics*, searched through drawers—for perhaps an hour I entertained myself this way. When the buzzer went off in the foyer, I found the control panel and pushed the "Gate Open" button without bothering to ask who it was.

"Don't do that," Sue Fontaine said. She had appeared at the top of the stairs wearing a sleep mask on her head, hair-band-style.

"No one else was answering it."

"I would have, eventually," she said. "If the wrong people get in, I'm the one he'll blame."

"The wrong people?" I asked, but she had turned her head at the sound of a car rattling up the gravel road. Her fingers tensed on the banister.

We listened together as doors slammed and men laughed and a

trunk squeaked open. A few minutes later, they exploded into the foyer, two men in topcoats, fresh from some city. They carried brief-cases and weekend bags and six-packs of expensive beer. Sue Fontaine's shoulders had dropped—by her general air of relief I guessed that these men did belong.

"Hey, Doll," the taller one called to her. He must have been about my age, though he moved with the athletic grace of a young jock. "Are we the first?"

"No," she said, gesturing at me with a sideways tip of her head. "There's a new guy."

"Are you Teddie?" the taller one asked.

I shook my head.

"Did you go to Dartmouth?"

"No," I said, standing up. "Why?"

"Everyone went to Dartmouth," Sue explained wearily. "That's where we all met Phil."

I reached out to shake the hands of the tall one and the short one, and we made introductions all around. Then, because I was thinking of other things, I forgot their names.

"Speaking of Litminov, have you heard anything?" I asked. "Is he coming soon?"

The taller guy twitched a lip, a look of disgust so fleeting that I nearly missed it. "Patience," he said. "You need to learn some self-control." Then he turned his back on me.

The other one adjusted his bag on his shoulder. "Hey Sue," he said, "what's for dinner?"

"Fuck off," she said.

He guffawed.

"I left some frozen pizza here last time," the taller guy said to his friend. And they were off in a swirl of black coats and swinging bags, heading around a corner. Sue Fontaine and I remained silent for a moment, listening to the noises from the other end of the house— the slamming of the refrigerator door, laughter, the ker-fizz of a beer bottle opening.

Then she sank down to sit on a stair, her arms wrapped around her knees, her cheek resting against one of the posts of the banister. Something about her stuck me as wrong—she could barely seem to support the weight of her own head.

I took a step toward her, then hesitated, not sure what to do. "Are you all right? You look like you're going to faint."

"I'm fine." She rose wearily. "I'm just going to lie down." She dragged over to the sofa, settled in with her feet on a pillow. She pulled her sleep mask down over her eyes, so that now she resembled some emaciated, weary superhero.

I settled into a plump chair nearby, flipping through a *Reader's Digest* version of *Moby Dick*.

After a few minutes, she said, "Are you still here?"

"Yes," I answered.

"Good," she said.

· · · · ·

Litminov finally showed up some time after ten that night, bursting in the door with a camera tripod under his arm, his jeans half-tucked into motorcycle boots, and Andrea trailing behind. He wore no coat over his t-shirt, and his arms had turned blister-red with cold. A Russian fur cap—the kind with earflaps, favored by members of the Soviet politburo—hid his eyes.

"Hey honey, I'm home," he boomed to the house in general, and then he whirled past me, leaving behind a smell of stale sweat, and headed for the kitchen. Seven or eight guys—they'd arrived over the course of the evening, with their bottles of liquor and their overnight bags—were having a party in there.

"Phil, you made it!" I heard one of them crow.

Sue Fontaine blearily lifted her mask from her eyes. She smoothed down her hair, slapped at her sweater to get the dust off of it. "The moment we've all been waiting for," she said dryly.

I stood up. My heart pounded. The asshole! How dare he make me wait all day and then ignore me. I headed down the hall to the kitchen but did not enter—instead I leaned against the doorframe, fuming. All the things I wanted to say formed a tight bubble in my chest.

The men stood in a knot around him. They were offering beers, backslapping, laughing at jokes he hadn't told yet.

"Hey Phil," one of them said, "look what I found." He pulled a threadbare baseball cap out of his back pocket.

Litminov took it and studied its insignia. "Cool," he pronounced, and then threw it on the counter.

He leaned against the stove, drinking a beer. The others chattered about some guy they knew who'd bought a thirty-foot sailboat and planned to live on it. Litminov yawned and then examined a piece of notepaper he pulled from his pocket.

I stayed in the doorway, considering my options. I wanted to give Litminov a piece of my mind, but I couldn't seem to find the proper opening. It's more difficult than you might imagine to get angry at someone who is acting as if you don't exist; there's the danger that they might continue to ignore you, in which case you'll look ridiculous.

Better yet, I could leave. Just walk through the living room, climb into my car and drive away. I put my hand in my pocket and felt my keys, the jagged edges digging into my palm, the cold of the metal.

And then, just when I'd given up on him, Litminov nodded in my direction. "Hey Duncan, you ready for our little experiment?"

"What?"

He stuck out his tongue and tapped it with one finger, as if dropping a pill there.

"Now?" I said, ashamed of my own voice, which turned high and nasal at moments like this, just when I wanted it to sound like a growl.

A few of the men laughed, but in a strained way that sounded like barking. Others traded glances. They jiggled their beers and waited for my answer.

"OK," I said.

"Let's go upstairs where it's quiet," Litminov said and cast an accusing glance at his entourage. A few of them tittered with laughter.

"We're not so bad," the tall guy said.

"Yes you are." Litminov pushed past them and towards me. "Come on," he commanded.

Then I was hurrying to catch up with him as he tromped through the living room, up the staircase, and along a dimly lit hallway with a deep carpet that muffled our footsteps, past prints of poppies and hydrangeas, the stems creeping to the edge of the frames. He stopped short and I nearly ran into him. "This'll do," he said and pushed open one of the doors along the hall.

The only light glimmered from the iridium-green face of an electric clock that seemed to peer at us out of the dark, and from the moon that branded itself, like a glowing sickle, in the top pane of one window. As my eyes adjusted, I could make out the slab-like shape of a bed, the moonlight cascading over the tops of three pillows. Litminov seemed perfectly comfortable in the murk. He stalked across the room, and I heard a "thunk" as he put his beer down on some table I couldn't see.

I groped along the wall until my fingers encountered a switch. I toggled it, but nothing happened. "The light won't turn on," I said. I wanted desperately to flash brightness in here, to dispel my unease, the claustrophobic intimacy of two men in a dark bedroom.

"The bulb burned out a while ago. That's fine with me," Litminov said. "You start taking Mem, you get so you hate the light."

I shuffled into the room, one hand out in front of me, feeling into the velvety dark. "So this is it?" I said peevishly.

"What do you mean, 'This is it?'" Litminov landed on the bed. The mattress creaked and chattered and seemed to suck for breath under him.

"This is where we're doing the grand experiment?" My voice shook. "In a bedroom with the light burned out?"

"Yeah," he snapped.

"You told me it would be a lab."

"It is."

"You said a lab," I insisted, my voice rising. "With doctors and heart monitors and beakers."

"I *never* mentioned beakers, my friend."

I was standing over him now, my arms crossed, gazing down at the pale blur of his face. His smell wafted up—sweat and something else. Pine pitch.

"Why didn't you just tell me the truth? OK, so it's not a lab, fine. But why tell me to be here six hours before you even show up?" I said. "I busted my ass to get here."

He laughed and the whole bed shook, creaking and squeaking underneath him. "Oh, he's berating me for tardiness. That's funny, considering you're the one who stole rare pharmacological samples from my apartment. Do you have any idea how much those pills were worth?" He threw a pillow at me. It hit me in the leg and landed at my feet with a sad, wilted plop.

My breath came out of my throat loudly. "Oh," I said, "that."

"Yes that, my friend."

"I'm sorry," I finally said. "I was going to send them back to you, but. . . . Listen, I still have one of the pills left. It's in my car. I'll get it right now."

"No," he said. "Don't. Sit down."

I looked around at the vague shapes that hovered around us in the room. "There's no chair."

"Sit on the other side," he said.

And so I stumbled around the end of the bed, and perched on its edge, leaning one arm awkwardly on a pillow.

"You know what happened in this bed forty-one years ago?" he asked, gazing up at the ceiling, his tone turning thoughtful, yet also, in its own way, menacing.

I made the smallest of sounds in my throat.

"I was conceived right here." He threw his arms up and the mattress twitched underneath me. "This is where sperm met egg, DNA raveled together, I came into being."

"You mean that this house. . . ?" I began, but didn't know how to end the question.

"I grew up here."

"So that's why," I said, suddenly sure I had gotten it, the key to all Litminov's contradictions, the reason he'd called this house a laboratory, even his initial obsession with developing a memory drug. "There's something here, some memory connected with this house, that compels you," I went on. "Something happened here."

"No," he pronounced. "That's just dumb." He reached for his beer on the bedside table, took a gulp. "Listen, forget the house. I'm tired of the house. I want to know what you did with the pill."

"I told you—it's in my car."

"No, damn it. The other pill."

"Well," I said, feeling my brow furrow, "I took it."

"I *know* you took it. But where did you go once you were high? You could relive any moment in your life. So what did you choose?"

I opened my mouth, and no words came out. Finally, I said, "I just ended up somewhere randomly."

He took another plug of beer, waiting for me to go on.

"I was six years old, in a canoe."

"Yeah?" he said. "And?"

"I peed in my pants."

He laughed. "See, Duncan, this is why I keep you around. You could have lost your virginity all over again; you could have won that award again. What was it called?"

"The Whitman," I supplied.

"But instead you pee in your pants." He started to laugh.

I cut him off. "I saw my mother, alive again." For a moment, the air in the dark room vibrated with that statement, with the echo of my mother and her sunglasses, the nervous way she'd gripped the oar. "She was younger than I am now. And so convinced she would go on living." I could hear the urgency in my own voice. It was an enormous relief, I realized, to be able to discuss this with someone else who'd done Mem—even if that someone was Litminov. "I got this incredible urge to tell her how she was going to die."

Litminov chuckled. He was resting his beer bottle on the rise of his stomach, rubbing his thumb tenderly over its neck. "That's just how I felt the first time I saw my mother alive again."

"So why is there that incredible urge to tell them? Even if you could, they wouldn't want to know."

The fabric of his shirt whispered as he shrugged. "After you've taken the drug enough, you get over that."

I slid further onto the bed, crossed my legs, leaned toward Litminov. Suddenly, there was so much I wanted to ask him. We would figure out this drug, the two of us. "I wrote down everything that happened when I was on the Mem," I told him and then explained the notations I had developed in order to describe my experiences—Win-6, Win-32, Win-40, etc. I was talking fast now, taking shallow swallows of air, because I was excited, finally, to be able to spill all the ideas I'd been keeping to myself during these last days. "This drug could change the way we regard the self," I went on, feeling myself grow professorial, the bed transforming into my podium, Litminov into an audience of worthy colleagues. "On Mem, you become several different selves collaged together, mixed up like samples on a hip-hop album. It lets you understand that there's no unity to consciousness, only bricolage. It's the most postmodern of drugs."

He laughed appreciatively. "Oh, you're good, Duncan. That's why I brought you in. Do you think any of those bozos downstairs cares what the drug *means*? No. They just want to get high. But you see it."

"I hope so," I said quietly. It was the first time in years that I had felt I'd found a job I could do better than anyone else: I could figure out what Mem meant. And isn't the great desire of human beings, beyond all else, to do what we are fit for?

"Are you familiar with Thomas De Quincey?" I asked. And then, because Litminov obviously wasn't, I told him about how De Quincey swilled up to ten glasses of laudanum a day—but unlike the other addicts of the time, he had recorded his experiences, combining scientific and poetic insight to draw a portrait of the drug. I told him that *Confessions of an English Opium Eater* became an international bestseller; and that even though De Quincey said he had written the book to warn people away from the drug, he'd also made opium sound so intriguing, so much a tool of self-understanding, that the book had the opposite effect—in the years after its publication, opium use tripled in England. "In one fell swoop, he completely changed the way we see drugs, forever," I said. "He created a new literature of pharmacology."

"And," Litminov interrupted, "You want to be De Quincey."

* * * * *

For weeks, I'd been burning to find out what, exactly, Litminov planned to do when we took Mem together. He'd mentioned some wild night we'd shared years before, some event of enormous significance.

Now, in the moonlit dark, he held out a tiny pill to me, pinched between finger and thumb. I cupped my palm so that he could drop it there. He announced his plan. It was hugely disappointing.

"We broke into fucking Low Library," he laughed, his voice high and eager, a boy's voice. "Remember? You were going to wimp out, but I convinced you to go through with it. We stole some kind of ancient manuscript."

I winced. "Yeah," I said. This was the big event? I remembered Litminov showing up at the door to my apartment, at 1 AM, dangling a ring of keys in front of me—the keys to the library.

Only a few months before, I had won the Whitman—the top humanities prize at Columbia. Ever since, certain people tried to collect me, as if I myself had transformed into a golden trophy. Litminov was one of those people. He always seemed to be catching up to me on the pathways that wound through campus. He called. He dropped by. I had been too lazy to resist the slow encroachment of Litminov into my life. I found it handy to borrow his vintage Yamaha motorbike, a little James Bond machine. And he fascinated me: he was nothing like the other people I'd met in grad school, so in thrall to their dissertations and their job interviews. He was exotic, in that his life was so much easier than mine. We had become friends.

So when Litminov showed up with those keys, suggesting we break into the rare books room at Low Library, I said yes. I'd been scribbling all night, and I was restless, and I didn't think that the keys would work. But we had broken in, and we'd had fun, I suppose, though I couldn't recall the details.

Now, Litminov tilted his head backwards and threw the pill into his mouth. "We should start in the library."

"Sure," I nodded, and then took my own pill.

He lay back onto his pillow, staring at the blackness above us. "You were so uptight back then. But I helped to loosen you up. You were my project, Duncan. I decided 'I'm going to teach this kid how to steal.'"

"Oh," I said, noncommittally. I was beginning to understand why that memory of Low Library was such a big deal to him: he saw himself as the hero of that night, the hero of my life story. Litminov had told me once that taking the drug with a friend made it more intense—now I guessed that this setup might be a lot better for him than for me. He was getting comfortable now, wrestling with a pillow, making the bed shake. "We'll start on the top floor of the library," he instructed. "Let's skip all the stuff that happened before that."

"You've already been there? On Mem, I mean."

"Of course, I've been there," he said, pausing to glug some beer.

Already, the Mem was beginning to tangle my thoughts. I closed my eyes and a vision seemed to crash over my eyelids; I was a small boy, bobbing in the waves at Nag's Head, splashing, making drops of water fly up so that they dangled a moment in the sun; my small chest puffed out to contain the ache of my joy. Christ, what a relief to be back on the drug. Like walking into your house after an awful day. Home again. "I have to stay high forever," I thought, quite distinctly, as the boy levitated on a wave, because it seemed intolerable that I would be banished from this place ever—I had begun to think of all the memories I visited on Mem as rooms in one big house, my house.

A voice boomed over the waves: "Duncan! Where are you?" I thought at first Litmonov's voice must be issuing from huge speakers on the boardwalk. And then I understood that he was talking to me from a few feet away, on a bed in the future, in upstate New York. My eyes fluttered. I saw the hump of his shoulder, glowing in the moonlight, and felt the swaying of the mattress under me, so that I still seemed to be floating on waves.

I had come back into the "present"—but not with any conviction. I was not this man slumped in a bed with his shirt tangled up into his armpits. In fact, I was no longer an "I" but instead a collection of memories that played themselves over and over. It was as if I'd found a way to live as a song or a film or a book. I remembered my father saying to me, "Kid, the world is your oyster," and now, finally, I felt it was, that I had been hardened down to some pearl-ish essence of Win Duncan.

"Duncan?" Litminov said. "Talk to me. Are you in the library yet?"

"No." My mouth, which seemed not exactly to be mine, moved of its own accord. "How?"

"First of all, don't go wandering off. Pay attention. You've got your hand on the—what do you call that damned thing?—the banister. I'm a few steps ahead of you."

As soon as he'd mentioned the banister, I'd felt a memory of it on my fingers, the cold oiliness of the marble that slid under my fingertips as I climbed in the dark, feeling for each next step with my toe. The beam from a flashlight made a polka dot of brightness on the stairs ahead; the light stretched itself over the bends and curves in the stairs and then leapt up to a wall. The young Litminov carried it. I couldn't see much of him except the outline of his body against the flashlight beam. "Look," he said, pointing the beam at a dictionary stand, which leapt up in the light, its fluted column mysterious with shadows. "This place is boring in the day, but not now," he said.

"Yeah," the young Win answered, and the word seemed to reverberate—I realized that I was talking with two mouths, that the Win Duncan who lay in the bed in upstate was speaking along with his younger self, reciting the words he'd said so many years before.

Now, we had stopped before a door, and Litminov pointed the flashlight at its key hole, and I could finally make out his face—his scrawny, beardless cheeks and his forehead, smooth as if he'd had a Botox treatment, but, no, it was no Botox, only time gone backwards, peeling away his worry lines, and mine too, I supposed. "OK," he called in a loud whisper. "Here we go." And the whisper seemed to rumble through my body, because the Litminov who lay beside me on the bed many years in the future said the exact same thing at the same time. And as he did so, the flashlight beam grew a deeper yellow, the jingle of his keys more crisp, and the forgotten smell of coffee that used to float up from my own skin became stronger. I understood now: when we talked along with the memory, we could make it more intense. This is why Litminov needed me. This.

Now Win-28 leaned against a shelf of books. He listened to Litminov scraping a key into the lock. He felt pleasantly jazzed up, alive.

Litminov found the right key, and a bolt turned with a metallic snick and the door to the Rare Books Room cracked open. Litminov dissolved into the darkness within. The young man, me, hurried to catch up. As Win-28 plunged into the room, the air suddenly turned dryer in his nostrils—humidity control. He could sense those ancient books all around him in the profound blackness, inscrutable as stars. The flashlight illuminated one of Litminov's denim thighs and the nubbly surface of the carpet.

Then a voice thundered—at first I thought it came from loudspeaker in the library. But no. Once again, it Litminov was speaking to me from that house in upstate New York, from the future. "Remember what we found? That was one of the fucking weirdest things I ever saw in my life."

As if on command, my memory skipped forward. Instead of standing in the doorway, Win-28 was leaning over a table. Just like that. No transition. A lamp spilled its glow all over the oak tabletop and onto one of his hands—a hand that I hardly recognized as my own, with its thin fingers and yellowish skin stretched over the knuckles, not a wrinkle anywhere.

Next to the hand lay a desperately old folio, bound with a ribbon. We had discovered it squirreled away in the bottom of a locked metal case, with papers scattered over it, as if some librarian had hidden it there. Litminov worked the ribbon off, and ever so carefully, using the tips of his fingers, lifted the first leaf. The thick surface—more like muslin than paper—boiled with an intricate etching. A giant snail slithered over a woman who embraced its fat head. A man received sexual favors from a wild boar. A dwarf with a boot on his head brandished a giant penis that was also an earthworm descending into a hole in the soil. The etching could have been a hundred years old or six hundred; it could have been a masterpiece or a copy. Litminov settled into a chair, using a magnifying glass to study the fine lines. He turned the pages, exclaimed over each one.

Win followed along with him for a while, and then wandered away, curious about what other treasures he might find. He fingered the leather spines on the shelves, pulling out a book now and then without even bothering to read its title, examining the marbled paper and the whispering tissue that protected engravings of sea shells and bewigged men and galaxies.

"There's some amazing stuff over here," he called.

"Wait a sec," Litminov called back.

Now Win opened a book at random, to a flyleaf, where he came across a signature: "T. De Quincey." Win knew of him, but had never been interested. Now, though, it was as if he'd glimpsed something essential about De Quincey in the way that signature slanted perilously on the page, as if it was about to tumble out of the book entirely.

The hair prickled on the back of Win's neck. He touched the brown T with the tip of his pinkie. This is why he'd gone into history—for these moments when he seemed to travel backwards in time and visit the dead.

Win lifted his eyes from the page. He surveyed the labyrinth of shelves, the aisles that disappeared into gloom where the light from the desk lamp couldn't reach. All of a sudden, he knew he would write a masterpiece one day. The future would unfurl before him like a red carpet. Applause would thunder. A woman would stand on her tiptoes to adjust his tie for an awards dinner. Win touched his tongue to his upper lip, the soft unpuckered flesh of a young man's mouth.

"Hey, check this out," Litminov called to him from the other side of the bookshelf. Win slid the book back into the slot. He found Litminov kneeling on the floor, his army jacket splayed before him; he was busy taping one of the etchings onto the fabric, so he could wear it out of the library. Win watched him crawling around on the floor with the tape, without really seeing what was before him. Win felt giddy, still, with his sudden knowledge of how tremendous it would be, his life, for all the joys that hovered before him. Do you know what that's like, to taste for a moment a twenty-eight-year-old's arrogance when you are forty? It is beyond delicious.

• • • • •

I woke from a profound, bland sleep. My eyes ached. Hoisting myself up to lean against the headboard, I tried to remember where the hell I was. How had I ended up in this strange room with the cracked walls and a door opening into a pink-tiled bathroom? It took a long time for me to piece together the answers: It was morning in upstate New York and I'd just slept off a Mem trip.

Litminov had vanished from the bed, leaving behind nothing but creases in the coverlet. After we had come down from Mem the night before, he'd handed me two sleeping pills and a bottle of flat beer. "Better take these," he'd said, "or you're going to feel mighty twitchy."

"That happened to me last time," I had said, guiding the pills to my mouth in the dark, tasting them, bitter, on my tongue. "It was awful. I thought I'd scratch my skin off. Why does it do that?"

I had heard—rather than saw—Litminov shrug his shoulders, the rustle of his shirt against the headboard. "We think it's got something to do with the way the drug excites your nervous system. Memories aren't just stored in your brain, you know; they're in your hands and arms and the muscles of your back." He went on like that, explaining in a low, even voice—not the least bit twitchy himself. Before he got to the end of his lecture, I had fallen asleep.

Now, I sat up. The room, which I had come to know in the darkness, revealed itself in the dove-gray light of morning. It was almost bare, except for the bed and a dresser. The only sign of Litminov was one motorcycle boot on the floor, tipped on its side.

I leaned over to check the clock on the bedside table: it was just after five o'clock. Awfully early. Aside from some murmuring from far off, the house was silent, as if it too had been dosed on Mem and was dreaming its past. A bird swooped across one of the panes of the window, and I noticed that the sky did not look right for morning. All of a sudden, my sense of time, of where I floated inside the day, shifted. It was five o'clock in the evening.

I'd been unconscious for maybe fifteen hours. As this realization sunk in, my cheeks got hot and my heart banged. I'd forgotten to do something, something important. It took me a minute to figure out what was wrong: Edie had promised to call me this afternoon. I'd missed her.

I could picture the cell phone lying on the seat of my car, half-tucked into one of the cracks in the leather, its red message light flashing like a tiny emergency. An hour ago that phone had rung and rung. What had she thought, when I wasn't there to answer? Had she called Dad? Or had she simply shrugged and gone back to her manuscript, the Xeroxed copy of the madwoman's scrawl, over which she marked notes in red: "Tittup" = a horse's canter.

I had to tell her the truth. I'd put it off for weeks, but that wouldn't work anymore. It was time. I would call her now. "Edie," I rehearsed silently to myself as I searched for my shoes, "I'm not with Dad. I'm in upstate New York."

I slid my feet to the floor, and a wave of nausea hit; I had to breathe deeply until it passed. I hadn't eaten last night; I'd taken three pills and slept for half a day. Downstairs, in the kitchen, I found a loaf of bread and wolfed down a few slices. I hadn't been this hungry in a long time, and I'd forgotten how desperate an act eating could be. Where was everyone? The living room was empty, my coat crumpled under the piano. I shrugged it on, opened the front door. The cold hit me like a punch in the face. My little Saab hunched under a bare tree. As I walked toward it, the world lurched around me—gravel, branches, darkening sky, shrubs, tire tracks frozen in mud, cracked birdbath. The passenger door squealed as I swung it open. I grabbed the phone and scrolled through the messages. They were all names I didn't recognize—Edie's students, I assumed. Edie herself had not called. Not at all, even though she'd promised. I tried her at her office. She did not pick up. I left a breathless, strangled message. Then I leaned against the side of the car and tried to calm down. It was OK; she'd be back soon. She'd gone to the gym or to meet a friend at the Thai place for dinner. Maybe she'd called but hadn't left a message. Surely, there was some explanation. She was not having an affair, I told myself, and it was stupid to jump to that conclusion. But I remembered catching sight of her a few weeks ago, walking across the quad with Gerry McBride, Dean of Humanities, our boss. Her hands had been flying in the air as she explained something to him, and he'd leaned in close, and there'd been a moment when I wondered, "Is that why she's been so distant?"

The passenger door was still open, shivering on its hinges when a gust of wind came up. I leaned over to close it and noticed the gleaming gold key stuck in the lock of the glove compartment. I'd put my last pill inside there, next to the car registration. Now, I felt I should have the pill in my back pocket. The next time I saw Litminov, I could offer it to him, a formality so he couldn't say I'd stolen it. I knew he'd let me keep it.

So I opened the glove compartment, found the envelope, stuck it in my wallet. Then I headed down the hill behind the house, shoes skidding on the stiff grass. The pond had frozen around its cattails, darkness seeping into the surface of the ice. I stood with my hands shoved into my pockets and listened to creaking noises. Looking out at that pond, I remembered another pond a long time ago, on the Cape, where Edie and I had skinny-dipped under a moon so big it seemed to have been plucked from a Mother Goose book. I wanted her now. I wanted everything to be OK. The freeze had crept into our marriage so slowly I hadn't noticed at first, but now it had come to my attention that I might lose my wife. I needed to leave this place tonight. I would find Litminov, tell him I was leaving, and then I would drive home to Edie.

I made my way toward the house, navigating the lawn by the light that spilled out of a picture window. I let myself in through a back door. Heat hit my face. I seemed to be in a basement storage room. Someone was moaning. The sound led me to a hallway, lit with one bulb. I heard it again—a woman's groan followed by a few indistinct words. I crept past a bathroom that smelled of chlorine and mildew. Ahead, through an open door, I could just discern the flash of white skin, naked people on a bed.

"Good, good," came a voice that I knew—Litminov. "Now under the table. Catch up with me," he commanded. It was just the way he'd spoken to me last night when he was high on Mem. He sounded like an indulgent, drunk father issuing an order to his child.

What were they *doing* in there? I stood just at the edge of the doorway, squinting into the gloom. Litminov was stretched out on his back, a woman beside him, half-hidden behind his bulk. At first, it was hard to look at anything but Litminov's belly, that obscene bulge of flesh bisected with a line of black hair. Then the woman squirmed around in his arms, and I saw her blonde hair. Sue Fontaine. She was naked, too, her skin almost bluish, with her eyes squeezed shut and her face tipped up to the ceiling. She appeared to be trying to read something on the inside of her eyelids. She mumbled something in a low voice, almost a whisper. And now she sat up further and I was able to see her chest.

She'd been scooped out. Where her right breast should have been, she was hollow. Nothing there at all, except for a shallow depression. Even more troubling, a crooked pair of lips grimaced near her breast-bone. No, not lips. It was a scar. I tightened my grip on the doorframe; I did not want to see this, but at the same time, I could not turn away. She lifted an arm, and the lips stretched into a leering smile.

"Just relax," Litminov said and he reached up and cupped her only breast. The bear paw of his hand swallowed it.

Her eyelids fluttered. "Hold them both," she murmured. "Play with the nipples."

Litminov lifted his other hand to finger the breast that wasn't there. "Mmmm," he groaned as he fondled the air.

My eyes, seemingly of their own accord, watered. I was moved by Litminov's gesture. It was the last thing I'd expected from him, the way he gave that breast back to her. And now I was retreating from that bedroom, moving toward a flight of stairs, which I climbed in darkness, as quietly as I could, to keep from disturbing them.

I trudged down the hall to the living room. Two men were slumped in armchairs, meditatively sipping from highball glasses. I nodded to them as I hurried past and jogged up to the bedroom where I'd just slept—I wanted a shower, or something. I wanted water on my face at least. It was dark now, nighttime and there was, of course, no way to turn on the light so I found my way along in the gloom with one hand on the wall, across a floor turned silver by moonlight. In the bathroom, I felt along tile on the wall until I hit the bump of a light switch. This one worked. When I flicked it on, the light was sudden and surprising, bouncing off the pink bathtub, gleaming in the medicine-cabinet mirror. I turned on a tap and water splashed into the sink, the color of urine. When it ran clear, I washed my face. Inside the medicine cabinet, there was no aspirin, just boxes and boxes of sleeping pills.

Red prickles of five-o'clock shadow had crawled up my cheeks. I looked god-awful. I stared into my own eyes in the mirror, but it was Litminov's fingers I kept thinking about, how he had stroked the invisible nipple with such tenderness. Maybe, because of the drug, he really could see that breast. He might have been making love to the seventeen year-old Sue Fontaine, or the twenty-five year-old. There had been such an air of comfort in that room, as if the two of them had found a home in each other. When had I last known that kind of ease with another person?

Christ, how I wanted to time-jump back to that studio apartment on West 114th, where years ago Edie and I slept until noon under cowboy blankets she'd brought from Montana. That tiny apartment had wrapped around us like a shell, cupping us in our own, newly discovered universe. In those first feverish weeks we had been together, we only used the lamp with the yellow bulb in it, and I got used to seeing Edie's face half-lit, in a chiaroscuro glow, her indistinct eyes peering up at me, her mouth a blur. Then the yellow bulb burned out and we replaced it with a white one, her face suddenly vivid before me, still beautiful, but with the ti-niest wrinkles and blackheads. We fell into ordinary love, serviceable enough to keep us happy. And then years later, we lost even that.

I drained the water in the sink, watching it glug-glug away. There was a towel hanging in the shower, and I reached in to dry my hands on it, waving them around in the terry cloth. It was then, with my hands moving around abracadabra-style inside the fabric that the idea struck. Edie might be fucking someone else right this very moment. I might have lost her. Our marriage might have already, for all intents and purposes, ended. But did it matter?

I owned her past. I had Mem. I could summon up the girl in the yellow light, or the woman who pranced beside me down Mulberry Street, or the wife in the blue wool hat. And I could edit her. All the Edies who'd delighted me, I would revive; and the other Edies would dissolve into forgetfulness. With a flourish, I let the towel fall back into place, and adjusted the hard-on that pressed against my zipper. I reached for my wallet as I padded back into the darkness of the bed-room and lay down on the mattress.

Now I had the pill pinched between finger and thumb. I could go to her right now, that young Edie who'd once reared over me on a fu-ton, that girl who would do anything for me. Or to earlier girlfriends. I could cheat on Edie with the ones who came before her, Julie and Laura and even sixteen-year-old Shauna.

The pill was on my tongue now, a hard little bump. I pushed it against the roof of my mouth, savoring that familiar, pungent flavor. It tasted of sex.

• • • • •

"Want some?" someone said.

"Huh?" I peeled open my eyes. Sue Fontaine hovered above me, proffering a bag full of what appeared to be tortilla chips. I struggled to a cross-legged position on the bed. Christ, was I naked? I glanced down and was relieved to find that I wore khakis and a white shirt, even though the last I remembered, I'd had on nothing but a wristwatch, crammed into the backseat of an Impala sedan with my high-school girlfriend, receiving my first ever blow-job.

"I thought you'd probably be hungry," Sue Fontaine said, and took a step toward me so that she could drop the bag in front of me.

"Thanks," I said, reaching out for them. I was ravenous.

As I stuffed chips into my mouth, she regarded me—and I suddenly became aware of how grungy I must look, the stubble on my cheeks and the slept-in shirt that clung to my unshowered skin and my bare feet with yellow toenails. She crossed her arms over a fisherman's sweater—pristine, cream-colored wool. "Just because we're abusing drugs doesn't mean we should neglect personal hygiene," she chided.

"True." I snuck a glance at her chest. Underneath the heavy sweater, she seemed to have two completely normal breasts. Maybe she was wearing some kind of prosthesis. "Where's Litminov?" I asked.

"That question again. Everyone's always asking that question," she shook her head, in mock dismay. "He's gone. Back to the city."

"Already?"

"He had things to take care of."

"This house," I said. "His parents left it to him when they died. When he was in college."

She nodded.

"It looks as if he hasn't changed anything since."

"He hasn't," she said, folding her arms even tighter against her chest, as if she was cold.

"So. . . ," I said, readjusting myself on the mattress, trying to make sense of this information. "So the house. . . . The drug. . . . What's the deal?"

She rolled her eyes, and shook her head, theatrically fed up with my questions. "As if I'm the authority. He's crazy. That's the simple explanation."

"How do you know him anyway?" I leaned toward her, pushing the bag of chips out of the way—I'd been wanting to ask her the question ever since I met her.

"You're wondering why I'm here, aren't you?" She was squinting down at me, her head tilted. "I'm not the kind of woman you'd expect to find tagging around after Phil. I speak four languages. I used to be a rarities collector for one of the biggest antique houses in New York, for God's sake. I'm better than all this. Is that what you meant to say?"

"I suppose so." I realized why she'd been so annoyed with me that first time we met: It was not that I had asked too many questions but that I asked too few. I hadn't bothered to notice her. "So what *are* you doing here?" I asked.

She took a deep breath. "Cancer." She let the word reverberate in the room for a moment before she went on. "They say it's all through my body. But there is a chance I can beat it."

I nodded, because Sue Fontaine seemed like a person who would scoff if I offered an "I'm sorry." Instead, I let the silence of the room speak for me, the hum of a heater in the basement offering my condolences.

"How old are you?" she asked, narrowing her eyes.

"Forty."

"I'm thirty-eight." It was an accusation. "Younger than you. Can you imagine what it must be like?"

I ran my hand over the stubble on my cheeks. "No, I can't."

"If you knew you might die, wouldn't you take Mem every chance you could get?" Now she had fixed her gaze on a corner of the room where weak sunlight hovered on the floor. "I was on the track team in high school. Long distance. I had incredible endurance. Grit, my coach used to say. He wanted me to go to the Nationals. So that's what I do on Mem. I run as hard as I can in that healthy body. It's fantastic."

"And that's all," I said. "You take the drug and you just . . . run? Don't you do other things?"

"Sometimes," she said, blinking slowly. "But I'm always disappointed. Running is the best."

I held her gaze. "What about when the Mem wears off? I would think that would be kind of awful."

"Why?"

"Well," I began, not sure how to put it without offending her. "One minute you're running, and then you wake up and you're here. . . ." I made two chopping motions with my free hand, by which I meant to show the distance between a girl running and a woman with cancer, the expanse of desire in between.

She shook her head slowly. "You've got to understand, Duncan. The drug is merciful."

I started, a little, at the sound of my own name—she might be calling me by my last name, but still it sounded strangely intimate on her tongue.

"After you've taken enough of it, the present moment begins to seem . . . arbitrary," she went on. "I can be that girl flying around the track whenever I want. So who cares about all this?" she flicked her hand to indicate our general surroundings. "Who cares that there's dust all over this bureau? Who cares that I can't do my job anymore? That's only the future. The more I take the drug, the more I become myself—that jolly girl who has her whole life ahead of her."

"So you use it as a kind of pain killer," I said.

"It's more than that. It fills in some hole that's opened up in me. It's not a pain killer so much as a prosthesis."

I tried, then, to resist the impulse to glance down at her breast—the one that I knew wasn't there.

"Phil wants me to write a statement," she went on. "He wants me to document how Mem has helped me. 'Get everything on paper, now, before you're too sick to write,' he says. Moments like that, you almost want to throw the pills in his face. But, still, he's right. When the trouble starts, he'll need all the statements and testimonials he can get."

"Trouble?" I said.

"He's handing out the drug to every loser who shows up at his door. I've told him to be discreet. But that's not his way. How long do you think all this can go on?" She waved her hand in front of her, as if to indicate the entire house, sweeping it all away with one dismissive gesture. "Anyway, Phil can take care of himself. But the drug—oh, the drug is going to need a lot of help. It will need our protection, Duncan. What happens when everyone else finds out about it? They'll want to ban it. Make it illegal."

"Maybe they should." I was standing up now, leaning against the wall. Sue Fontaine was a tall woman, but I was taller still, and I could see the top of her head, the bits of scalp that showed through the spiky blonde hair. It must have grown back only recently, I realized, after the chemo. "We don't even know yet how safe it is. I would have to understand far more about this before I took a position on it."

She fixed me with those startling eyes—pale, pale blue, as if sickness had soaked the color from her. "Are you so cruel," she said, "that you would keep this drug a secret from a person like me, a person suffering? I don't know how I would have gotten along without it in the last few months. Every cancer patient, every AIDS patient, everyone in pain should have it."

"Yes, well," I stuttered, "but that's different."

"Not different. Because if it's made illegal, then no one will have it, even the people like me. Right now, before that happens, we have a responsibility to tell everyone what it is. If I have to present myself as the pathetic victim of cancer, well so be it. We have to give this drug a human face."

I leaned forward. "You keep saying 'we.' You want me to do something. You want—what?"

She pursed her lips, considering how to put it. After a moment, she said, "You could be a lot of help to us."

I stuck my hands in pockets, rattled my car keys. "But how?"

"You've got that look. That TV look. And you're a professor. And Phil says you've won all kinds of prizes. You could be the one who goes on the ten o'clock news and makes the public see the value of this drug, everyone, even the healthy people." She had taken a step forward, and now stood just a smidge over the line of my personal space, so that I had the urge to back away. But I was against the wall and I couldn't.

"I hate to break it to you, but I have zero influence. I'm just a washed-up academic." I was, suddenly, exhausted. Out the window, the sky had turned white, as it does on winter mornings; the branches of bare trees covered it with cracks; the world out there, all fissures and fractures, and people dreaming of escape, seemed way too inscrutable, too huge, for me to affect in even the slightest way.

"You could do it if you wanted to," she said. "You're perfectly capable."

"No, I'm not."

"Yes," she said. "You are."

Chapter
6

I drove back to New Hampshire. When I took the turn into my own neighborhood, the car glided past hills of snow. Every house had its own pile out front, so much extra snow that no one knew where to put it, snow that had gone gray as newspaper, snow in lumps like the pills on old sweaters, snow that kids didn't even want to play with because there was too much of it.

In front of our house sat my own personal pile. How many hours had I spent shoveling, my shoulder aching, ice water seeping into my boots? And after all that work, it had snowed while I was gone. The first week in April might as well have been goddamned January. The driveway had turned white again, and I had to shift into first gear to get up the incline. I rolled into the garage, angling so I could fit my Saab beside Edie's car. For a moment, I stayed packed into the seat, listening to the car creak and groan as it cooled. It seemed to me as if I had taken a wrong exit back in New York somewhere. If only I'd turned off onto another highway, I might have driven to that studio apartment on 114th Street with its murky yellow light. Or maybe I could have returned to the apartment on 95th where I scribbled on legal pads and lived on takeout from La Taza De Oro. I belonged in those places. Not here.

I sat, parked in my own garage, staring through the windshield at all the equipage of my own recent past—boxes piled up in the corner with my labels on them, the paint can with red drips down its side, the brass fixtures that I had bought at Home Depot—but none of it made sense to me. Why had I cared so much about those hinges? Why had I bothered to make a box for extension cords? My own life was a foreign country where I did not speak the language. I wanted to go home, to my real home, which was not this place but somewhere long ago.

Wearily, I stepped out of the car, and made my way across the yard, toward the back door of the house. Halfway there, I stumbled. Something had tripped me up, something black and half-hidden under the snow. I reached down and lifted a corner of the thing, and it unfurled underneath my hand—a pair of pants, my dress pants to be exact, wool with chalk pinstripes. I shrugged and slung them around my neck like a scarf. Inside, I draped them across a chair to dry.

"Edie," I called, but got no answer, so I trudged upstairs. I roamed all through the house until I found her in the extra room we used as an office. For a moment, I lingered in the doorway and watched. She wore headphones, nodding to music that I couldn't hear, leaning toward her computer monitor, typing in intense bursts. The light fell into the hollow of her cheekbone, and I saw what a sharp-edged woman she had become.

It had been so different the night before, when I'd been high on Mem. She had rushed toward me—that lost, long-ago Edie—with a suitcase dangling from her hand and a black cap hiding her hair. "Oh," she had said, "Win. You really did come." She seemed to taste my name in her mouth, a delicacy. Her face had been rounder then, with glasses that were always in danger of sliding down her nose. You could still see a shadow of the awkward teenager she'd once been back in Montana, when she worked the register in her father's bookstore. She dropped the suitcase on the carpet and made a movement toward me, as if she wanted to fall into my arms, but then stopped herself. "You didn't have to meet me," she said.

It was true. I didn't have to. We'd only slept together once so far. But I'd ridden the subway out to the airport anyway. I reached down and picked up the suitcase—so light it had seemed like a prop in a play.

Then, suddenly overcome by emotion, Edie had grabbed my arm and hugged it. "It's good to see you. Tell me what you did while I was gone. Tell me everything," she said. And so, striding along, I regaled her with details of my research, and in her company I felt myself transforming into a more fascinating man, my coat swirling around my knees, my ideas curling out all around me like a filigree, like the halos that saints wear in medieval paintings. She had walked beside me with a quick skipping step, adjusting her glasses, laughing.

How I wished I could find that Edie in the house now. But no, the cadaverously beautiful woman in the desk chair—with her naked eyes and her velvet jacket and her jagged profile - was not my Edie at all. And now she pivoted in her chair and caught sight of me.

"Oh." She pulled off the headphones. "You're back."

"Yup." I took a few steps forward and leaned over her to kiss her.

She pulled away, wincing. "Don't."

And then I knew. I'd been trying to convince myself, during the five-hour drive this morning, that everything would be OK, that Edie still didn't know and I would have a chance to explain myself. But now I saw that everything would not be OK. Not at all. "You're mad," I said.

She hauled one booted foot onto the desk and then the other, leaned back in her chair and glared up at me. "You know when I figured out you were lying? When I saw you putting maps in your suitcase. Since when do you need a map to drive to Manhattan?" Already, something fundamental had shifted between us. We were, for an entire string of seconds, not a couple anymore. "As soon as you were out the door," she said, "I called Bernie."

I let myself fall into the other desk chair, which bobbed underneath me in a series of panicked creaks. "Bernie," I said.

Now she'd turned away from me; she was speaking to her computer monitor. "He didn't want to rat you out. But in the end, he did. Litminov. I can't believe you've gotten tangled up with that creep. And your adventures in pharmacology." She made a clicking sound, as if to say that she had no words for her disgust. "At first I didn't believe Bernie; I didn't think you'd lie to me, not like that. And I didn't see how a drug like that could exist. But it does exist, doesn't it? This memory drug."

"Yeah," I said, and the word seemed to shrivel in my throat.

"Oh yeah, and I just bet the memories are real. Like when an acidhead finds out that the universe is made out of rubberbands. Yeah, that's real too."

"No." I said. "Bernie didn't explain it right. He just doesn't get it."

"Oh he gets it. You wouldn't believe the excuses he made for you. You've had a terrible year. You're going through a crisis. You need my support. I should just be patient. Etcetera." She swiveled toward me. "Patient," she said and shivered at the word. "You've been mean to me for the last year. Always sniping."

I took a deep breath. "Did you bury my pants in the yard?"

She crossed her arms, let her head drop back, seeming to consult the ceiling for an answer. "No," she finally said. "I didn't bury them. That would be going entirely too far. I threw them out the window. I was going to throw the rest of your clothes out too, but then I stopped myself before I turned into a cliché." She let her boots drop to the floor—bang! bang!—then leaned forward, regarding me through narrowed eyes, and I was afraid for a moment she'd burst into tears. But she didn't. "You lied to me," she said. "And *why*? So you could go take drugs with *Litminov*? What the hell has come over you?"

"You've got to understand. I've stumbled onto something huge here, Edie." I went on like that, trying to make her grasp the enormity of the situation.

She sighed impatiently, waiting for a moment when she could interrupt.

"Look," I said, in a final bid to win her over, "why do you think I tried so hard to get my hands on this drug? Because of you, Edie. I wanted to go back to those times when we were happy. I wanted to be with you."

"Me." She covered her eyes with one hand. "You used this stuff to. . . ." Her words trailed off.

"Remember that old apartment on 114th, and the studio you had downtown. Christ, Edie, that was so amazing." I was speaking loudly now, the way I did when I lectured a class on a point that the students were too obtuse to understand. "You've forgotten what it was like. But I've been back there; I've seen it. You have no idea what we've lost."

Edie had curled into herself, one elbow against her chest, her hand still obscuring her face. "You're giving me the creeps." Finally, she let her hand slide down to her lap and stared at me absently. "So you took this drug," she began, slowly, "and you traveled back into your memories, like when we first met and that crap."

"Exactly."

"Did you have sex with me?"

My cheeks grew hot. "Well, yes, among other things."

She closed her eyes. "That's such a violation," she said.

"No," I began, "you don't get it."

But she was already on her feet, holding her chair in front of her legs, like a shield. "Oh yes, I get it," she said in a flat tone, resigned more than angry. "It's porn. You take that pill and you watch me, over and over."

"It wasn't like that," I said. "I was remembering *you*, not just your body."

"And for your information, I was miserable back then."

"You were?" This caught me by surprise—I had always thought of New York as the Eden from which we'd been exiled, that golden light of her old apartment, the sound of traffic in the rain like distant applause as we drank coffee and talked, endlessly, of who we would be. Could Edie possibly have been unhappy back then? "Just the other day," I protested, "you were saying how much you missed that Indian place, with the old man who read palms at the table."

"I miss that," she conceded. "But not the rest of it. Win, I was such an under-confident little *shlump* back then. Remember the anxiety attacks I used to have?"

"That didn't happen very often."

She snorted with disgust and glared beseechingly at the ceiling. "Well, clearly you have invented your own version of the past."

"I was just there, Edie. I saw you. But you don't want to hear that. You don't want to remember the good parts."

She exhaled a long sigh. "I'm going out," she said.

"Out? No." Now I was standing too, leaning toward her, as if I meant to follow. "Where are you going?"

"I don't know. School."

"You can't just leave in the middle of an argument."

"Yes, I can." She grabbed her sweater from the desk, put it on, fussed with the zipper, then glared up at me. "And Win? You're not going to like this, but I want you to stay somewhere else. For a couple of days."

The words didn't make sense to me at first. "What?" I said stupidly.

"I need a break from all this. And you do too. Even if you don't know it yet."

I found myself blinking furiously. "So what are you saying? You want me to move out? I can't even sleep downstairs?"

Her eyes darted away from mine. She nodded.

"This is all because I lied?"

"Not just that," she said. "Because we're miserable together. *You're* miserable with me, even if you won't admit it. It's been this way for a long time. We need to be apart to figure out what we're going to do. We shouldn't be this unhappy." She had regained her composure now, and spoke with a rehearsed dignity, as if she'd practiced this speech in her imagination many times.

"It's my house too," I said. "You're just going to kick me out?"

"I'm sorry. I really am, Win." She pursed her lips, as if holding in the rest of the words. I waited, my pulse pounding in my temples, a headache already throbbing, for her to finish. Finally, she said, "I've already talked to Bernie. You can crash at his place. Just for a few days, like I said, then maybe we can work things out." Now she held onto the doorframe as if she might fly away. The room seemed to have elongated so that she stood at the end of a tunnel. I took in all the familiar landmarks of my wife—the knot of hair secured with a chopstick, the sleeves of the jacket that she'd pushed up to her elbows, the long legs in black jeans—but every detail seemed too small and too crisp. It was as if I were examining her in an old photograph under a magnifying glass. Then she slipped around the doorframe and winked out of sight. I heard the scrape of her wedding ring on the banister as she descended the staircase. Then silence. She'd gone.

• • • • •

That night, I crammed myself into a tiny bed with a pink coverlet and teacups dotting the pillowcase. The headboard clawed my back and my feet stuck out past the end of the mattress. I was trying to read *The Economist.* Across the room, a silver mirror and comb lay just so on top of the bureau; a poster of some pop singer hung crooked on the wall; a pair of flip-flops nestled together, yin-yang-style, on the floor of the closet.

Bernie kept this room ready for his daughter. Once a year, his ex-wife would drop her off for a few days and then head to an ashram in Vermont. Bernie's ex-wife was a meditation junkie.

"Alice spilled some perfume last time," Bernie said, apologetically, when he showed me to the room. "I can't get the smell out."

I could picture his girl—eight or nine years old—standing by the window, her head pressed to the glass, like some child in a Grimm Tale, abandoned by her mother. Even more than her honeysuckle perfume, the room reeked of her homesickness. But no, I would not think about Bernie's daughter. That only made it worse. I squirmed in the bed and finally wedged a stuffed monkey under the pillow in order to prop my head higher. I returned to *The Economist,* my eyes marching along the page dutifully. I didn't absorb a word of it.

My mind was chattering to itself, repeating the news over and over again: She'd kicked me out. A kind of raw fear hovered somewhere in the back of my mind waiting to escape. If I lost Edie, I might lose everything else, too: house, job, snow shovel, coffee maker, TV, compost pile, workbench. Without her, my future could be anything I wanted. And what the hell did I want? The truth was I didn't want a future at all. I wanted to go back to the way it had been eight years ago, wanted to live in the cracks of my past happiness, to make a home there. Blood beat in my forehead, my jaw. I flipped to a new page in *The Economist,* staring at the photo of a world leader with his fist in the air. Maybe a half-hour went by. The phone rang. Far away in the house, Bernie's footsteps pounded.

"It's for you," he called up the stairs.

I regarded the phone on the bedside table: a pink princess model decorated with a heart-shaped stickers.

"Win. Get the fucking phone," Bernie called again.

As soon as I put the receiver to my ear, her words started. "There's something I haven't told you," Edie said. I pictured her in the kitchen, the phone cord swinging back and forth like some pendulum ticking out the finite minutes that two people can stand each other. "I haven't been entirely honest."

"All right then, who is it?" I heard myself say.

"What do you mean 'who is it'?"

"The person you're sleeping with," I said dully.

"No one. You."

"Then I don't understand. What's the secret?"

"Not an affair," she breathed, nervous. "It's not anything like that. It's more, something worse maybe. I feel bad about it, terrible. I've divorced you."

"Divorced," I repeated. It was a word like a blade, a needle of pain masquerading as a bit of vocabulary. "That's impossible. You can't divorce me without my knowing it."

"An imaginary divorce," she said, impatiently. "I did it back in August, almost a year ago. We were having such an awful time, remember? You got turned down for that grant and you wouldn't talk to me for days. You threw the alarm clock against the wall."

"I remember," I said, and I knew I should offer up some kind of apology for the rage I'd flown into, when that envelope had arrived with another no, one more no in a long summer of letters that fell through the mail slot with a series of small plops, no, no, no, while Edie scribbled away upstairs on her goddamn opus.

"You were being so difficult," she said.

"It was marriage," I said, my jaw tight. "Just ordinary marriage."

She sucked in a long breath. "I should have told you," she said. "I'm sorry."

My hand had tightened on the pink receiver. "You're not making any sense."

"I'm making perfect sense," she said, "if you'll just listen. I'm trying to apologize. I divorced you, in my mind, and that's a terrible thing to do to someone."

Her words pounded against my ear like little blows. My eyes were closed. I was studying the after-image of the bedside lamp, the way it faded into a yellow blur. "When did this start?" I asked. "Don't say 'August.' Tell me the exact moment."

"I don't know," she whispered. But then her voice came back, strong and sure. "I remember that I'd been to the lake that day, and when I drove up to the house, my skin was still buzzing with that feeling you get when you've been outside for hours. I remember I was walking across the yard, trying to hold onto that bliss. Then I looked up and saw you moving around in the kitchen. Suddenly, I could not go inside. I could not make myself go through that door. It was too small in there, and I wouldn't be able to breathe. We'd end up squabbling, and my lovely mood would be gone. I just couldn't do that one more time. I couldn't have that be my life.

"So right there in the backyard, with a wet towel and a bathing suit in my hands, I thought, 'I'll get a divorce.' And an image came to me immediately: an evening gown, a midnight-blue sheath with cap sleeves. My divorce. I let it fall over me, the way a silk dress does. It was something a young woman would wear, Audrey Hepburn in *Breakfast at Tiffany's*, but I looked smashing in it. That's the very word that came to me: smashing.

"And as soon as I had the gown on, I knew I could go inside. I headed right into the kitchen. You said, 'Where the hell is the mustard?' or something like that. You had the door of the refrigerator open, and you were pointing at an empty space. I might have been drawn into the argument. But now the gown protected me. It made me bullet-proof. Smashing. 'Oh dear, I don't know where anything is,' I said, as if I was French movie star who'd wandered into this house when I really should be riding horseback down a beach in Monaco. And so that's how it was. I absented myself. I learned how to be elsewhere."

"Christ, Edie," I moaned. "We should have talked. You should have told me."

"I meant to. But I kept thinking maybe I was wrong. Maybe things would get better."

"We had sex. Many times," I said. "Were you absent then? Did you have your gown on?"

"I don't know. It was so confusing. I thought I was going through a phase, a mid-life something."

"Let me ask you this," I said, and now my throat seemed to have closed up, making it hard to squeeze out words. "Are you wearing the gown now? Right this moment?"

"Yes," she whispered.

That's when I hung up.

• • • • •

The ambient noise in the faculty dining hall: clatter of trays, clang of utensils, and hubbub of voices. I kept a book open and my gaze drilled onto the page, feeling the ping of curious stares on my back as I hunched over my chicken noodle soup. On a small Catholic campus, you have no secrets. They all knew: Edie had kicked me out. On certain days, I couldn't imagine ever trusting her again; on other days, I wished I could crawl back into marriage like it was an unmade bed, the sheets smelling of last night's sleep. I was tired. Too tired to begin refashioning a new life for myself.

"How *are* you, Win?" the department secretary had wanted to know this morning, her eyebrows pointing upwards with the strain of her sympathy. "Fine, fine," I'd said, bustling by. I'd been staying at Bernie's place for two weeks now, pulling clothes out of a suitcase so that I came to school rumpled and smelling of his daughter's honeysuckle perfume. When I hurried down the hall, the other professors gawked at me for an instant and then snapped their eyes away, shocked at my changed condition. Much as I hated to draw their disdain, I still did not bother to shave most mornings. It exhausted me even to think about dragging the razor over my cheeks.

Now, the peppershaker on the table caught my attention; I picked it up, weighing its surprising heaviness in my palm. Lately, the most ordinary things had begun to strike me as miraculous, all these objects that had surrounded me for years without my noticing them. I had slurped chicken soup in this cafeteria hundreds of times without tasting it; I'd drawn the curtains in my office every day without knowing whether the fabric was blue or beige; I could tell you a Latin phrase was inscribed in the eaves of the college chapel, but I had no idea what those gold letters said.

I had thought this place would bury me under, that I'd die in New Hampshire, but now the opposite turned out to be true. I would be banished. I doubted very much I'd get tenure. Even if by some miracle I did meet with the committee's approval, I couldn't stay here, with Edie working two floors down and the secretaries baking me casseroles and cluck-cluck-clucking.

A month ago, I believed that I hated Mercy College, but the truth was I hadn't known it; after eight years, it had become invisible to me, and I'd inhabited only my idea of it, only its ghost. But now that I knew I would leave, a funny thing had happened: this kingdom of gothic spires and students waddling around in down jackets and Jesuses hanging in every corner with their toes *en pointe* like ballerinas, this Mercy College had turned vivid and beautiful as any lost land, any place you possess only in memory.

I held the peppershaker a few inches from my face to study the fluted column pocked by years of service in the dining hall, with an inch of brown powder on the bottom and a scrim of pepper dust clinging to the glass near the top. It gave off a faint smell of sneezes. The peppershaker hummed with the maudlin beauty of an object plucked from another time; it might have sat on the dining room table in my family's house in Greensboro when I was six years old. I might have glimpsed it when I was high on Mem. Perhaps, years from now, I would. I might take the drug and decide to return here, to the peppershaker, with its sad load of gunshot-colored dust. But more likely, I would not, and it would vanish down the drain of forgetting, along with the rest of the dining hall, the maroon sweater vest on the retarded boy who wiped a table and the sign over there that said, 'Monday special: stewed beets.' I curled my fingers around it, so tightly that the glass bit into my skin. Even this—my clasped hand with the butt of glass sticking out, my efforts to hold on so tight to this one small object—would be gone, forgotten someday. All lost, all banished, nothing, in the end, ours.

That day, I locked the door to my office and called Litminov's cell phone number. I'd tried a few times before with no luck. But this time now, for once, I got him. Litminov barked, "Duncan? What's up?"

"I wanted to ask you—" I stammered.

"Yeah, I know." He sounded out of breath, as if he were walking somewhere. "You want to know how you can get more. They all do."

"Not exactly," I began, but he was already talking over me.

"And here's what annoys me most. You probably want it so you can go back to some milquetoast memory. You want to feel sweetly nostalgic all curled up in some nursery room. But the drug can do so much more. If you're not afraid of your demons, Duncan, if you're not a pussy, you can. . . . Hold on a minute."

He seemed to have walked into a crowded room; now I could hear the half-bleats of other people talking in the background, the staccato of ambient noise.

"Yeah. That's right. How much?" Litminov said, talking to someone else, his voice faint now.

"Where are you I asked?"

Fumbling noises, a crackling sound, more hubbub.

"What?" he said.

"Where are you?"

"Gun store," he said.

"Christ. You can't buy guns in New York."

"I'm not in New York," he said. And now I thought I heard wind in the phone. Or was it traffic noises?

"Where are you?"

"Never mind that," he snapped. "Anyway, what was I saying?"

"Demons," I reminded him.

"Oh, yeah. So yesterday, I discovered the real potential of this drug. It was incredible, Duncan. I went into the *dark* zone, shot right back to a memory that scared me shitless. Not the big worst one, mind you. But one of the worst ones. It fucking sucked; when I came to, my shirt was drenched with sweat."

"You did this on purpose?" I'd been keeping still, hunched over my desk, as if, even though he couldn't see me, any movement on my part could cause him to hang up. My hand, clamped around the receiver, throbbed.

"Are you not listening, Duncan? Have you not heard me? Yes, I did it on purpose."

"Why?" I asked.

"Number one, to prove I could. Number two, because of how I feel now. Like I've burned all the dirt out of my system. No, that's not it. I feel invincible, fucking invincible." His mouth seemed to be right on top of the phone; I could hear his tongue slurping when he talked, hear the wetness of each glottal stop. "I've discovered a whole new side of the drug. The dark side, Duncan. The terror may be great, but the rewards are vast."

"I'd like to try that myself," I lied. "To relive something awful. See if I can endure it."

"Well, you'll get your chance, Duncan. Give me a call. In a few weeks. Don't bother me before then." Then he hung up.

The next time I tried the cell phone, it had been disconnected.

• • • • •

"Do you want any?" Edie asked me, as she poured herself some iced tea from a red pitcher that I had never seen before. I'd been living at Bernie's, sleeping in his daughter's tiny bed night after night until my back was twisted into a permanent S. Today was the first time I'd so much as been through the door of my old house—already I thought of it as the "old" house—and I was here now only because she needed to tell me something.

I noticed that our wedding photo had vanished from the side table. My favorite chair, the one with the ripped cushion, had disappeared too, banished to the basement, I supposed. I sat on the hard-back rocking chair I'd always hated.

"Sure," I said, "some tea would be good." When had she begun drinking iced tea? She used to think it was foul.

She handed me a glass so cold that it made my hand ache.

"So what is it?" I asked. "The thing you couldn't tell me over the phone?"

"First of all, I wanted you to know that my Uncle Lester abused me," she said, sitting on the edge of the couch, one black-jeaned leg crossed over the other, appearing to be utterly at ease. "Not that I want to play the victim. But it did happen. It did affect me."

"Oh, OK, but I already knew that," I said. "You told me a long time ago."

"Yes," she said, "but you never understood."

"Understood?" I said stupidly, still trying to adjust to the absence of my chair from its usual spot. I felt awful and I desperately wanted a drink. Instead I forced myself to march along through the conversation. "I'm trying to understand," I told her, "but you can see why I might be confused. You told me about all this years ago."

"I've been thinking about Uncle Lester a lot lately. Re-thinking, I should say. How I was molested. Constantly. Over several years." She appeared to be perfectly calm, with one arm slung across the back of the couch, but the ice rattled in her glass.

"You always laughed about him. Uncle Letch. You always acted like it was no big deal," I said in my own self-defense. Ten or eleven years ago, when she first told me about him, I'd wanted to fly to Montana and punch the old slime bucket in the teeth, but she'd assured me that wouldn't be necessary. Uncle Letch, she had pronounced, hadn't scared her in the least; even at ten years old, she had known he was a buffoon. "You said you never let him get to you," I added.

"Well, he did get to me. He really hurt me. You didn't—" she began, and then crimped her lips together, as if to trap some accusation of me before it flew out.

"What?" I said.

"Never mind," she shook her head, took a careful sip of tea.

"Tell me."

"All right. How do I say this?" She was bent forward now, one hand pressed into the fabric of the sofa, which absorbed it, made it disappear. "You never noticed anything, Win. You were oblivious. I told you that I was molested as a kid. Yes, it was a big deal. A huge deal."

My heart beat in my mouth, in my tongue. It was all so unfair, this. "You didn't *want* me to do anything."

She waved one hand in the air, her gold band flashing in the light from the window—she still wore the wedding ring, at least. "Listen, I didn't mean to get into this. Whatever's wrong in our marriage, that's not important right now." She leaned back, regaining that eerie calm again. "I just wanted you to know that I'm doing work on myself."

"Doing work?" I said, jerking my head back. "Christ, Edie, you sound like someone else."

"I know." She held my gaze, as if waiting to watch the reaction she was about to have on me. "I'm in therapy. Unfortunately, it causes me to sound like a walking cliché sometimes."

"You? You were always so scornful of stuff like that. You were the one who said therapy turns big existential problems into bland suburban tropes."

"I know. I still believe that. But for some reason I decided to try it anyway. And the weird thing is, it has helped. A lot."

"When?" I said. "When did this start?"

She sidled her eyes away from mine. "September," she said in a low voice. "I started going in September."

Of its own accord, my hand flew up to cover my eyes. "That's more than six months ago," I said, weakly, staring into the dark of my own fingers.

"Yes," I heard her say.

I rubbed my cheek now, the stubble that made scritch scritch sounds against my fingernail. "You didn't tell me. You, basically, lied."

"I did not lie. Though it did feel a little like I was having an affair. Sneaking out to meet with Dr. Brenner. Who is a woman, by the way."

"I never noticed you being gone," I said. "When did you go?"

"Thursday mornings. I would have told you I was in therapy, if you'd asked."

"So I suppose I'm the monster," I said.

"What?" she looked at me side-long.

"In your therapy sessions. You talk about all the things I did to you. How I failed you." And then, as if for emphasis, I reared back my head and sneezed. I grabbed the damp wad of toilet paper I kept in my pocket and sneezed again, into it. I'd been sick for days.

"It's not like that," she said, running a hand through her curls, adjusting them. "We haven't even gotten to you yet. We're still doing childhood. It could take years to get to you."

"So that's why Uncle Letch," I said, wiping at my nose and wishing we could find our way into the conversation I had intended to have with her when I came here. To wit: Edie, when can I move in again? When can I stop sleeping on a twin bed in Bernie's house?

"It's amazing," she said. "Before, if you'd asked me whether I'd been molested as a kid, I would have insisted I wasn't. I worked so hard to make my pain gothic and twisted, to transform it into some kind of Jane Eyre-like secret. Something literary, for god's sake. I didn't want to be just another adult child of alcoholics who suffered some abuse. But it turns out I'm just like everyone else. Boringly screwed up."

"So your therapist thinks what Lester did—that was sexual abuse?" I felt my forehead wrinkle.

"Yes, of course," she leaned forward now, speaking urgently. "He'd corner me in the back of Dad's store, tell me how he wanted to jerk off on my breasts. Maybe he never touched me. But Win, it was still abuse. I was a kid. I didn't have breasts. He infected me. He's been dead for years, and I still can hear him telling me what he wants to do to me."

"You're right. It's horrible," I muttered, dutifully.

She interrupted. She didn't want my sympathy now, only to talk. "I never told you this, Win. He's the reason I made up Eglantine. What I always told you about having an imaginary world, that it was some fey little girlhood fantasy—that was never true. I made up Eglantine to survive. When he was leaning over me saying 'cock' and 'pussy' I'd be in my palace in Englantine, pruning the topiary. Maybe that's why every girl invents a secret world. I don't know." Now she stared out the window at the fir trees, her eyes glossy with reflected light. "I think I married you because you let me stay in Eglantine. Don't take this the wrong way, Win, but you didn't pay much attention to me. And that's what I wanted years ago."

I snorted disdainfully. "So I am the monster."

"No. I didn't say that. You're not listening." One tear appeared, like a glass bead in the corner of her eye. She wiped it away, and then stared at the dampness on her finger, at its shine, as if she had made something beautiful. "I wasn't happy. That girl you met in New York? She was a mess."

"But you were happy," I said. "You were always laughing. We'd just hole up together for days, with our books, some takeout food, and the futon on the floor. That's all we needed. It was so . . . great."

She gave her head a little shake, making the curls shiver. "That girl is gone, Win. I've sent her packing, off to Billings, Montana. She's living upstairs from her mother, cowering under a quilt made by Grandma Sidle, reading all the works of Charles Dickens, one by one. She's gone. Let her go." Edie had slid toward me on the couch; her hands cut the air as she talked; one curl fell over her forehead and she slapped it away, as if it were a mosquito.

"You can't just get rid of who you were," I protested.

She put her glass down on a table so carefully that it never made a sound. "Let's not argue about it," she said.

"But we do need to talk about what's going on now. What we're going to do."

"OK," she said. "You start."

I opened my mouth, took a breath, but no words came out. She let the silence fill up the room; she seemed to own that silence, as if it were that red pitcher that I'd never seen before, hers alone. My heart bashed around in my chest. Finally, I said, "The thing is, what are we going to do, Edie? I can't stay at Bernie's forever. I want to come back." I couldn't bear to look at her as I said this—begged, really—so I studied the patch of sunlight that fluttered on the wall, just under the windowsill, like a sick butterfly.

I heard her rustling, adjusting herself on the couch. "I'm sorry, Win. I'm not sure whether you should move in here again." She had steepled her fingers under her chin, and she touched her pursed lips with the top of the steeple, and I could tell she was trying to figure out how to drop some final bad news on me. She drew her breath. She slid her hands along the thighs of her jeans. "I've been thinking a lot about my childhood, actually, because I might want to have a kid."

"You do?" I'd always told her that if she wanted to get pregnant that would be fine with me, all she had to do was say the word, but she never said the word, and so we hadn't even talked about it for years.

"It's now or never," she finally said. "My eggs. My stupid, stupid eggs."

"All right. We'll have a kid," I said.

"I didn't mean it like that. I meant—," here she waved her hands in the air, as if to scoop the right words into them.

"Oh," I said. "I see." This is why she'd gone into therapy; this is why she'd have to get rid of me. Sweat broke out on my back, and the fabric of my shirt prickled horribly. "You think I'd be a shitty father."

"Win," she said, "No, you'd be a great father. But I'm not sure our marriage is strong enough. What if I had a kid and then we broke up a year later? I have to think about this. I need more time."

"No," I said, and now I was standing in the middle of the room—I'd leaped up from the rocking chair with such forced that it davened like a frightened old man behind me. "I know what you're doing. You've got someone."

"No one," she said, "I swear." And now she was standing too, rubbing her forehead. "I'm so tired."

"Me, too."

She looked up at me, jaw tight. "Look, let's just get the worst part over, don't you think? So it will be behind us."

Then, before I quite understood what had happened, I found myself heading upstairs with two black trash bags crinkling under my arm. They smelled of chemicals and the faint ghost of garbage-to-be. We were separated, and so I'd need more clothes. All the time we'd been talking, those trash bags had been waiting for me on the kitchen table. She'd put them out for me.

At the door to the bedroom I paused. It looked nothing like the room we'd shared, the place where I'd dreamed for thousands of hours and performed hundreds of sex acts. That room had been a nest, papered with coffee-stained journals, padded with dirty clothes, the smell of skin and sleep lingering everywhere.

Now it looked like a goddamned Howard Johnson's. She'd made the bed and the cleaned the floor and banished the papers. The walls, which used to be crowded with framed photos, had turned stark white. For a moment, I leaned against the doorframe, and my stomach felt so scrambled I thought I might throw up. Only six years ago I'd stood in this exact spot, gazing at the bare wood floor and the dresser that the last owners had left behind, and said to Edie, "We should put the bed in here." What had happened in between? I couldn't understand how I'd traveled from that moment to this one; or rather, how I'd transformed from one man into another. For a moment, an awful moment of clarity, I knew exactly how Edie saw me now: a man who shambled around with one shoulder bent under the strap of his leather bag, under the weight of the book he'd never finish; a man who would not cheerfully change diapers at two in the morning, oh no, far from it; a whiner, a wreck, a ruin, a liability, a pill head; a man like her father, who had been too drunk to protect her from Uncle Letch. The garbage bags made sad little rattling sounds as I moved my arms.

Enough, enough. I took a breath and plunged into the bedroom, as if I were diving underwater. As quickly as I could, I pawed shirts and jackets out of the closet and into the bags. I stepped into the dark, wrestling with a coat, to see what I could find in the back of the closet. Something clattered to the floor—one of the photographs that had been on the wall. She must have shoved them in here, all the mementos of me. I reached for the picture that had fallen between my shoes, and then ducked out of the closet, so I could see which one it was. Oh yes. My father took the picture, years ago, and sent it to us as a present. He'd included a joke, I remember, about how he might use Edie and me in his next ad campaign. And it was true, we had looked like an ad for something, sitting on the tailgate of an old VW, our tan legs dangling, with the beach behind us. She leaned, as she used to do, against my arm. We exuded the air of two people for whom everything has come easily—good looks, love, a beach house, the summer off.

I dusted the glass with my shirtsleeve, and after a moment of consideration, placed the picture in the dead center of the bed. She would wander in here after I left and find this photograph, and she would have to pick it up. She'd have to put her hands around the silver frame, and she'd have to look at my young self, who would be staring up at her, me with golden-red hair down to my shoulders. That would be my revenge. She'd have to look at who I was, and why she had loved me. At least for one moment, she wouldn't be able to hide it in the closet. Notice, Edie, how your fingers curled loosely on my bare leg. Look at your tan. Your post-coital grin. We both know what that means. You can't deny it. I have proof. You were, goddamn it, happy with me.

• • • • •

Bernie leaned forward in the easy chair with bald spots on its arms; blue light from the TV flashed across his glasses. Now that the Knicks held a four-point lead, I balanced on the edge of the cushion, curled into myself, watching Spree dribble down the court. It was the first time I'd felt decent in weeks. For entire minutes, I could lose myself in the simple urgency of willing the Knicks to score, trying to muster whatever mojo I possessed to push at their tiny bright bodies around the court on the TV screen.

"No!" Bernie screamed as they lost the ball to the Lakers. A stack of journals on the coffee table teetered and then slid to the floor. Bernie didn't notice. He lurched forward in his chair. "For fuck's sake, don't mess this one up!"

We kept on the Knicks like that, pushing them with everything we had. An hour later, they won by six points. Bernie high-fived me, danced a little salsa, his bathrobe swinging around the legs of his sweatpants. With the cloth belt dragging behind him like a tail, he headed off to the kitchen to bring back some celebratory beers. On the way into the living room, he halted in the doorway, staring at me. I was sprawled on the couch with my head propped up, a tissue poking out of one of my nostrils—a few days ago my cold had turned into a sinus infection, a lump of pain that lodged in my jaw and wouldn't move.

"What?" I said.

"You look like shit."

"I've looked like shit for weeks."

He scratched his cheek with the cap of one of the beer bottles. "True. But this appears to be more serious."

"I'm fine."

"You should go to the doctor."

"I've been. They gave me stuff. It didn't work."

He lumbered over to his easy chair and collapsed into it, the beer on his lap.

"Give me one," I said, making a half-hearted grab for the beer.

"No. Aren't you on antibiotics?"

"I'm serious, Bernie. Give it. It's my property. I bought it."

He sighed and handed me a beer, then reached in his pocket and tossed me the bottle opener too. "Suit yourself."

For a moment, we sipped in silence. I could feel the worry in Bernie's brain circling like the blades of a fan, humming, agitating the air in the room.

"When do you finish up?" he finally said.

"Next Thursday is my last class. But then I've got the grading. And then I'm done, and I mean really done, because they're probably going to fire me."

"You don't know that." He paused, and we both pretended to watch the mute TV. After a few moments, he said, "So what about the summer?"

I blew my nose and when my ear unclogged, my hearing became very precise—I could pick up the ticking hum of the refrigerator in the kitchen. "Next week, after my last class, I'm driving straight down to Manhattan. I can stay at Dad's place while he's away."

"Away?" Bernie said, with a note of concern in his voice. "So you'll be there alone?"

"Yeah. Dad's going to some Caribbean Island where people play golf. A whole month."

"You should go with him," Bernie said, pointing at me with the tip of his beer bottle. "Get some sun. You might even consider playing golf yourself."

I snorted, nearly spitting up beer. "You're serious?"

"Absolutely."

"I thought you were going to lecture me about how the United States holds those islands illegally."

"Normally, I would," he said. "But you shouldn't be in New York alone for a month."

"Why not?"

He shrugged, became absorbed in one of the ads that flashed silently on TV. After a moment, he said, "Litminov."

"You think I'm going down there to score some drugs. Is that what you really think?"

He sighed, rolled the bottle between his hands, shook his head ever so slightly.

"Listen, Bernie. Litminov's gone. I've tried every one of his phone numbers. They're all cut off." This was true. But it was also true that I knew where he lived, and I planned to find him. Indeed right now I had no other ambition.

"I wonder what's happened to him," Bernie mused.

"Guess we'll never know," I said, though according to my own fantasies, I would track down Litminov and force him to answer all the questions that nagged at me—for instance, how he'd come upon the drug in the first place, and what, exactly, he had meant by the "dark side." And I would also procure more Mem. Lots of it.

"I need to go check my email," Bernie said. "She might have written back by now." A week ago, he'd met some woman—a postdoc from Yale, to be exact—on an internet dating site. They'd been exchanging long messages that I gathered had recently turned intimate. He spent hours now in his office upstairs with his face a few inches from the screen, typing and erasing, the white light reflected in his glasses.

"Yeah," I said, "I think it's already been a whole forty-five minutes since you checked."

But he didn't hear me. He was already thumping up the stairs. I blew my nose. Nothing came out except a small spatter of blood. I groaned and closed my eyes, lying back on a pile of pillows, sucking breath through my scabbed, polluted nasal passages.

When I craned my neck, I could just see the clock on the kitchen wall, its hands moving implacably, shoving me into the next moment, whether I wanted to go or not. Christ, how I wished I had a dose of

Mem. I clenched my fist and imagined that I held a pill, a tiny hard nub pressing into my palm. I lifted my hand to my mouth and ate the pill that was not there. I waited. Nothing happened, except that the clock in the kitchen tick-tick-ticked, beating out its trudge into what will be. And I, Mem-less, had no choice but go forward with it.

• • • • •

A few nights later, I skidded to a stop in front of Edie's office in the humanities building. I rapped on the door, hard, so that it swung away from my hand, revealing Edie at her desk, half-hidden by her computer monitor.

She glanced up, her face lit by the white-blue glow.

"Oh," she said. "You scared me."

The smell of leather, that smell I had forgotten, her smell, hit me. "You busy?" I said.

"Sit down." She waved at the metal folding chair kitty-corner from the desk.

I fell into it. It was too small for me and my legs spooled out over the floor. I squirmed around, trying to get comfortable. Meanwhile, she appraised me, her chin rested on one folded-up hand. She wore her curls swept back, smoothed against her skull. She had a sleekness about her, an air of uncomplicated contentment. It seemed impossible that I was now legally her husband, or that I had ever been.

"Win," she said, narrowing her eyes, "are you drunk?"

"No. Just a few beers." I had in fact spent the last few hours in my car, parked above the town dump, staring out at the refrigerators and mattresses and kid's shoes piled against the side of the hill, all the detritus of other people's ex-lives. I'd sucked on a bottle of bourbon, the very same brand that I used to steal from my parent's liquor cabinet when I was in high school. I'd made it a third of the way down that bottle, and then, weaving along back roads with the prissy caution of the very drunk, I'd driven here.

"You look like you're going to fall out of that chair," Edie said.

I shrugged. My hands, cradled behind my head, felt numb, and the fingers only seemed to be there in theory. "What's that?" I nodded in the direction of the stacks of paper that she'd arranged on a low coffee table by the radiator.

She followed my gaze. "What do you mean? It's my book."

"No," I said, staggering out of the chair and onto my feet. "The black thing."

"What black thing?"

I paced over to her book, all spread out so neatly, all ready for publication, and braced my hands on my knees to lean over. She'd put a stone on top of each pile, using them as paperweights—those smooth gray stones we'd collected on a trip to the Cape, years ago. Except on one of the piles, instead of a stone, sat a black iron cat with an arched back.

I picked it up, holding it around the U of its torso; it turned out to be far heavier than I'd expected. "This," I said. "Where'd this come from?"

"Paul found it in some thrift shop. It's supposed to be a bookend."

"Paul?"

"The guy who does tech support. He fixed your computer once, remember?"

The thing suddenly felt poisonous in my hand, the way the iron fur bit into my palm. I let it drop. It fell onto one of the chapters, knocking the papers askew.

"Hey," she protested. "What are doing?"

I couldn't answer. I couldn't seem to tear my eyes away from that cat, with a yellow eye of dabbed-on paint. It struck me as exactly the kind of quirky object that a young man picks out in order to charm a woman into bed.

"How old is he anyway? Twenty-five?" I finally said.

"I don't take your meaning." She ran one hand across her smoothed curls.

"Are you fucking him?"

"No."

"But you could," I said, "If you wanted to."

"I suppose." She sounded exasperated, as if seducing a lithe young fellow with long sideburns would have added to her list of chores. "God, Win, stop staring at that thing. I'm not interested in him, truly. If I slept with him, he'd make me read his science-fiction screenplay."

I put my hands up to my face, rubbed my forehead, took in a deep breath between my palms, which smelled sharply of bourbon.

"Really," I heard her say, "he's a nuisance."

Without bothering to answer, I headed over to the window behind her desk, cupped my hands so that I could gaze out at the line of poplar trees that stood out against the stars, marking the edge of a hill. The trees had just begun to bud out; even in the dark, I could discern the flecks of leaves shining amid the soot-black branches. In a few weeks, the apple trees near the football field would dazzle the grass with their white petals. The campus had already lost its mud and ice, soon it would shake off its trudging students and their demands. It would transform into a shaggy pastureland with fringes of forest, here and there a gothic spire needling the blue sky; it would become the New England campus you dreamed about as a boy, when you dreamed of reading leather-spined books underneath the violet shadows of the elms. I had always loved Mercy College during the precious three months of summer, the stone buildings turned monastically cool inside, and the views of green that shimmered in every window.

"I met with Father Sullivan today," I said, turning to face her, arranging my arms across my chest, trying to appear unperturbed.

"Oh?" she said, cocking her head. I could tell by the ways she clutched the edge of the desk, the muscles standing out in her forearm, that she was listening with all she had, and she was afraid to hear what was coming next. "So what did he say?"

I swallowed. The pleasant haze of tipsiness evaporated. All of a sudden, I'd gone stone-cold sober. It was the first time I'd told anyone, and the words didn't come easily. "He said. . . ," I took a breath. "He suggested that I start looking for another job."

"He *said* that?"

I let out my breath, nodding. To my surprise, I felt enormous relief. She knew now. It was over. I'd done the last thing here in New Hampshire that I had to. I was through.

"He can't say that." She'd shot to her feet.

"Please," I stretched one arm out toward her, as if I meant to stroke her back, calm her down, but I was too far away for that. "We knew this was coming. It's not a surprise."

"Yes it is. He can't tell you to leave, not without letting you go through the tenure-review process," she fired back. "You could sue him for that. Goddamn it, you have to fight for yourself."

The more fierce she grew—her necklace swinging, thumping against her chest like an errant heart—the calmer I became. "Edie," I said, stretching out the two syllables of her name, taking all the time in the world, and I was suddenly, startlingly, the one who controlled the room. "He told me off the record. He said—quote unquote—'If you want to, Win, go ahead and submit your tenure box in the fall. But I'm telling you, as a friend, that you should start looking elsewhere.'"

She blinked up at me, and I thought she might cry. "But why?"

I rubbed my chin. "Probably because I blew off a meeting with the Curriculum Review Board last week, which I'm supposed to be chairing. That was pretty much the *coup de gras*."

"Oh Win," she cried—not too loudly, of course, because there might be other professors eavesdropping from their offices down the hall. "So what are you telling me? You want to be fired?" she staged-whispered.

"I guess I must want that. That must be the explanation." I was aware of the cold air coming off the window, making the skin on my back goose-pimple.

Edie sucked in a gasp of air. "This is awful," she said, and then smeared her tears across her face, impatiently, ashamed to have me see her cry.

I sidled behind the desk, toward her. She flinched away, but when I smoothed her hair from behind, she let my hand stay, and I thought for a moment she might fall against me, her back against my stomach, the way we used to stand at the window sometimes. I had forgotten how small she was, how her skull—her brain, everything that was her—I could cup between my two hands. I began massaging between the little bird bones at the back of her neck. For a few seconds she tolerated my touch; then she grew still and watchful; finally she hunched her shoulder to shake my hand off. "Don't," she said.

I was left standing behind her, with my arm hanging awkwardly. She bent away from me, opened a drawer, snatched a Kleenex out of it, and from the little furtive movements of her elbows, I knew that she was tending to her face, getting it cleaned up. I stared out over her head, at the journals crammed in a line at the top of her bookshelf. Even from across the room, I could tell she'd put them in chronological order, be-cause I recognized the small red book at the end—her first triumph, which we had admired over dinner maybe ten years ago. "I'm actually real," she'd said, running her fingers over her own name on the page. I could imagine her standing on tip-toe to add the latest journal to the display. I felt, all of a sudden, sorry for her. She'd worked so hard and for what? Paper on a shelf.

"How are you doing?" I whispered. "Edie? Talk to me."

She sniffed. "I'm fine." She crumpled up the Kleenex, tossed it ex-pertly into the trashcan across the room, and then stepped backwards, away, to face me. "So what are you going to do?"

"Like the man said, I need to get a job somewhere else."

"You're really going to do that? Leave?" She searched my face.

"I have to," I said, and then tried to smile, but it came off as a wince.

"You know, Win, I was trying to help, without you knowing it. I was doing everything I could for you." One of her hands flew up; now she was carving the air in front of her, describing the shape of something. "I was pulling strings. If you'd just played it straight for a few more months. . . ." She shook her head, disgusted by the waste of all that effort. "I could have made sure you got tenure, Win."

That last bit pissed me off. "I just came here to tell you what happened, that's all," I tossed over my shoulder, as I threaded my way around the desk. "I didn't want you to *fix* it. I'm not in need of saving. I'll do fine on my own." I headed for the door.

"Wait," I heard her call from behind me.

I turned and we faced off from opposite sides of the room.

"I want to help," she said.

I shook my head. "You can't."

Chapter
7

My father called it a period of adjustment. "This could be the best thing that ever happened to you. Think of the opportunities you have now. The opportunities!" He'd been cutting up a steak as he said this, and now he stared petulantly down at his plate. "Goddamn it, why don't they have all the utensils here? Excuse me, Win." He raised one hand with a half-cocked finger to summon a waiter. Within seconds a mustached fellow in an achingly white shirt hovered over our table. My father leaned toward him conspiratorially. "I need a marrow spoon, if you've got one."

The waiter hurried off. "Now where was I?" Dad said, staring down at the bloody shreds of meat to get his bearings. Around us in the dim light, old men in crisp suits drooped over their tables, faces flickering in the candlelight. They conversed in the languid way of the retired and wealthy.

"I know you're reeling now," my father said, "but I think this was the right move. You weren't happy up there in New Hampshire."

The waiter materialized beside my father, proffering a linen napkin, on which glittered a tiny spoon.

"Ah!" my father said, taking it from its pillow. He dug it delicately into the joint of the T-bone, scooping out gooey marrow, put a morsel in his mouth.

I scowled. "That's disgusting, Dad. You're going to get mad-cow disease."

"Oh, don't be so damn dark. This stuff is full of vitamins. It's what keeps me going. Ask Gloria. Your old man has not slowed down one bit." And then, as if the subject of his sexual vitality reminded him of what he'd wanted to ask all along, he slid his wineglass into the exact center of the table, and cleared his throat. "So, by the way, why did you and Edie split up?"

I hunched my shoulders. "Well," I began, picking up my knife and studying it, the pieces of myself—nostrils, stubble, arched eyebrow—that flashed across its polished surface.

"You have a girlfriend," Dad supplied helpfully. "A student maybe? Listen, I wouldn't condemn you for it."

"No, there's no girlfriend," I said, placing the knife just so beside my plate, the steak that I'd painstakingly cut up and then left there. I didn't eat much these days, because of the chewing. It seemed like too much work.

"Oh, come on!" my father exploded. "No girlfriend?"

I gazed past his shoulder, to the spray of flowers spot-lit in the center of the room, petals casting dramatic shadows on a white-linen tablecloth. The worse my life got, the better the restaurants he took me to. "No," I said, "no girlfriend."

"Well, what then? There's got to be some reason you're not living with your wife anymore."

I shrugged. "It's hard to explain."

"Try," he said.

"She doesn't like me."

"Hmm." He began digging with his spoon again. He'd hoped that I would confess to a nineteen-year-old ballet dancer, a motel, lingerie, secret phone calls—anything, anything that would prove I had an appetite like my old man. He wanted a son with teeth. But instead he'd ended up with me, a man who'd married a feminist and gotten his goddamn balls cut off, a man who knew nothing about fly fishing and tended to take his bourbon with water.

"Ah Win!" he said sadly. "You've always been so good."

"But I'm not," I wanted to say. "I've been experimenting with drugs, hanging out with Litminov, lying to my wife." In some odd way, my old man might have been proud of my recent misdeeds. For a moment, I considered telling him everything.

"Dad," I said, and a story about Mem swirled around in thoughts, taking shape. Was there some cleaned-up version of my last few months I could tell him? He'd be fascinated. Maybe a bit envious. He might even want to try the drug.

"Yeah?" he said, scraping at the bone with his small spoon, all concentration.

"I don't think there's anything left inside that carcass," I said.

"Guess you're right." He rooted around in the breadbasket until he came up with a biscuit, took a bite of that. "So when are you going to come work for me?" he said, with fake nonchalance. "You've thought about my offer, right?"

"Yeah, thanks. It's not for me."

"I don't think you're understanding this, Win. You'd run a whole division. Do you know how many guys would kill for that?"

I opened up my mouth for a rebuttal, but Dad was already talking.

"Maybe you imagine this is some make-work job I'm creating for you because you're my son. But that's not it at all, Win. I *need* someone with your skills. We've been talking about this for years, Harry and I, how to crack the academic market." Now he was on a roll, his words pounding out. He'd torn his biscuit in half, and he used the mangled piece of bread to point at me. "Most universities do their publicity in-house. But what if we changed that? We could end up handling half the schools on the East Coast. I've met them, Win, these guys in their blue suits with the brass buttons and their university ties. They think that if they hire a big-name ad agency, it will make them look desperate. They see us as tacky. Years ago, I sat down with a dean at Columbia University, yes, your old school, and I explained that we'd be the perfect agency for him, a tasseled-loafer kind of place, very classy. He wouldn't have any of it. But you, Win, you know how to wrangle these fellows."

"Dad," I sighed. "Please."

"All right." He tossed the piece of biscuit onto his plate. "Just think about it. That's all I ask."

And I did think about it, as we glided down Broadway in a cab. I slumped in my seat so that I could watch all the wonders above us, the crowns of towers lit up purple and gray and blue. "I would like to move back to the city," I said sadly.

Beside me, my father rocked forward and crossed one leg over the other, adjusting the fabric of his pants with little pinches, so that it didn't bunch. "Well, you could," he said, and let the rest hang in the air.

"I know, I know. I should take the job."

He patted his top leg, as if keeping time to a song that played in his head—absolutely nonchalant, refusing to let me see how much this all pleased him. "Whatever you want, Win. It's your decision."

"What would be the next step—I mean, if I were interested?"

His hand stopped its patting. He seemed to be listening to me with his whole body. "If you were interested?" he said, lightly. "It could all be very informal. We could go out for drinks with Harry and Alan and some of the people who'd be on your team. See whether you click."

"Just drinks?" I said.

"Sure. I could set something up when I get back into town."

"We'll see," I said, and my chest ached with the dull twinge of diminished expectations.

• • • • •

And then my father flew off to St. Bart's, and left me alone in his apartment, standing in front of his coffee maker as it gurgled out its morning complaint. The numbers on the side of the machine glowed the time: 10:14. I had the whole rest of the day stretching before me, in fact, a whole month in Dad's apartment.

I watched as 10:14 on the coffee maker melted into 10:15, hoping this new minute would bring some relief. When I was in New Hampshire, I had thought that if I could only jump the gray stone walls of Mercy College, I would feel better. But, in fact, I felt exactly the same, that knot of heartburn-ish dread that had been lodged below the fourth button of my shirt all through those weeks in New Hampshire was still there. I poured myself a cup of coffee and fell into one of the Dad-sized leather chairs, picked up the paper, pushed my eyes across it.

I was feeling middling bad, and then, suddenly, a wave of profound awfulness hit me. It started as nausea, a clawing in my stomach, as if something in there wanted to escape. I clamored out of the chair and paced to the other side of the room, trying to outrun it. I found myself in the bathroom, where I lathered up a washcloth and scrubbed at my face. I shut off the taps and examined myself in the mirror, those eyes staring back at me, pupils absurdly large, drops of water catching in the red and gray stubble on my cheeks. One worry line, like a third eye, sat just at the top of my nose. I looked old. I looked like my father.

Then I scuttled out of the bathroom, scanning the apartment for some sort of relief; I wanted anything, anything to push away this awful mood that clawed at me. By the door, my father's dry cleaning spilled out of a bag; he'd commanded me to take care of this before he came back into town. The sleeve of a white shirt caught the sun, its cuff holding violet shadows in a hollow of fabric. It reminded me of something I couldn't quite identify—some moment, white fabric glowing in the light, connected with an evanescent happiness.

If I'd had a dose of Mem in my hand I would have slapped it right onto my tongue and flown back to it, whatever it was. Out of nowhere, I felt sick with longing for the pill, glossy as a chestnut, with flecks of black. I had to find some Mem. Now. The need for it moved my legs; I was hurrying across the room, toward the door, suddenly purposeful. It might be hidden somewhere in this city, maybe in walking distance; so close, if only I could find it. I grabbed a coat and headed out, sprinted down the three flights of stairs. Then I was out on the street, with its smells of exhaust and Indian food. The wind grabbed the bottom of the coat and made it fly around my legs.

I was sprinting along the sidewalk, dodging across streets, heading downtown, to Litminov's place. The craving for Mem frightened me. I'd had bouts in New Hampshire, but nothing like this—I'd been too busy, too drunk, too something. I thought I could claw my skin off for wanting it. Blocks flew by. My legs ate up sidewalk. Now I pushed my way through the revolving door and into the lobby of Litminov's building, my teeth clenched, my jaw tight as a clamp. The doorman—young as one of my students—slumped in his chair.

"I want Phil Litminov in the penthouse," I said, towering over him, able to look down into his lap, at the newspaper spread out across his thighs.

He hopped to his feet, letting the newspaper flutter to the floor. He stood a good five inches shorter than me. "Yes, of course, sir." Then as my request sunk in, he tightened his eyebrows, confused. "Excuse me. Who?"

"Litminov. The penthouse."

"I'm sorry, Sir," he said, blinking up at me. "There's no one in the penthouse at the present time."

"No one?"

"No one. It's vacant. I believe the tenant will be moving in next month."

"Christ. When did he leave? Litminov. Where is he? You must have some forwarding address."

The boy glanced down at the phone on his desk, judging the distance between himself and it, making sure he could grab the receiver if need be. With my stubble and my hungry eyes and my height, I must have scared him. "Sir," he said, "I've never heard of—who did you say?"

"Philip Litminov."

He shook his head. "I've never heard of him. Are you sure you have the right building?"

"Of course," I said. "I was here just two months ago."

"And you're sure it wasn't the one next door?"

"Yes, of course," I said impatiently, though it occurred to me now that I might have made a mistake. Last time, there'd been no doorman. I'd just headed right for the elevator and no one had stopped me. "You must have a list of tenants somewhere," I added, in a softer tone.

"Sure." The kid, still watching me warily, flipped open a black-leather book on the desk. I noticed that he'd placed his other hand, as nonchalantly as possible, beside the phone. "OK. Here's the list of residents from last month," he said. "You can look through the whole register if you want." He spun the book a hundred and eighty degrees and pushed it towards me.

I leaned over his desk, squinted, picked up the book and studied the typed list that had been glued onto a page. "Penthouse," I read, "Tenant: James Rinehart." I dropped the book on the desk. Suddenly everything seemed up for question. Maybe I did have the wrong building. Maybe I'd imagined Litminov entirely. "James Rinehart?" I said. "Who's he?"

The kid was about to answer when the elevator made a ka-thunk sound, and the doors slowly parted. We both watched, as if the mysterious James Rinehart might make his entrance. But it was only a nanny, her head wrapped in an African-looking kerchief, pushing a stroller. She ignored us as she guided the stroller toward the door. The baby shook his rattle at me; his eyes locked onto mine, and for one discombobulated moment, I could imagine that he knew where Litminov might be, or that he himself might be Litminov, after one too many of those pills, gone backwards in time.

The doorman rushed off to help the woman angle her stroller down the front stairs. I was left alone in the lobby. The elevator made a groaning sound and the doors began to close. For a moment, I considered jumping on and pushing the P button; a number of stupid schemes flitted through my brain before I noticed the bronze walls. I knew the inside of that elevator, the way the light smeared across every surface, even the floor, catching in dented places, so the whole elevator appeared to be a glowing gold box. I had the right building. But Litminov had vanished. Even the memory of him was gone from this place.

"Sir," the doorman said, glancing over at me nervously, realizing that I stood nearer to the elevator than was comfortable for him.

"All right," I grumbled. "I'll go."

"Why don't you call the company that manages the building?" he said.

I waved that idea away. "No. They won't have heard of him either." And wrapping my scarf around my neck, I pushed through the door back out into the roar of the street. For a moment, I didn't even try to make sense of it—the paradox and impossibility of Litminov's disappearance. Instead I walked. I walked until I thought my shoe leather would peel away.

• • • • •

It was three in the morning and I kneeled in the living room of my father's apartment, surveying the line of photographs that stretched across the tan rug before me, the evidence of my boyhood running from the kitchen to the edge of a bookshelf. A few hours before, I'd come back to the apartment, still tortured by the absence of Litminov. How had he found a way to expunge himself from the building's records? Well, there was a perfectly sensible explanation for that: Litminov had money and connections. If he wanted to vanish entirely, he could. I should have been satisfied with that explanation.

But I couldn't help toying with another terrible possibility: to wit, that I had only imagined I'd been in Litminov's loft that day back in March. That my mind had lied to me. If that was true, then it followed that I might have never taken Mem at all, and many of the events of the last few weeks, the ones that seemed most compelling and true, were in fact delusions.

Maybe I'd cracked up. After all, I had no way of proving that Mem existed. Yes, I'd showed Bernie a pill once—but that could have been a nub of brown that I'd found anywhere, or even a speck of dirt that I'd carefully tamped into a ball.

All day, I'd been infected by the idea that I was going insane. As I walked around the city, I'd tried to shake it, but it had only gotten stronger. Now, when the buzzer went off in Dad's apartment, I toyed with the idea that the sound might be a hallucination, even though I'd just ordered Chinese food. I opened the door to a short fellow with a shock of black hair, carrying a paper bag that smelled of steamed mushrooms and sesame oil. I didn't speak a word to him, just handed over my cash. "Thank you," he said, nervously, and pocketed the bills, and I felt crazier than ever.

It was then, walking toward the kitchenette, that I suddenly remembered my mother's photographs. They had to be stored somewhere in this apartment. The thought of them was enormously comforting. If my memories of the last few weeks were wrong, at least there were some things I knew about myself, some facts that could never fall into doubt.

And so I'd left the bag of takeout on the counter and started digging through Dad's closet until I found the pile of photo albums. For years, my mother had fussed over these, arranging and rearranging the story of our lives. I flipped through the pages, examining the familiar shots of birthday cakes and baseball games, of my young father leaning against the flank of a Ford, and my brother Bruce dressed as a skeleton. My mother almost never appeared in our photos, but in a way, she was everywhere. She was the narrator of our lives. She told us how to pose, and when and what expressions to put on our faces.

I found myself taking the photographs out of their sleeves, so that I could examine the crabbed handwriting on the back of each square—my mother's brief commentary on the event. "Christmas. Both boys have chickenpox." "Winnie reluctantly boards the bus to camp." "Bruce scored the winning goal!"

And once I had the photographs free, why not lay them out along the rug, to see how they looked together, to construct my own story, a solid chronology of myself? So I knelt down on the carpet, and began spreading the photographs out like playing cards. I arranged them in order, a parade of cub-scout uniforms and stuck-out tongues and aviator-frame glasses and bad hair. The procession spanned the length of the living room, and stopped when I was seventeen, with the last photo she ever took of me. Maybe the last photo she ever took, period.

I picked up that final photo. A weedy boy with a red Afro (me) poses awkwardly beside a girl with a corsage clamped on her wrist; my skin looks clammy, almost shiny, as if I were running a fever, but perhaps that was the effect of the flash. I flipped over photo. "Win takes Cynthia to the prom. Our little boy is growing up!" Mom had scrawled on the back.

And that scrawl of handwriting brought her back to me, her voice, her sense of humor. "You're getting too big!" I could hear her saying, exasperated. She longed to stop time. In that way, she was the opposite of my father, a man always pressing forward, always sniffing out the next moment. Even now, at seventy, he kept his face pressed up against the window of the future, trying to peer at all the wonders he was sure awaited him. But my mother, she had been a thoroughly backwards-looking woman.

On the second of March, 1981, she carried a casserole dish into the dining room and then suddenly hesitated, gazing at my father and me as if we were vague acquaintances and she was trying to remember our names. My brother Bruce was then away at college, so it was just us, watching her from our seats at the dinner table.

"What's wrong?" my father said. "Is it the light?"

The chandelier in the dining room had shorted out that day, so my father had dragged a lamp up from the basement, perching it beside the table so we could see our food. The lamp cast weird shadows across the burnished wood; in that stark light, the ham that sat in the middle of the table shone, as if in a sweat.

"Yes, turn it off," she'd moaned. "That light is giving me a head-ache. It's going right through me." Tears had sprouted in my mother's eyes. The dish crashed around her feet, shredding itself across the floor in a semiology of broken pieces that I studied in that long fro-zen moment. "This whole house is giving me a headache," she wept. "This house is killing me." Those were her last words. She died of an aneurysm.

Maybe the house did kill her. Though my father and I never dis-cussed it, I think we both half-believed that the stucco ranch house, with its hot-as-Hades asphalt driveway and its rhododendrons darken-ing the windows, might be some kind of murderer. Within a month, we moved out. We got out of there so fast that I lost the comic books I'd hoarded since I was nine, and the Playboys stuffed in the secret shelf behind my bureau, and the dog tags I'd saved when we buried Comet, and my favorite pair of high tops. We fled that house like ref-ugees, with just a few possessions. We didn't look back. First we holed up in an apartment in Charlotte. Then, when I finished high school, we moved to Manhattan. I'd been accepted at Yale for the next year, but I didn't have the heart to go, to leave Dad alone. So I switched, at the last minute, to NYU.

Now, I replaced the prom photo where it belonged, at the end of the line on the carpet. These were my mother's memories of me. She hadn't known she would die at forty—at the age I was now—but she must have suspected that these photos could outlive her, and I would depend on them one day to reconstruct my boyhood. What she had not photographed, whatever she had deemed unmemorable, I had largely forgotten. Except when I was on Mem.

I squeezed my eyes shut and called her up, as she had appeared in one of the few photos we had of her: a woman with a beehive of hair like the frosting on a fancy chocolate cake. With all that hair, you barely noticed the face underneath, small and intelligent, the lips tipped into an amused grin.

"I'm going crazy," I whispered to her. "Mom, help me. I'm losing my fucking mind."

• • • • •

At the Columbia campus, I swish-swished across the quad, the fronds of grass licking my shoes. My stomach did a nervous flip as I jogged up the steps and toward the double doors of Low Library, which were flung open to warm air. I might have been on my way to meet an old flame, the way my hands shook as I unbuttoned my coat.

I had come here for proof. Litminov had vanished, but the memory of that Mem trip we'd taken together still haunted me. I planned to walk through the Rare Books Room, like a detective studying the scene of the crime. I would examine that door that Litminov had opened with his stolen key, and the table where he'd sat, and the book with Thomas De Quincey's signature in it, the scribble of brown ink that had set my course for the next fifteen years. I wanted to find these things again, to demonstrate to myself, if only in some small way, that it *had* happened. Mem existed. Litminov existed. We really had been taking the drug together. I was sane. My memories could be trusted.

Now, I grabbed the cool marble balustrade of the grand staircase and climbed up, floor after floor, just as Litminov and I had done that night, on the drug. When the stairs ended, I paused a moment, taking in my surroundings. It was all just as I remembered it, except that this time I didn't need a flashlight: a vaulted cavern filled with long tables and reading lamps, the hermetic smell of temperature-control in the air, the shelves that hid the entrance to the Rare Books Room. I threaded past armchairs and dictionary stands, and turned the corner, expecting to see those grand double doors.

They weren't there. Instead, white walls stretched up to the ceiling. It was as if the Rare Books Room had been erased entirely. I felt the blood drain out of my face. "Christ," I said softly to myself. First Litminov and now this. The sounds of the library washed over me—the squeaks of students' sneakers on the marble floors, whispers, rustles of paper. I didn't quite believe what I was seeing, that blank wall. It was simply impossible that what had been so solidly there would be gone.

Across the room, a sign said "Information." I hurried in that direction, catching the attention of the man behind a desk, a bow-tied little fellow with precarious glasses.

"Where's the Rare Books Room?" I demanded in a harsh whisper.

"Butler Library," he whispered back. "Across the quad. I can draw you a map."

"I know very well how to find Butler Library." I spoke in my regular voice now, which in this place might as well have been a shout. "I've just been there. Where do you think I got these books?" I indicated the three volumes about neurology that I carried tucked under one arm.

"Sssh," he reprimanded.

"It used to be right over there," I hissed, pointing at the wall. "They've changed everything around."

"No," he drew out the word. "Actually it's always been in Butler." With his tiny hands, he worried a pen.

I gripped the edge of the desk, bending over so that I was eye-to-eye with him. "Are you saying I'm wrong?"

"Sir, if you have a problem with the location of the Rare Books Room, then please take it up with someone else. That's not my responsibility."

"Fine, I will," I said, straightening up, giving him one last withering look, marching away, and jogging down the stairs. But as I reached the front doors of the library, I slowed. By the time I got out in the sunshine, I had stopped entirely, rubbing my chin.

A vague recollection had come to me—a memory entirely different from the cinematic productions of Mem, a memory faint and ghostly and hard to piece together. I could see myself climbing a flight of stairs that shuddered under my feet, past the bare light bulbs in the Butler Library stacks, entering a threadbare room with metal shelves. Was that the real Rare Books Room? Had Mem distorted the details, made them grander and more operatic, put the room in the wrong library, editing my own memories to suit some agenda of its own? Had Mem lied to me?

I lowered myself onto the stone stairs and squeezed my temples between two sweaty hands. The sun beat down on the back of my neck. It occurred to me that I should walk over to Butler Library again, go up to the top floor, see what the Rare Books Room really looked like and try to sort out the truth. But I didn't have the heart for it. Instead, I stumbled to my feet in the direction of Dad's apartment. Passing through the front gates of the university, I found myself on Broadway, feeling sick, poisoned, dehydrated. I waited to cross the street with my toes at the edge of the curb.

A bus thundered past me, leaving behind a whoosh of soot that gummed up my eyes. Cars flashed as they hurtled themselves uptown. The traffic whizzed, all sharp edges and sizzling tires.

One minute I was waiting for the light to change and the next minute my purpose had changed entirely. A rogue thought had entered my brain, accompanied by a great and terrible dread: Maybe I'd come to the edge of the curb to throw myself in. Now the thought seeped all through my body. I soaked in it, this conviction that I might, possibly, jump out into that howling traffic. This moment, right here, could be the end of the story. The sun on my black wool coat turned lethally hot. I watched as my foot lifted itself off the sidewalk. A cab sped past, so close I could see a flash of the woman in the back seat, bent into her cell phone, before she was gone. My toe dangled over the edge of the curb and cast its shadow on the asphalt. A rush of blood pounded in my temples and in my wrists; I felt alive and terrified and very curious about what would happen next. I stretched my leg before me, like a tightrope walker, and prepared to step into the blur of metal.

Then I was yanked backwards—someone had grabbed my coat and used it as a harness to return me to the sidewalk. Just behind my ear, a man's voice grumbled, "Don't be stupid." The books I'd had tucked under my arm flew from my grip and tumbled into the street. A van swerved to avoid them, saw there was no place to go, and ran them over. Then, as if some kind of taboo had been broken, the cars that followed thumped over the books, breaking their spines. A page broke free, flying up for a moment, and scuttled along the road before it was flattened.

This all happened in a few seconds. By the time I turned around, my would-be savior had disappeared. I wanted to pick him out of the passersby, run after him, to tell him that I hadn't really been serious, just playing a game. But it was too late. People rushed past me on the sidewalk, pointedly refusing to catch my eye. He'd gone.

When I turned back to the street, the traffic had stopped, waiting for the light. The books had been reduced to smashed paper, spread up and down the block like giant pieces of confetti. I crossed now, pretending that I had nothing to do with the paper strewn all over the asphalt, and then headed downtown toward the subway stop on 102nd street. The wool coat—my father's—flapped around my legs, way too hot for this spring day, but I didn't bother to take it off. My face itched. My shirt stuck to my back; I was grimy, sweaty, unshowered. At the next corner, I grabbed onto the side of a building, the rasp of brick under my fingertips, waiting out a dizzy spell.

The seriousness of what I might have done suddenly caught up with me. Would I have thrown myself into the cars, really, or would I have stopped myself at the last second? I didn't know. My thoughts rattled in my brainpan like a dry cough.

I began walking again. I took off that goddamn choking coat. Things started, in some way, to make sense again. That bad moment at the edge of the curb had been a warning, I decided. As long as I paid attention to the warning, I'd be OK.

"Bernie," I thought, as I plunged down into the darkness of the subway station. I would call him and tell him everything. Maybe he'd order me to go see a shrink. Or maybe he'd demand that I come back to New Hampshire and stay with him. At any rate, he'd have some plan for me. I'd do whatever he said. I needed help.

As it turned out, though, I never did talk to Bernie—not that afternoon, anyway. When I hurried into my father's apartment, the red light on the answering machine was blinking. I assumed the message would be from Dad himself, calling to check in. But when I pressed the button, it was a woman's voice that issued out of the tinny speaker.

"I'm looking for Win Duncan," she said. "Someone gave me this number. Win, if you are there, I need to talk to you as soon as possible. This is Susan Fontaine. You met me at the house. I need to speak to you," she said. "It's urgent." She left a number for me—Manhattan area code.

I slapped the wall, as if I were high-fiving it. Then, elated, I played the message over again and took down the number. It was hard to write. I was so excited that my hand shook. Sue Fontaine really did exist. Which meant that the house in upstate existed. Which meant Litminov existed. Which meant it had all happened, all that I remembered. I must be sane after all.

Chapter
8

A woman with red hair, slim as a cigarette and wearing some kind of Asian necklace with big knobby beads, let me in.

"I'm Mimi," she said, after I'd introduced myself. "An old friend of Sue's. I've been staying here while she recovers."

"Recovers?"

"From the operation," Mimi said, locking up the door behind me. "Didn't you know?"

I shook my head.

"You can sit here. I'll go get her," Mimi said, as she led me into the kind of room that belonged in a magazine, tall windows and antiques everywhere.

I did not sit. Instead, I prowled around, examining Sue Fontaine's possessions while I waited—rather a long time—for her to come into the room. A low bench decorated with Arabic script gleamed under the window. A black chair in the shape of a Z posed in front of a crimson wall. A mirror frame foamed with lacy curls of iron—up close, you could see it had been made out of rusty nails, bent and melted. Each object stood apart from the others, as if on display. The room declared Sue Fontaine to be an expert of some kind—and now I remembered what she'd told me when we were in upstate, that she had once worked for an antique trading house, roaming all over the Middle East and Asia to scout out treasures, that she'd loved to travel and now her traveling was done.

I heard her before I saw her, coming toward me down the hallway, a cane thumping and the friend whispering encouragements. The skin at the back of my neck prickled. From the sounds of her approach—the tortuously slow pace with which she moved—I knew that things must have gone terribly wrong for Sue Fontaine in the last month and a half.

"Oh damn," I heard her say, "my foot's dragging again."

"Here," Mimi said, "lean like this."

My eyes stung as I watched the hall, waiting for them to turn the corner. When I reached up to touch my cheek, I found that it was damp. For a moment I studied the sheen on my finger. A tear. I blinked the rest of the dampness way, and took in a diffident, professorial sniff of air. Composure restored.

Then she emerged out of the darkness and stood on the threshold of the room, leaning heavily on Mimi's arm. Sue Fontaine, once so tall and graceful, so proud and ethereally beautiful, had shrunk. A tweed jacket rattled loose around her caved-in chest. Beside her, Mimi's health—her flushed cheeks and toned arms—appeared almost obscene, a kind of pornography of well-being.

"Thanks for coming," Sue Fontaine said, rearing up as best she was able, pushing against the cane to struggle to her old height. Her voice, at any rate, had not changed. There was still the tang of her Australian accent, the old haughtiness.

"Of course," I said, and hurried over to her, intending to shake hands. But then I surprised myself by hugging her instead. She smelled of hospital and band-aids. "It's so good to see you," I told her, struggling to keep my voice steady.

Instead of leaning toward my embrace, she simply stood there and endured it. "And you," she said.

I straightened up again, touching the wall for a moment to get my balance. I felt off kilter, as if the room had tipped on its side. I had come here bursting with questions: Where was Litminov? Did Mem create false memories? Had it caused any mental problems? And, of course, where could I get more?

But now, I forgot all that.

"You don't have to pretend. I know how bad I look," she said, and thumped her way over to the nearest chair, her friend shuffling along beside her. A moment of quiet fell on the room as she negotiated her way into the seat.

"I'll leave you two to talk," Mimi said.

"Would you bring us some tea?" Sue Fontaine said, looking up pleadingly.

"Of course."

"Use the red tray."

Mimi laughed. "All right," and then she adjusted her necklace, setting it to rattle, and headed off down the hall again.

Sue Fontaine turned those pale blue eyes on me. It was the frank, searching gaze I remembered from the last time. "Surgery," she said. "Two days ago. I'm still recovering from the incisions and that godawful stuff they put in the anesthetic, so you're seeing me at my worst. In a week, I should be able to walk."

"You're going to be OK?" I had settled in the chair across from her, and was leaning forward, not quite daring to reach over and touch her hand but wanting to offer some kind of comfort.

"In a manner of speaking."

"You'll be well again."

She shook her head, with her eyes closed, as if she needed to give her full concentration to what she would say next. "The operation was just to relieve pain, pressure on a nerve. So, yes, I will get better. I'll have a few good months. And then, after that, I'll get worse. There will be nothing left to do then, but endure it."

"Oh," I said. I found myself blinking again, struggling to keep my composure. "I'm so sorry." And now I did lean over and put my hand on top of hers for a moment.

She opened her eyes again, chin lifted, staring me down as if she dared me to contradict her. "I'll make the best of it. I've always been good at that."

"Well -," I began, and felt my voice start to crack. I cleared my throat. "And then there's the drug. You said that helps you." It was a small consolation to offer, but the only one I could think of.

She shifted her gaze away from me, let it fall on the table beside the chair. She fiddled with a small bowl that sat there, adjusting it, as if something about its placement had suddenly bothered her. "Yes," she said. "The drug."

With her face turned away from me, the light from the window chiseling her profile, I couldn't read her meaning. I thought, then, she wanted my approval.

"No one would condemn you for it. Not in your situation," I said helpfully. "You should take as much as you want of it."

"Of course I should." Now she glared at me, shoulders up, so the jacket bunched around her neck, like the arched back of a cat. Then, after a moment, she dropped her shoulders and sighed. "I don't have that luxury. Duncan," she said, and now she leaned toward me as much as she was able, "I don't have any pills. They're all gone."

"But you—" I began, and a tremendous disappointment sucked at me, so much that I left my sentence hanging. I cleared my throat to regain my composure. "I'm afraid I can't help you. I don't have any either."

"I didn't expect you to have any," she said. "But still, you can help."

Just then the friend whisked into the room with the tea tray, placing it on the lacquered table that sat by Sue Fontaine's chair. Wordlessly, she handed me a tiny cup with a few mouthfuls of tea in it. The room filled with the smell of steam and jasmine and something else I could not name.

"Drink it," Sue Fontaine commanded. "It fights cancer. Everyone should drink this stuff."

I did as I was told, closing my eyes as I drained the cup. When I opened them, the friend had vanished.

Sue Fontaine was still sipping her tea with deep concentration, as if she could feel it healing her. Then she cradled the cup in one hand, regarding me. "You had something you wanted to ask me," she said.

"I did?"

"On the phone, you said you had a burning question. You thought it better if you asked in person."

I drew in my breath. "Oh, right, that. I wanted to know what happened to Litminov. I tried to find him a few days ago. It was the damnedest thing. The doorman in his building had never heard of him. As if Litminov never existed. I thought I must be going crazy."

For the first time, Sue Fontaine laughed, revealing teeth as spotlessly white as her shirt. They were the teeth of a beautiful woman. "Well you didn't expect him to rent the place under his real name, did you? That wouldn't be like Phil. He had some lawyer lease the place for him. And of course he's gone now." And here one end of her mouth twitched downwards, in a split-second expression of grief. "He's disappeared. It's terribly worrisome."

"When?"

She shook her head, looking off at a corner of the floor where the curtain fluttered, and pursed her lips, as if trying to master her emotions. Then she met my eyes, squarely. "He came by here a few weeks ago. He wouldn't stop pacing back and forth, over there," she indicated the other end of the room by raising her chin. "I kept saying, 'For God's sake, sit down.' He wouldn't sit. He said, 'I've figured out what I have to do. How to cure myself.' I kept asking him what he wanted to cure. He wouldn't tell me. You should have seen him. His shirt was *soaked*." She paused for a moment, cocked her head, regarded me thoughtfully. "Then he said goodbye. That was the last time I saw him."

My mouth had gone dry. "And you have no idea where he went?"

"No," she said. She cradled her teacup in one hand, looking off at the other side of the room, as if the ghost of Litminov still hovered there, pacing and raving, two pools of sweat darkening the underarms of his shirt. "The thing that worries me, that really. . . ." here her voice caught, and it took her a moment to go on. "He gave me the deed to that house in upstate."

"Gave you?"

"Yes. He sat down at that desk there and sold it to me for one dollar, the whole thing, the house and sixteen acres. I was pleading with him. 'Why are you doing this Phil? Tell me. Tell me.' He said he wanted it in my name, in case of trouble. He wouldn't say what. Just left it on the desk, kissed me, and ran out the door."

She fell silent, both of us did. The possibilities, the awful what-ifs gathered in the darkness under her chair and in the folds of the saffron-colored curtains. Finally, she said, "I do worry about him. He was my first love, you know."

"Litminov?"

"I know. Ridiculous. But there you are. I met him freshman year at Dartmouth. Phil was so different back then, so kind and sensitive. That summer, my first in the U.S., I lived with his family at the house."

"That house in upstate you mean?"

"Yes. His parents adored me. They hoped I would marry Phil someday." She laughed joylessly. "And maybe I would have. But then, the next spring, that horrible accident. I'm sure you know about that."

"Not much," I said. I was leaning forward now, toward her words. "He would never talk about it."

"They were in the Ukraine, on a pilgrimage to see the town where Phil's father grew up, driving on some tiny road that wound through a forest. It happened late at night; Andrei was driving; Olga was up front beside him. Phil was in the back. That's what saved Phil's life. He was behind his father. Cushioned by him, you might say."

I swallowed. "Oh. I didn't know. I had no idea he was in the car when it happened."

"Yes," she stroked her teacup. "Phil couldn't remember much about the actual impact, except that there were suddenly headlights, illuminating everything in the car. The truck that hit them must have suddenly come around a bend. It took Phil months to recover. He became a totally different person after that. He'd been so sweet before. Afterwards," she shrugged then shook her head at the shame of it. "I've always thought something in his brained knocked loose. Organic damage."

"Is that when he got the scar? In the accident?" I touched the end of my own lip, in the place where the white mark appeared on Litminov's face.

She nodded slowly.

Now I stood up and found myself heading over to the window to gaze down at the traffic on Broadway below, the burning spots where sun glanced off metal and glass. Poor Litminov, with his broken head. "You want me to do something for you," I said, staring at the sidewalk, where crowds moved along in bunches. "You have some job for me." And when I turned around, she had reared her head up imperiously. But her cane hung off one arm of the seat—it was the kind with a gray-plastic handle and a rubber foot, an ugly thing, and I could not help feeling pity for her.

"You want me to find him," I said, letting my back sag against the wall, and shoving my hands into my pockets.

She shook her head. "No, not that. I wouldn't know where to look. But I do have a favor to ask you. I want you to go see Dr. Banerjee. He was our chemist, the brilliant fellow who used to cook up the Mem for us."

"You want me to buy drugs for you?"

"I want you to buy a chemical for me." She stared at me, her hands quiet in her lap. "In the eyes of your government, it's not a drug. It's perfectly legal. Let's call it an herbal supplement. And it's the only thing I think about now. I need it to get through what's going to come."

For a long moment, we both fell into silence. Somewhere at the other end of the apartment, a faucet turned on and then off again. The friend, cleaning up. "You think it will really help?" I finally said.

"I know it will," she said briskly, as if to change the subject. "And don't worry. You'll like Dr. Banerjee. I met him a few times, and we had rather jolly conversations about art. A very nice man. I don't know how he ever got involved with Phil. He never seemed like the type. Well, actually I do know. Money. It's always money, isn't it?" She placed her teacup on the tray, and then skewered me with her gaze. "You have a car, right?"

"Yes," I said—in fact, I'd stowed the Saab in a cheap garage in Queens.

"It's about three hours away from here. Not too difficult to find."

I pictured myself on the highway then, speeding in the direction of Mem, toward the one man who knew how to make it. "All right," I said.

"I'll give you everything you need. There's a note in here for Dr. Banerjee." She reached into the pocket of her jacket and pulled out a thick envelope. "And money."

She held it out to me. I did not cross the room to take it.

"You're trusting me with all this? How come?" I wanted to know.

"Because who else will do it? My friends wouldn't understand."

"What if I cheat you?"

"I worked fifteen years as an antiquities trader, and I know swindlers. I can sniff them out. You're not one. You're decent. I see that in you." She had begun to droop in her chair, I noticed. She'd let the envelope fall into her lap, as if it were too heavy to hold up.

"I don't think I am a decent person," I said. "I'm afraid I might steal the pills from you."

She studied me with those white-ish blue eyes, this emaciated rumpled woman, hardly more than a pile of fabric. "No you won't. I can tell. Please. You've got to do this."

I unstuck myself from the wall then, and took a few steps toward her. I was not at all sure that I was a decent man; in fact, based on my recent behavior, it seemed likely that I would hijack the pills, maybe even disappear on her. With a doomed feeling, I reached down and let her hand me the envelope.

• • • • •

I pulled off Route 93 and downshifted the Saab, leaning forward to watch for the sign—a corporate logo that signaled the entrance to the office park. Finally, I found it. The name of the company would be thoroughly familiar to you; it's a word you've seen on bottles brought home from the drug store, a few French-sounding syllables. I turned into a long driveway and wound toward a slab of a building that squatted among carefully pruned stands of pine and scrub oak on a grassy hill. This was, apparently, just one of the company's research labs.

"There's a guard in the lobby. Phil and I always went around the back," Sue had told me the day before. And so I left my car at the nether end of the parking lot, half-hidden under the cruciform arms of a pine tree. Then I headed purposefully toward a door set into the putty-colored wall on the back of the building. I yanked on the metal handle. Just as she'd promised, it opened.

Second floor, she'd said. I eased open another door, to spy on the hallway, which was cluttered with cardboard boxes but empty of people. I slid out into the open. "Biohazard" blared a red sign on a door with a blacked-out window. Every surface in that hallway seemed to carry its own warning: "Caution - Lasers," "Emergency Shower," "Liquid Nitrogen." The place reeked of chemicals. I hurried to the end of the hall, number 217, and knocked. Up until that moment, I hadn't been particularly nervous, but waiting for a long minute out in the open, my blood began to pound in my hands and ears. The ambient noise around me, the groaning of machines and far-off murmur of voices, became sharp as I listened for approaching footsteps. What the hell would I say to this man?

Finally, the door jerked open. A short fellow with a potbelly, glasses hanging from a chain around his neck, peered up at me. "Yes?" he said.

"Dr. Banerjee?"

"Correct."

"Win Duncan. I'm a friend of Sue Fontaine's."

"I'm sorry. I don't quite. . . ." He raked his fingers through his hair and I noticed the fastidiously clipped nails and the gleaming cufflink at his wrist. A man who liked fine things. A man who, perhaps, could not live without certain luxuries.

"She used to come here with Phil Litminov."

He dropped his hand, and it made a little slapping sound against his hip. "Mr. Litminov?"

"Yes, but this has nothing to do with him."

He moved a step closer to me, blocking the entrance to the room with his cannonball of a body. "You tell your Mr. Litminov that I am not interested," he said, gripping the door with one hand, as if he were preparing to shut it.

"Please. I've come because Sue Fontaine needs—"

"Yes, yes, I remember Susan," he interrupted, impatiently. "But she always traveled with Mr. Litminov."

"Not anymore. Litminov is gone."

"Gone?" Dr. Banerjee reared his head back with surprise.

I did my best to explain, and as I talked, I watched Dr. Banerjee loosen his grip on his door. "Well, better not to discuss this in the hall. Come in," he said, and backed away so that I could follow him into a lab, a cavern full of shelves stacked with supplies, countertops littered with glassware. A window winked with light that filtered through the scrub oaks, and faraway, I could just make out the blur of cars on the highway.

"Curious," Dr. Banerjee was saying, shaking his head. "I myself have not heard from him for some time. We had a falling out, you see. He gave me headaches, your Mr. Litminov."

I pressed my lips into something like a smile. "Well I won't give you headaches. Nor will Sue. She's quite ill, you know. Cancer."

He nodded, absorbing this, and his face softened. "I'm very sorry to hear that. How bad is it?"

I sucked in a breath, making a sharp sound of distress, and blinked at the window behind him. I was remembering what it had been like the day before when I'd leaned over her chair and clasped her arm, guiding her to her feet. She had been as light as an empty suitcase. The feel of her—that nothingness when I had expected human weight—still haunted me. No grown woman should have weighed so little. "Bad," I finally said. "It's very bad. I have a note from her." I reached into my jacket pocket and produced it.

With one of those manicured fingers he cut through the seam of a thick envelope. As he did so, he wandered into another room. I took this as an invitation and followed him into an office, which was bare, except for a desk and a few chairs, a pen set. When he'd finished reading, he folded the letter neatly, and then tore it into strips. We both watched them flutter into the trashcan.

"Sit," he said, gesturing to a chair. He perched on top of the desk, making himself taller than I was. "I am sorry to hear about poor Susan. Indeed I am. Did she tell you that she offered to do me a favor once? I didn't take her up on it, but now, looking back, I think I should have."

"So you'll help?"

"I am no longer in that business," he said, curling his fingers together into an upward-turned fist, a kind of prayer position. "As you can see, I have a good job here, and I don't need any trouble."

I felt my jaw tense. "I can't go back to her without anything. You don't know what this will do to her." My voice sounded like a stranger's, and what I said seemed to come from somewhere just behind me, over my shoulder, just out of range of my vision. I was surprised to hear the proof, in my voice, of how much I cared about Sue Fontaine, how much I wanted to protect her from what was coming. It seemed that another Win Duncan lived inside of me, a man who knew how to be good; I wanted to let this man out, let him run the show.

"Look," I said, lowering my voice now. "I have to have something that I can give her, something I can put in her hand, and say, 'This will make you feel better.' If I have to drive back down to Manhattan and tell her I failed, it's going to eat me up forever." I said these words in the simple way you do when you know you are in the right. Because I did know. All of a sudden, I was certain I would do whatever I could to protect Sue Fontaine from more suffering.

Dr. Banerjee blinked a few times. "I do not doubt that you are in earnest, Mr. Duncan. But you should consult her doctors about palliative treatment—the traditional painkillers would be best. I am just a chemist. I don't have anything for you."

"The drug," I said, and then cleared my throat. It was the first time I had mentioned the reason I was here by name, and I almost regretted unloosing the word into the room. It seemed crass, somehow, to say "drug" in front of Dr. Banerjee with his striped Oxford shirt and the tasseled loafers, his air of being above all this nasty business. Still, I barged along. "The pills you've made, the Mem—"

"Mem?" he interrupted. "Oh yes. That was Mr. Litminov's fanciful name for it."

"All I know," I said, "is that your pill has been a godsend for Sue. It's the only thing that seems to comfort her. She's terrified of. . . ." Here I paused, searching for the words. I found myself staring out the window above the desk, watching the birds that wheeled through the ugly whiteness of a twenty-first century sky—smoky with pollution, pocked with ozone holes, sweaty with greenhouse gases. The injustice of Sue Fontaine's lot, of my lot and your lot and everyone's lot, seemed to be written in that sky. My eyes had gone wet. "She's terrified to die the usual way. It's barbaric, when you think about it. To be stuck here in the present, watching your body get eaten up. The pill is her only way out. She doesn't think she can bear what's coming unless she has a supply of it. It helps her let go."

"Does it?" he said, touching his lip. "That's interesting."

"Imagine you only had a week left to live. Would you want to spend that week in bed with tubes coming out of your every orifice? Or would you rather be young and healthy—your best self? That's what she wants."

"Interesting," he said again and studied me for a long moment, with his arms crossed over his plump chest, the red pinstripes of his shirt showing through the lab coat, ghostly. He breathed in and out, unashamed to stare at me, taking that as his right. "How do I know that your Mr. Litminov really has gone? You seem very sincere, but still, before we enter into any kind of agreement, I would like to be sure."

"Call any phone number you have for him. They're all disconnected."

"That proves nothing," Dr. Banerjee said

"Well then you'll just have to trust me."

"Hmmm." He rubbed his chin. The whisper of traffic filled the room. A machine somewhere in the building began to throb. "You must understand something, Mr. Duncan," he finally said. "I was badly used by your Mr. Litminov." He paused then, as if he were deciding whether to confide in me. I knew better than to pry or prod. I simply sat. It was a trick I'd learned from teaching. When no one in the class would raise a hand, I used to slump in my chair and watch them, refusing to speak, until the very air ached with the silence. Now, I used the same tactic. I rearranged my hands in my lap and cocked my head, gazing up at Dr. Banerjee expectantly.

It worked. After a long, awkward moment, Banerjee cracked. "Look," he finally said, "if I tell you what happened, it must not leave the room. Is that understood?"

I nodded. "Of course."

"Your Mr. Litminov never found the drug to be strong enough, you see. He wanted it to last twelve hours instead of two. He wanted stronger hallucinations. 'This is baby aspirin,' he used to say. He told me once that he'd tried to take three doses at once and vomited them all up. He was always after me to 'tweak' the drug, as if I only had to take a pair of tweezers and pluck out a molecule. I refused. Even if I'd known how to make the drug stronger, I wouldn't have done it. Too dangerous. As it is, even in this relatively mild form, I wondered if it could harm people. I don't think it's physically addictive, but it does seem to exert a strong psychological hold."

"Has it hurt anyone?" I asked. "Sue told me it was pretty safe."

He shrugged. "It would take millions of dollars to determine that. But I can tell you this: People have been using a mild form of TR-12 for centuries. That's its real name. TR-12. It comes from a plant. A shrub."

"A . . . shrub," I laughed. The word, for some reason, caught me off guard.

Dr. Banerjee did not see the humor. He kept on lecturing, his arms folded over his fat chest. "I learned about it during my childhood. We had a shrub growing in the rocky outcrops near our village in the Indian side of the Himalayas. It's a high-altitude plant, a form of rhododendron actually, with long roots that spread out over the rocks. Old men would cut twigs off this plant and gnaw on it until their teeth turned orange. It was known to be a folk cure, like the coca leaves in the Andes. Or poppy tea that the Russians drink when they have a toothache. For hundreds of years, the people in my region used this plant to soothe the melancholy of old age. I supposed nowadays you would call it 'senior-onset depression.' The twigs seemed to help—it seems that, for old people, a robust memory is essential to mental health. So several years ago when I was working in Madras, I thought it would be interesting to isolate the psychoactive component of this plant."

"You were the first one?" I asked. "Nobody had ever bothered to study it before?"

"As far as I know."

"That means you invented it."

"Bah," Dr. Banerjee spat out. "No one invented it. It's a shrub, Mr. Duncan. All I did was separate the interesting chemicals away from the bark and the cellulose. There's not much art to that. I manufactured a pill that was only a few orders of magnitude stronger than what people had always used. It was something of a hobby, you see. I used to hand out samples of it to friends—other chemists, pharmacologists, people who would be interested in it from a research angle. I had hopes that the drug might have some kind of commercial application. Unfortunately, I think there's little chance of that. But my pills did create something of a sensation among a small group of chemists. And that, I suppose, is how it fell into Mr. Litminov's hands."

"You gave him a pill?" I asked.

"No, no, no. He showed up here, three years ago, unannounced. He had already tried the drug—I don't know where he found it—and he wanted me to make it for him. What he proposed was perfectly legal. And he made me a very generous offer.

"I have five daughters, Mr. Duncan, beautiful young women who graduated with top honors from Harvard, Yale, Stanford. It is expensive to have such outstanding children. There is medical school. And law school. And weddings that go on for weeks. I was not in a position to turn down Mr. Litminov's offer.

"For a while, it worked out very well. He flattered. He made promises. And then the promises stopped. He began to quibble about the drug. He wanted it this way and that way. And stronger, he wanted the drug stronger.

"Finally I said to him, 'If that's what you want, Mr. Litminov, I suggest you find another chemist.' And he said, 'I already have' and stormed out. He never paid me for the final batch. And he suggested that he might try to get me in trouble somehow. But that was the last I saw of him." Then, Dr. Banerjee slid off his desk and stood, thinking along with the tum-tum-tum of his fingers drumming on the lab coat. "But I can see that you are a very different kind of man than Mr. Litminov. Perhaps I could help you. Of course, it depends on what you could do for me in return."

It took me a moment to take his meaning. "Yes, of course," I said, and reached into the pocket of my jacket for an envelope bulging with cash, which I placed on the desk. "That's from Sue." I slid the envelope a little further from me with the tips of my fingers, as if it were slightly repulsive. "I think you'll find she's been very generous."

"Under other circumstances, I would refuse any payment. But my expenses," he said, "are astronomical." His hand rose to his hair, to adjust the lock that fell across his forehead. His eyes skittered around the room, moving everywhere but to the white rectangle of the envelope, which was indeed very fat. "A minute." He held up a finger and hurried out of the room. I heard some drawers open and close in the lab, and then he returned with a glass vial in one outstretched hand. "There you go," he said. "There's a good fifty doses at least. That's all I can give you for now."

It was cold to the touch, the size of a film canister. "Wonderful," I said, as Dr. Banerjee escorted me to the door, and we shook hands curtly, like two businessmen.

• • • • •

Back in my car, I sat with one hand on the steering wheel, the engine off. Pine needles had spilled from the branches above and stuck to the windshield. The air had thickened, and I could smell a storm coming up. The pills rattled as I rolled the vial around and around, trying to spy on them through the glass. These were green instead of the brown I was used to. "I found a way to make them cleaner," Dr. Banerjee had said just before I left. "That should help with the unpleasant side effects."

I sat in my parked car, afraid of what I might do. Cleaner, I thought. Imagine: Mem without the skin-crawling anxiety afterwards, without the tight jaw and the tics and all the rest of the horrors. It seemed too good to resist. I turned the glass bottle around again, noticing how it magnified my fingers so that they looked fat and strange. Ever so carefully, I pulled the stopper out and sniffed—yes, I knew that smell of new-mown hay. Then I forced myself—it took all I had—to stop up the vial. My craving for Mem had come and gone over the past few weeks; sometimes I wanted it horribly, sometimes not all. But now I couldn't seem to put the bottle away. I held it to my eye, squinting into it, as if it were a telescope. Each pill became huge, an out-of-focus green glob that would contain a world of pleasure and of revelation. I wanted one so terribly that I can scarcely describe the want.

I could pop a pill in my mouth right now. Sue Fontaine would never know that I'd taken one. But *I* would know. If I took one now, I would be the man who'd snitched a pill from a dying woman. To do so would be to cross a line; to step into a moral country from which I might never exit. As I turned the vial this way and that, the pills fell into a heap against the glass, and I could almost imagine that they were conspiring together. I closed my eyes so that I wouldn't have to see them.

The rain began to peck at the roof of the car. The sound of it reminded me of her cane, the stuttering thump of it as she'd dragged herself across the room. "You're a decent man," she'd said, as if she could read it on my face. I wanted to be that man. I felt myself stretching toward him. And it was thinking of that man I would be—Win-42, Win-45, Win-50—that helped me muster my strength. What I did now would determine whether I would become a better man or a worse one. My fist was squeezed around the vial. I opened the glove compartment and tossed it inside, so I wouldn't have to look at it anymore.

Then I let my head loll back on the seat and waited out the craving, let it wash over me and subside. And to my surprise, after a few minutes it did let up. I turned the key. I drove. I kept my eyes riveted straight ahead so that I could not see the glove compartment.

On Route 93, the rain came down for real, a sheet of water pouring over the windshield, melting the world for the instant between every sweep of the wipers. They were whacking back and forth furiously, beating out a rhythm. "Decent man, decent man, decent man," the wipers sang to me. I clenched the steering wheel and peered at the road through the dazzle of rain, racing to get back to Manhattan before temptation made a fool of me.

Once I was in the city, I thought it best to go to her apartment directly, so I parked in a lot, spending twenty bucks just so I wouldn't be alone with the pills a moment longer than I had to. As I stood waiting for her to answer the door, I tried to pinch my rain-soaked shirt away from my chest; it was sticking to me like a clammy plaster.

She opened the door a crack, leaning heavily on the cane, her eyes bruised with fatigue.

"How did you manage with Dr. Banerjee?" she said, following me with her eyes as I came inside.

I produced the vial from my shirt pocket and held it up above my head, hero-style.

"Wonderful," she said laughed. "You're fabulous. Thank you so much."

"Where do you want it?" I said nonchalantly, as if the vial of pills was enormously heavy, a piano or a sofa, and I would have to haul to the right spot for her.

She was lurching away from me toward the bedroom. "In here," she said. "On the table."

I followed her into the room. It was filled with antique mirrors—cracked, yellowed, bubbled. Orchids, a dozen of them or more, hung from the ceiling, stretching their finger-like roots out into the air. In the middle of all of this sat a bed with a chocolate-colored spread.

She climbed onto it and lay back on the silk pillows. I put the vial down beside her lamp, but I couldn't seem to let go of it. My fingers stayed pinched around its neck.

"You should take a pill home with you. For all your effort," she said.

My mouth watered—it actually watered, as if I'd just smelled meat—so that I had to smack my lips. I helped myself to one of the pills, wrapping it in a discarded foil from a chocolate truffle that I found on the bedside table. I put it in my breast pocket, that little gold ball, and felt it throbbing there, full of possibility.

When I looked down at Sue, she was scrutinizing my face, those pale eyes roving back and forth as she tried to read my expression. "So," she said, "what did he say?"

Haltingly, I told her what I'd learned from Dr. Banerjee—that Litminov might have hired another chemist, might have found a way to produce another kind of pill, far stronger than Mem. "Who knows what he was up to," I said, slumping into the chair beside the bed.

As she listened, she held a paper napkin in one hand, crumpling and crumpling it until it disappeared inside her fist. "This is not good," she said when I finished. She pressed the napkin against her one temple. "I have a terrible feeling. Why did he give me the deed to the house? I keep puzzling over that." She had fixed her gaze on the mirror across the room, talking to the reflection of gray sky and window shade. "It was almost a little ceremony. He handed it over and said, 'Goodbye, Susie. Goodbye.'" She shifted her eyes toward me, and we stared at each other in silence.

I couldn't think of a thing to say. I raked my hands through my hair, across the stubble on my neck. Somewhere outside a car alarm went off, like the cry of a startled bird. She lay back down on the pillows. "We'll make sense of this later. Now I need to sleep."

"Do you want me to stay?"

"That's all right. One of my girlfriends is coming over soon. Duncan, thank you. You've been wonderful. I have to come up with some way to thank you properly for all you've done. Actually, you should take more of the pills."

"No," I said, wrestling my way out of the chair and finding my feet. "One's enough."

• • • • •

Back at Dad's apartment, I flopped down on the couch, intending to watch a baseball game, but I ended up falling asleep. Hours later, I woke with my face in a leather cushion, the room glowing white from the TV screen. It was the phone that woke me.

"I'm sorry. I know it's late," Sue Fontaine said. She sounded entirely different than she had earlier that night: determined, calm. "I just wanted to tell you that I'm embarrassed at how I behaved today. I get like that sometimes—all weepy. Hate it. I'm sure Phil's fine, wherever he is."

"OK," I said, blinking furiously to get the blur of sleep out of my eyes. And now, I spotted a gold bit of foil on the coffee table, shining in complicated crinkles. My pill. "Did you take the drug yet?"

"Not yet," she said.

"You think these pills, they're really OK?" I was leaning over that gold foil that smelled, ever so faintly, of chocolate.

"Yes," Sue said, with some force in her voice, so that I imagined her lying on the bed with the vial of pills gripped in her fist. "I've seen people take it hundreds of times. No one ever got sick."

"Sue," I said, and that one sibilant word cut through the air between us. It was the first time I'd used her name. "Tell me something."

"Yes," she said.

"Why do you want it so badly? I would think that you'd want your mind as clear as possible," I meant to add, "when the end comes," but those words had jammed in my mouth. I swallowed hard. "I know you've told me before. But tell me again."

"Because," she said, and then faltered. She tried again. "I have to have something to look forward to. There's going to be a time when I know I can't walk or move around, and that's when I'll start dosing myself. I'll use the drug to stay in one moment, the exact moment that is my favorite of all. I'm seventeen, running with the track team. And I've just won the scholarship to Dartmouth. I know that soon I'll be off to the States. And because I'm the fastest sprinter in my high school, and because I'm pretty enough, and rather precocious, I imagine that I'm going to have all kinds of adventures. I'm so excited to find out what will happen to me." She laughed self-consciously. "Actually, it sounds stupid, doesn't it?"

"No," I said. "Not at all."

"When I was a kid, I thought I'd be enormously rich, wear caftans, live in Hawaii, and date rock stars. It seems silly now, but was so delicious back then. I owned the world. I miss that so. Especially now. With so little to look forward to."

Then I understood, in one sudden convulsion (the foil clasped in one hand, the phone receiver in the other) what she meant. "You want to remain yourself," I said.

"Yes," she said. "Exactly. All this nastiness I've been through with the cancer, it's killing my spirit. I won't let that happen. I am going to retain my dignity."

"I think that's why I wanted the drug too. Why it's had such a hold on me. When I'm on it, it seems to restore my dignity. My sense of meaning." Now, I was thinking of the Rare Books Room, how I'd touched that signature's of De Quincey's and seemed to know who I was again—that feeling I'd had of coming home.

I told her about that—and also about the awful day when I'd gone back to find the Rare Books Room and discovered a blank wall instead. "I was shocked when reality didn't line up with what I'd remembered on Mem," I said. "I thought I was going insane. I walked out to Broadway, and I nearly threw myself into traffic."

She laughed. "Oh dear God, Duncan. Well, I'm glad you didn't."

And then I found myself chuckling too. "Nearly ended it all."

"How melodramatic."

"That is what scares me about the drug," I said, turning serious. "You think you're seeing exactly what happened in the past, but you're not. It lies to you."

"You could say the same of ordinary memory."

"Yes, but still. . . ." I hunched further over the phone, intent. "That moment you want to go back to, when you were 17—maybe it never happened."

"It is real, even if the facts are mixed up. The sense of who I was back then. That girl *is* the real me. This woman with the cane and the bad hip and the terrors at night—she's an imposter. I don't want to be her at the end, Duncan."

We both fell silent, for a long time. The line hissed between us. "I'll help you," I finally said, "when it's time."

"You will?"

"Yes."

"You damn well better. Now that Phil's gone, no one else can do it. I'll have lots of people around, of course. But none of them know. You'll have to help me take it."

"I will," I said.

"Thank you, Duncan." Her voice wavered, and I was afraid she might begin sobbing. But instead, she turned formal. "That gives me great peace of mind. It's damned decent of you."

A half-hour later, I lay in bed, trying to fall asleep, listening to the rumblings and honks of 21st Street. My mind felt unusually calm. A single beam of light glowed through a chink in the curtains and lit up the wall like a tiny spotlight. I watched the dot of light pulse on the white paint. I felt myself concentrating down into a single speck of resolve. I would throw myself into the one good thing I knew to do right now—help Sue.

Chapter
9

"Not the opium-eater, but the opium, is the true hero of this tale," Thomas De Quincey wrote in 1821. And with that, he announced a unique experiment, never before attempted in the annals of science or literature. De Quincey would let a drug speak through him. It would guide his pen; he would merely serve as the amanuensis, the Boswell to its Samuel Johnson. The glass of laudanum in his hand would dictate a message.

This was an experiment borne of his desperation. In the summer of 1821, creditors were scouring London in pursuit of Thomas De Quincey, threatening to lock him in debtors' prison. He had promised *London Magazine* a scientific article on opium, but one small article would not pay enough to keep him out of chains. He needed to produce a literary sensation, a book that all of London would talk about, that would earn thousands of pounds. Sitting in the lobby of an inn, he dipped his quill into ink and let it hover of the page. What to say? In the summer heat, his shirt itched. He sipped his tea that he'd ordered on credit. He contemplated the weave of the blank page.

It was then that De Quincey saw how to make a smash: He would not just write *about* opium. He would turn his words *into* the drug. He would write a book that was itself a little cake of opium, a perfect simulation of the high, all its terror and joy

The book that resulted, *Confessions of an English Opium Eater*, became an international sensation. Baudelaire plagiarized it. Scientists studied it. Moralists banned it. The book sold like opium.

It could be considered the greatest marketing feat of the nineteenth century. Before De Quincey published his slim volume, the English thought of laudanum a.k.a. opium as nothing more than a toothache remedy, a brown bottle you kept on your medicine shelf, not terribly dangerous, about as exciting as aspirin is to us now. After De Quincey, opium was hailed as a key to enlightenment, a scourge, a destroyer of souls, the door to paradise, wonderful and terrible, but certainly not boring. He'd invented a drug that already existed.

And now I planned, as best as I was able, to replicate his experiment. I sat at my father's desk with one green pill before me—I'd placed it on top of an eraser, so that I wouldn't lose it. Next to it, a little white pill, Xanax, waited at-the-ready. Sue had given it to me. "It's a much better chaser than the sleeping pills," she said. "Take it when you feel the high letting up. Don't wait too long, otherwise you'll get the horrors."

Beside me, a legal pad waited, along with a stack of sharp No. 2 pencils. I'd taped a sign on the inside of the apartment door, "Don't Leave." I was determined to write all though the high (if that was possible), to record every last detail.

With my fingers digging through my hair (grown long now, and a bit greasy), I stared down at that green dot. I didn't have the least desire to unearth a missing fact from my past; nor could I necessarily do that, since the drug sometimes got its details wrong. And unlike Litminov, I thought it better to stay clear of the darkest memories. What I wanted was to return to the most ecstatic moment, the most transcendent joy, I had ever known.

I picked up the pill, felt it as a hard little knot between thumb and finger. When had I been happiest? I didn't know. The pill, even though I hadn't taken it yet, seemed to talk to me then—to transmit a message through my fingers like a little radio. "Take me," it said, "and you'll know."

"3:25 PM: It seems important to place the pill on the exact center of my tongue. I can feel it melting now, spreading into a circle of flavor, the bitter chemical taste that's peculiar to all pills, mixed with something else, something sweet."

"3:47: I think I feel the first twinges. Just now I closed my eyes and the back of my eyelids became a wall covered with graffiti, insistent colors glowing in the sunshine, a wall that I used to pass every day when I lived on 114th street. But that's not where I want to go. I can sense something better waiting for me in further-past, when I was a boy in green high-tops, and I seem to be wandering. . . ."

"3:54: Daddy."

That's where my notes leave off because I was too overcome to keep writing. The top of my head seemed to have turned to glass; I saw not with my eyes (which were closed), but with my whole skull, all around, in every direction: a patch of sunlight scalding a porch floor, a tiny scabbed and hairless knee with a Band-Aid flapping off of it, a bit of the chair with the daisy-patterned fabric of a chair—oh, Christ!, it had just come back to me that my mother had the chair re-upholstered to make it "cheery," but somehow it had failed her, and she'd put it out on the back porch like it was a bad dog.

I had become a solid lump of nine-year-old boy, with his chin resting on one tucked-up knee, smelling the salty skin of himself, and peering at a red model car that he balanced on his hand. "Porsche," said the gold plastic script on the car's trunk. "Poorsh-Ah," the boy whispered to himself, pronouncing the way Daddy had taught him. When he said the word, as if by magic, he felt a down-low throbbing, delicious, along his legs and up into his belly. I, Win-40, understood what must be the achy and sweet stirrings of a pre-pubescent hard-on. But the boy assumed that this new sensation was just part of his new life, which would begin when everyone else woke up and climbed into the car, the real car, with the cooler in the back, and they flew down the highway toward the beach, Daddy smoking a cigar while he palmed the wheel.

Yesterday had been awful. Daddy had still been gone, and no one knew when he'd come back and Mom lay in her bedroom with the curtains drawn and said, "You boys amuse yourselves," and nothing had happened, all afternoon, nothing, nothing. Win-9 and his brother had roamed around the block, searching out kids, but everyone else had gone to the beach, so they had explored the dark-eyed houses, yards with no dogs, driveways without cars, and they'd pretended it was the end of the world and all people dead but them, which began to seem more and more true. A horrible blah-ness, a dread, a doom, had gathered in the shadows under the bushes. Daddy had been gone for weeks, and now Win-9 wondered whether they'd ever had a father at all, or whether he'd only imagined that man.

But then, last night, Daddy had burst in the door with chocolate coins in his pockets, and a model car under each arm. Win-9 had clawed open the package. And Daddy stood over him, breathing out his grown-up breath, bourbon and the stench of dead leaves. "When you're old enough, you'll have a real one," he had said. Win-9 had known then, with a great bang of his heart: Daddy would stay. It would all be different now, forever. Daddy would sit in his rightful spot, behind the steering wheel of the Olds; and that awful blah-ness would evaporate into the steamy August air, poof.

Now it was the next morning, and they all slumbered in rooms invisible above the porch ceiling, and for another hour he'd have the house to himself. Win-9 held the car high in the air, watching green reflections of trees sliding over its hood. Giddiness gripped him, clenched his chest, goose-bumped his skin. It came on him like a fever. And it pierced Win-40, too, for a few seconds, that joy so strong it scrambled his stomach, like a sudden liftoff in a jet. The boy stared down at the iron birdbath in the yard below, noticing how it leaned into his own happiness, holding it in a blue circle of water with flakes of light floating on top, as if you could walk right up to that birdbath and pick the light out of the water and pop it into your mouth and it would melt like candy. The boy imagined that he owned happiness now, that it would be his forever now that he had learned the trick of it. And he tightened his fingers around the red car until the door handles and side-view mirrors pricked deep into his skin. And I, the man, sank down to the floor, lying on the uninteresting carpet of my father's apartment, but just when I'd grasped onto that bliss, just when I thought I had it and could keep it, it faded out like a radio signal. The boy guided the car along the floor and up over the speed bump of his foot. I could feel that tickle of tires as they rolled over his skin, but what I really wanted, the heroin of lost happiness, floated just outside of my grasp, and I wished desperately for a dial somewhere so I could turn up the drug. This is what Litminov wanted, too, I suddenly understood. More.

And then I whisked away to five years later, a basketball court, me dribbling and then leaping into the air for a layup, and I forgot everything else as the ball thunked on the backboard and swished through the net, and I landed on those young, miraculous legs, and sprinted away.

* * * * *

When it was over, I wanted to bolt, to run downstairs and take a cab to the airport and fly somewhere far away, maybe Morocco. I headed for the door, reached for the lock, and then I saw the sign I'd made for myself, "Don't Leave" and so I forced myself to sit back down at the desk, and then for good measure, I tied myself into the chair with a sweater. I thought about taking the Xanax, but then, instead, I picked up the pen, not exactly sure I'd be able to write, because if I could channel all this energy that would be excellent, and yes, I found myself scribbling furiously, in handwriting that didn't look like my own—a tiny panic of script.

Maybe Dr. Banerjee had indeed made improvements in the drug or maybe I was developing a tolerance. Anyway, I had no horrors. No facial tics. No thoughts of death. None of that awful aftermath I'd experienced the first time I took Mem. Instead, I felt as if I were on speed—a good dose of clean methadrine. I wrote until my right hand ached; then I switched to the left, then switched back. Scritch, scritch, scritch, the pen said, and I knew exactly how to move it. Night came and I flicked on the desk light, and the entire world became the pen in my hands and that yellow pad with its blue lines. I made an espresso and drank it down to its silty dregs. At two in the morning, I typed the best of what I'd written into my laptop. By the time the window began to blush with light and trash trucks groaned down the street, I had finished up the account of what had just happened to me and added some explanatory notes about Mem. I sent it off in an email to Edie, and Bernie, and an old friend of mine who's a physicist in London, to colleagues in the history departments of a half-dozen universities, and to a woman I dated in college who now works at a publishing house.

I would reprint it here, except that I no longer like it so well. My first attempt to grapple with Mem was full of dry theories, pronouncements and pontification.

And now, nearly a year later, I'm still struggling to get Mem right, to transform a small green pill into words on a page. I'd like to say that I have, like De Quincey, found a way to turn my words into the drug itself, that this book is a pill, that reading it gives you a contact high. But no. I have not the art. All I can do is tell you what happened next.

• • • • •

And what happened next was this: A few days later, Sue Fontaine called, waking me from a long and groggy sleep, and insisted that I meet her in Central Park. "Have you looked out the window recently, Duncan? It's glorious. We've got to go."

"How?" I croaked into the phone. "How will you get there?"

"Oh, I can gimp about on my own now. I'll take a cab."

A half hour later, I found her on a bench by the 86th street entrance. She'd replaced the hospital cane with an antique walking stick, but she barely seemed to need it as she stood up to greet me with a peck on the cheek. She was still gaunt, but elegantly so. You might take her for a model just past her prime, all spiky blonde hair and jutting cheekbones, those perfect teeth that appeared now and then between the fire-engine lipstick.

"You look so well," I said. "You look gorgeous."

"Yes, don't I?"

"And have you heard anything more about Litminov?" I asked.

"No," she said, walking beside me now. The cane gave her the air of an English baron surveying his grounds. "But I have been thinking about poor Phil quite a lot. I'm mourning him, I suppose, because it's finally sunk that he's gone. I might never see him again."

"You don't know that."

She limped along beside me, silent, and the cane answered for her, a slow thunk-pause-thunk. We stopped on an overlook beside a hillside covered with rocks and ferns, with a sparkling stream below.

"How about the pills?" I asked. "Have you taken any yet?"

"Not yet. The doctors told me that this last operation would give me some relief. And it has. I'm almost like my old self. And I want very much, for the moment, to *be* here." She raked my face with those pale blue eyes to see whether I understood what she meant.

I nodded, squinting because of the sunlight. "Yes," I said, as if I got it, though the truth is, I couldn't begin to imagine what it must be like for her to totter about in this fragile sunshine knowing it might be her last June, last fern grove, last stream, and I the last man with whom she might flirt.

"What about you?" she said. "Did you take yours?"

I nodded again, closing my eyes now, letting my head loll back to bask in a warmth with some bite in it, the hint of what might be a sunburn tonight.

"You don't waste any time," I heard her say, and though I couldn't see her, I knew she had pulled one side of her mouth up into a roguish half-smile, her trademark. "So how was it, this new batch?"

I opened my eyes onto the spangles on the surface of the stream and the wet rocks, little shards of light that tattooed themselves on my vision, so that when I turned to Sue, I saw them superimposed on her face, spots, ghosts, as if she were in a movie that was burning up on the screen, holes opening up in her skin the moment before the film snapped and she disappeared.

"It was great. And actually," I said, "there's something I've been meaning to tell you." I crossed my arms, nervous about saying what had to come next. "I wrote up a kind of rant about Mem, and I sent it to an old friend of mine, an editor, and she wants me to turn it into a book. So it's a done deal now."

"A book?" she blinked. "How wonderful, Duncan."

"I still have to write the thing, of course."

"Well," she said, tipping her head to one side, as if doffing an imaginary top hat to me. "Congratulations." And then halfway through the gesture, she seemed to forget what she was about to say. She'd noticed something that had distracted her. She crossed her arms, cocked her head and examined me up and down. "Duncan," she said. "What happened? You're not wearing your wedding ring anymore."

I examined my left hand. My ring finger was indeed naked, the skin paler where the gold band should have been. "Weird," I said. "I must have lost it. Or—I know what happened—I took it off when I was high. It was bothering me, I guess. It's got to be in Dad's apartment somewhere."

"Hmm," she said, and peeled away from the railing to walk, her heels clicking on the asphalt, and the cane moving as regularly as a metronome. "Lost it," she said, musingly. "That's interesting. I didn't think people lost wedding rings anymore. So tell me about this mysterious wife of yours."

"I already did tell you. We're separated," I said, as if that explained everything.

"So why wear the ring at all then?"

"I never thought about it, to tell you the truth. Is that what separated people do? Take their rings off?"

She paused, let her head fall back to gaze up the canopy of branches overhead. "Damn, this is beautiful. I feel like I've been let out of prison. Oh, I don't know, Duncan. I don't know how people are supposed to behave. When my ex and I split up, I kept the ring on for years, because it made me tired to have men looking at me."

"She called me yesterday," I said.

Sue lowered her head and gazed at me with that flat, almost mannish stare of hers. "And?" she said

"She wants me to drive up to New Hampshire and have a talk. No agenda. She just wants to hash everything out. Sort out our finances."

"And what do you want?"

I sighed, stepped off onto the grass, thrust my hands into my pockets. "I don't know. When you're taking Mem, it's hard to have any kind of normal relationship. I'm not sure how I feel about Edie—the real Edie who exists now. I know that I love the person she used to be, but that person's gone, except, of course, when I'm high."

"Yes," Sue said. "That's how it was with Phil. When we got back in touch, I found him . . . distasteful. But, when I was high, I could see the boy in him again, sweet and awkward, a little bit worshipful. So I couldn't help it. I began to care about him all over again."

She sighed, rubbed her face, nearly lost her cane.

"You look tired," I said, taking her elbow to support her.

"I'm completely nackered, actually," she said, as she limped over to the nearest bench. "I'd like to just lie down right here, but that wouldn't be very dignified. I suppose I've overdone it, once again. I'm always pushing myself too hard."

Around Sue Fontaine I always knew what to do next. She had a way of turning me into a hero, a swain, a knight in a white t-shirt. The man I'd been a few months ago—Edie's boor of a husband, to be introduced reluctantly at cocktail parties—had vanished. I was brimming with generosity and useful ideas. I found her a cab and helped her into it and rode with her back up to 93rd Street. And then once we had passed through her apartment door, I rushed around, gathering Tylenol with codeine, a bottle of sparkling water, and a teacup made of delicate white porcelain.

"All right, that should be everything," I said, standing over her bed, feeling thoroughly healthy and competent.

"Thank you," she said, rolling her head on the pillow to gaze up at me, revealing a long white neck with strands of blue vein shot through it. "You've been so kind."

"Not really." I splashed some water into the teacup, and she sat up to take a Tylenol. For a minute, before she drank, she held the cup to the window, where it caught some sunlight and turned into a glowing half moon. "Bone china," she said. "So delicate. You can see my fingers through it." She dangled two fingers inside the cup, just the tips of them so as not to touch the water, and they turned into shadows I could see right through the hard porcelain.

"Nice," I said. "But where are your bones? When you said 'bone china,' I thought it might work like an X-ray machine, and I'd be able to see your skeleton."

She laughed, took a sip of water, admired her cup again. "They call it that because the china's made of bones. And paste, of course."

"Whose bones?"

"Oh," she said, placing the cup back on the table with the great care, "Tories, Republicans and One Nationers. I believe there's some Rupert Murdoch in there too." She settled back onto her pillows, and folded her arms over her stomach. "Ah, that's better."

"I should go and let you sleep," I said, but somehow I did not go. I ended up seated on the edge of the bed, looking through her photo album, while she told me salty stories about her aunts and uncles and her old mother back in Perth.

"Don't you want to be with them, when—you know—you get sicker?" I said, and the mood between us turned serious, the sheets sending up their medical smell of starch and hospital beds.

"No, they're going to come here, to see me. My brother, bless him, is flying out in a few weeks." She pulled up one leg and the next, so she lay with her knees pointed up to the ceiling—as if to relieve some secret ache that she would not bother to tell me about. "This is my home. I'm not going anywhere."

Then I was lying beside her, on top of the covers, my head on a pillow, my hands cradling the back of my neck. "You're able to be happy," I said, "despite everything."

"Today has been a good day."

"Yes," I said, "it was." We lapsed into silence, and I studied her ceiling, the blankness of it, clean and white and spare. The woman breathing only a foot away from me would probably vanish before the year was out. She would wither first; nurses would hook her up to machines; then her heart would stop; and then she'd begin to decay. It didn't seem the least bit real. She was, if anything, more passionately alive than I.

I let my head fall in her direction. She had closed her eyes, but her knees still thrust up in the air. Her pale skin, stretched over a graceful arch of her cheek, was the color of the teacup on the table behind her. "Bone china," I thought to myself, and reached out to brush the rise of her cheek with one finger.

She startled, and her eyes snapped open. "Oh," she said. "You scared me."

"Sorry," I said, but I did not take my hand away. Instead I traced the rim of her eye and her eyelash.

"Um, lovely," she purred.

"OK, now I really should take off so that you can sleep," I said, my voice gone scratchy with tenderness. And I did.

• • • • •

I was trying to write about Mem, to start the book, but found it impossible to think in Dad's apartment with its monstrous leather chairs and the chaos of takeout containers in the kitchen. The apartment knew me too well; it had seen me asleep on the floor and crawling around in search of my wedding ring—which still hadn't turned up—and I needed to go to some café.

At the door, I paused. "Don't Leave," the sign commanded, still there after a week. I ripped it down. I left.

Hunkering in the musty sofa in the back of a coffee shop a few blocks away, I read through the email again, instructions from my editor. It had been fine to imagine myself pontificating about Mem, but now that I had the chance, it scared the hell out of me—what if I couldn't get it into words? The laptop hummed, waiting for me to type.

"Could you plug this in for me?" a female voice said from somewhere above my head. When I looked up, I saw she was standing over me, dangling a laptop cord, a young woman with velvety black hair. She wore a baggy sweater and no shirt underneath; her V neck plunged low enough to expose the pearly skin of her cleavage.

"Sure." I took the end of her cord, threading it behind the sofa toward the outlet. Then came the embarrassing moment when I had to shove the prongs into the holes in the wall; I think we both became a little red-faced by the act of penetration, at the way I had to become intimate with her laptop cord. At any rate, when I sat up again, she had turned away from me, busying herself with a pile of library books.

"That should do it," I said.

She flashed me a sidelong smile. "Thanks."

"You're working on your dissertation," I said. It was not a question. I knew as soon as I saw the books on her table, bound in canvas, bristling with yellow scraps of paper.

"Actually, yes." She laughed.

"I've been through it myself. Years ago. What's your topic?"

She shook her head, and that heavy black hair fell like a theater curtain over her cheek. "Oh, God. Don't ask. Sleep disorders in Gulf War veterans. Officially, I'm getting a Ph.D. in psychology, but I'm interested in public policy, too."

"Sounds like a promising subject."

"You think?" She leaned forward, one slim hand covering her notebook. "Sometimes I want to drop out. I could be working right now, and instead I'm amassing this huge debt." She fixed me with her dark eyes, suddenly serious. "Do you think it's worth it, getting a Ph.D? Actually, pretend I never said that. I've put a three-month moratorium on asking that question. Of course it's worth it."

She couldn't have been more than twenty-six, lovely in a way that reminded me of the women of my youth, not just Edie, but all of them. Now that they were older, they were encased in tweed jackets; now they had titles before their names and husbands that frightened you a little, patent lawyers and cardiologists; now, they spoke fast, rat-tat-tat, because they were so very busy with their gifted children and their deadlines. But once they had been like this girl, laughing with their mouths open and wanting you to tell them it would all be OK.

"So you work in academia?" she asked.

"Used to," I said, and flipped down the lid of my laptop, settling in for a conversation. I launched into the story of Mercy College, mining it for whatever humor I could. She laughed at my jokes, and when she laughed, a necklace glistened on her chest.

"What are you planning to do next?" she asked.

I was surprised at how authoritatively the answer came to me. "I'm going to take care of a friend of mine. She's dying. That's my first priority."

The girl's eyebrows pulled together. "Oh," she said. "Oh. How kind of you."

"It is?" I said. "I guess maybe it is. I haven't really been thinking in those terms." And then, to change the subject, I got her talking about her dissertation again.

She laughed. She explained. Her hands described arcs and roller coasters in the air, and her necklace sent off sparks. Diamonds, I thought. She had so many years ahead of her, so much future, and she wore all that luxury of time the way she wore her necklace—forgetting it was there, oblivious to its beauty.

"Nice necklace, by the way," I said.

"This?" she fingered it, as if to remind herself which one she'd put on that morning. "Rhinestones. They're not worth anything."

"Hmm," I said. It would take very little effort to get her into bed— I knew that. I would sleep with her, and I looked forward to that. But I wanted something else, too, beyond just the sex, wanted to run my thumb over that broad, unlined brow and remember all the other girls, wanted to see her take off that necklace and leave it curled on a night table, the fake diamonds gleaming for both of us.

"Let me buy you lunch," I said. "There's a decent place across the street."

"Cool." She stuffed her books into an enormous canvas bag, and followed me out the door. Yes, it was that easy.

• • • • •

Back when I'd lived in New Hampshire, all through those many summers of tall grass, I hardly ever wheeled the lawn mower out of the garage. On a block where everyone else pruned and clipped until their bushes resembled green poodles, Edie and I used to let everything go to hell. Weeds used to form rat colonies around our house, sprouting up into spindly towers and vomiting their seeds everywhere in the fall. Someone once slipped a note under our door, accusing our lawn of bringing down property values. Edie and I had a good laugh about that one, and then went back to our respective offices, to bury ourselves in work again, lawn forgotten.

And so the last thing I expected, when I drove up to the house in New Hampshire, was to find myself confronted with a wall of hedges straight out of Disneyland and a rose-covered arbor—is that the word? Arbor?—that I had to pass through to get into the yard, and once inside, a lawn that stretched up to the house, seeming to invite croquet players and tea parties. A smell emanated from the ground, an intoxicating a smell I'd forgotten all about after the long winter and a month in Manhattan: mowed grass.

As I climbed the steps toward the porch, the door opened, revealing a slice of darkness, and then she slipped out, tugging one of her curls behind her ear, wearing what she always wore: blacks jeans and a billowy shirt. We hugged, chastely, and for a second I suffered a sharp nostalgia for the time when I might have kissed her on the mouth.

She gestured out at the yard. "A bit much, I know." And now she was talking fast, waving her hands around, the way she did when she was nervous and wanted to smooth over the situation. "I bought the hedges from the Anuccis three blocks over. I was driving past, and old Mr. Anucci was out there pruning them with his cigarette hanging out of his mouth, and it was obvious that those hedges were the bane of his existence. And all of a sudden I wanted them, you know, because they looked so old-fashioned and they sort of suggested a new identity to me, a new person I could be, and I thought 'I could be the woman who lives behind the hedges.' So I pulled over and offered to buy them. Now I'm regretting it. What a crazy idea. It cost a fortune to have those things transplanted."

"The yard looks great, Edie," I interrupted.

"Yes, it does, doesn't it?"

"It reminds me of. . . ," and here I hesitated because I didn't know exactly what I meant to say, but I felt the idea coming toward me, swimming from mind to mouth. "Eglantine," I finally pronounced.

She blinked, staring around at the hedges, the deep greens of them, the black and secret places where their roots met the earth. "Eglantine," she repeated, the name of her own country. "Funny. I hadn't thought of that."

"You always described a lot of topiary. English gardens. That kind of thing."

"Yes," she said, her face softening. "I can't believe I didn't see it myself." She turned and melted through the door. "Come on in," she called. "I made some iced coffee, just the way you like it." And then, trailing the end of her sentence behind her like a scarf, she headed off toward the kitchen.

I followed her down the hall, past the coat rack, past the stained-glass window striping the carpet with red, the stairs and the dingy rose wallpaper, and I seemed to step right back into the feeling of that house, the Sunday afternoons working through a mountain of *New York Times* sections as I put off stumbling upstairs and grading a pile of freshman papers. I felt the house pulling at me; it whispered to me of drowsy afternoons, of that half-sleep I'd lived in for so many years. And for a moment, I suffered a pang of longing for my old life and for Edie, who knew me so well.

"So," she called from the kitchen, "I liked the article you sent me." When I entered, she was taking a pitcher out of the refrigerator. "You know I wasn't thrilled about you getting so involved with the drug; I really thought you might be heading for a crack-up. But now I think I understand. You're really on to something, Win. I must admit, I was kind of jealous when I read what you sent me. I thought, 'I wish I were out there having adventures.'"

"You've got your mad women," I said, leaning against the wall. I wished she would stop flitting around the kitchen, that she would stop and just look at me. But now she was stepping back to the refrigerator, a paper towel crumpled up in one hand.

"Oh, yes, my mad women." She opened the door of freezer and her head and shoulders disappeared behind its white façade. "I was so absorbed with them. But I just handed in the manuscript."

"You're going to be famous," I said.

She shrugged. "So what else is going on? Give me the full report."

"Well," I said, "I just signed a book deal. About Mem. I've already started work on it."

The freezer closed with a smack. Edie stood across the room with an ice tray half-forgotten in one hand. "Really?" For years, she'd been hovering over me, worried, as I tried to finish that damn De Quincey book. And now here I was signed up for another book, and I could see the flicker of doubt pass across her face.

"You don't think I can do it," I said, letting the back of my head fall against the cool surface of the wall, as if I might retreat into the mortar, pass through the shell of this house and out into the shadow of the fir trees in the side yard.

"Of course you can do it," she said, and turned away. "That's fantastic. Listen, let me just finish this up and we can go out into the backyard."

I watched as she whacked the ice tray against the counter and then turned it upside down on top of one splayed hand, and I tried an experiment. I tried to become her. With a great effort of imagination, a tensing and straining of all my mental equipment, I attempted to leap through the bone of her skull and into the labyrinth of brain tissue, to feel what it must be like to be Edie. She held two ice cubes now, and I imagined my hands as her hands, the burning cold on my palm, a drip of water down my finger. And then I strained to go beyond that, to inhabit all the memories and ideas that floated in her mind: the gin bottles that her father used to bury out in the backyard when she was a little girl, and what they looked like when she dug them up, soil crusted on their mouths; and her madwomen whispering to her from manuscripts, speaking to her of Victorian rooms where clocks ticked incessantly; and the tower in Eglantine where she leaned out of a window and surveyed her own land, the topiary hedges and then a field of heather stretching to the beach, and ships crouching in the ocean, waiting for her to imagine them into the harbor. I tried to hold all of this in my mind at once, but I couldn't do it. She'd spent years trying to explain herself to me (and I to her), but in the end, it had all been for nothing. I could recite her memories, but I could not feel them. She was another country, and I would never travel there.

"OK, that should do it," she said, walking toward the back door carefully with a tray, ice clinking demurely against the sides of a pitcher. I followed her out into the sun, and we lay on lawn-chair recliners. The sky was a child's drawing of blue. Lounging side by side, I could imagine us on a cruise ship together, very old, reunited and reminiscing about our lives, as if our marriage had been a long, long time ago and was now a matter of historical record.

She took a sip, and then asked, in the coolest voice possible, "So have you met anyone?"

"Not really. Nothing serious."

"That means you have," she said sleepily with her chin pointed up at the sky, her eyes half-closed, making it clear just how indifferent she was to my exploits. "I knew you would."

"We've only been seeing each other for a few weeks," I said.

"You don't have to downplay it, Win. Tell me about her. What does she do?"

"She's a grad student at NYU," I said.

"Oh, a *grad student.* I see." And all the rest of what Edie might have said hung in the air, vibrated in the distant buzz of an airplane.

I immediately felt the urge to apologize for Melinda's age. But I decided against it. I stared up at the branch above me, the chinks of blue sky showing through the leaves. "How about you?" I said, in an effort to change the subject. "Are you seeing anyone?"

"It's complicated." She turned in her recliner, knees pointing at me, gold hair blowing into her eyes so that she had to swipe it away.

"This is the thing you needed to tell me in person, isn't it?"

"Yes." She pressed her lips into a rueful little smile. Finally, she said, "I'm trying to get pregnant."

"Christ." I felt beads of sweat break out on my upper lip. "I can't believe this. You've got some guy already."

"No," she said. "Sperm bank."

"Goddamn it, Edie. You know I wanted a kid."

"You didn't really," she said.

"Don't tell me what I wanted. You don't know."

Her jaw was tight, the muscle working in her cheek. She wouldn't look at me. "At some point, I decided to do it on my own. It seemed easier."

I rolled my eyes, and sound came out of my mouth that I hadn't made for months, a gasp of fury. "Fuck you," I mumbled.

"What did you say?"

We had dropped through a hole, a breach in the universe, time-traveling backwards into the moist hellish armpit of our marriage, into fights we'd had years ago. But it only lasted a few seconds, that flashback, and then I came out the other side, back to the deck chair, the branches nodding drowsily overhead, the smell of grass.

"Let's not do this," she said, and stood up. She took the glass from my hand, and poured me more iced coffee from the pitcher—the iced coffee, I have to say, was excellent, made with pure cream and lots of cracked ice.

She lay back down again, raised her chin to the sun. "That's better," she said.

"So have you started your treatments? Is that what you call them? Treatments?" I managed to sound civil, friendly even.

"I start this week," she said. She opened one eye, let her head loll over my way.

"And you're going to do it all on your own?"

"Yes. Well, actually, no. I plan to have excellent childcare." There was something in her voice, a little hiccup, a suggestion of laughter, that I hadn't heard in a long time.

"You'll be great." I was surprised to hear the words of a magnanimous man bubbling up from inside of me. Whoever had spoken, he was not the guy who'd been Edie's husband for the last few years, the wounded prick who'd scuttled to and fro in his Saab, seething over his wife's success. He was gone, that man. Just another self I'd shed. Win-39. Dead.

She looked over, using one hand to shade her eyes. "You're going to be great too."

Chapter
10

It's May now, almost a year after Edie made that prediction, and I'm typing in the library of the Litminov house in Upstate, a blanket wrapped around my shoulders. Out the window, the skeletons of cattails quiver dryly in the wind. The pond has flooded its banks and spilled into the meadow, seeping through the grass in rivulets and estuaries, where it reflects the sky, covertly, in little surprising streamers of blue. On the wall across the room, over a white mantle, a portrait of Litminov's father hangs, Andrei, this man in the chalk pinstripe suit, with his hands folded in his lap, who watches me so intently. He's become a friend, of sorts.

In 1988, Andrei Litminov, his wife and their son drove in a rented Renault in the western part of Ukraine; twelve miles away from the town where Andrei had been born, the car collided with a delivery truck, and Andrei, died immediately; his wife Olga held on for a few days in a nearby hospital, and then also succumbed. The truck driver survived, as did young Phil Litminov, a twenty-one-year-old student. I know this because I found a folder with the newspaper clippings and funeral notices stuffed in the back of a drawer.

I met Philip Litminov about six years after the tragedy, but he never spoke of it to me, would clam up whenever I asked him about his family. Funny that we never talked about what happened. And now I live in the house where he grew up, presided over by the spirits of his dead parents. I type these words into a laptop under the gaze of

Andrei's black eyes, and occasionally I glance up when I'm stuck for a word, as if I might ask him for a suggestion. He was, after all, an international financier. I'm sure his advice would be helpful.

I did not end up living here all at once. It happened in dribs and drabs, in spare weekends. Sue Fontaine first gave me the key to the Litminov house in the summer, asked me to collect the mail, check on the leaky faucet, and then, because I had nowhere else to live, I just kind of stayed. She didn't mind.

In the fall, I drove into Brooklyn every week or so to see my girl-friend Melinda. She'd fret over how thin I was getting—it is her belief that I can't feed myself properly when I'm on my own, which is prob-ably true—and she would pull some kale soup or roast chicken out of her old-fashioned refrigerator, and the kitchen would fill with steam as she heated it up for me.

And always during those visits, I'd check on Sue, who was declining with heartbreaking speed. Once, in August, she managed the ride up to this house with me, and even was able to pick her way through the meadow to the pond. I can still remember how she looked that day, her button-down shirt billowing around her thin frame, one hand raised to shade her eyes against the sun that bounced up from the water. I watched from about twenty feet back, not wanting to in-trude—we both knew it was the last time she'd see the place. In No-vember, when she found it difficult to walk, she checked herself into a hospice. A few weeks later, I was up here at the Litminov place, and I called Sue's room; one of the nurses told me that she'd been hooked up to oxygen. That's when I packed my clothes and climbed into the Saab, steered down the gravel road, made sure the front gate was tight, and then took off.

I was the only one who knew about the stash of pills in the drawer by her hospice bed. I would have to be the one to help her get them into her mouth when she couldn't do it herself. I would have to be there, right through the end.

That all seems like another time now, though it happened only five months ago. When I remember those awful last days, I see myself in a hard-backed chair by the bed. Other people swirl in and out of the room—nurses with trays, her brother with his guttural Aussie swear words, friends with gifts of orchids. But always, I stayed, because I'd made a promise to her. In secret, so the nurses wouldn't see, I kept track of the Mem she'd taken on the flyleaf of the book I'd brought with me. I watched over her, as her legs twitched and she murmured to herself, and when I glanced up, I never knew whether the moon

would be hanging over the city or whether the sun would be insinu-
ating itself through the slats, because I'd lost all sense of ordinary
time, of the people out there on the streets, honking and revving their
engines. The world had retreated to nothing but a distant roar. An
intense, almost athletic focus came over me during those last days. It
was as if, instead of being trapped on the twentieth floor of a Midtown
building, I was rowing a dingy across a great ocean, moving slowly,
slowly to a distant light, carrying Sue with me to a place of safety. I
heaved at the oars; I kept my eyes locked at that light that appeared
and disappeared over the churning waves. It was mythic and awful.

• • • • •

One night, just before the end, I woke up in my chair to find all the
visitors gone and the room illuminated by the faint red glow of the
clock radio. Sue rustled in her sheets.

"Hey." I sat up, rubbing my neck, "you OK?"

"Davy?" she said, calling me by her brother's name.

As my eyes adjusted, I could make out her face in the blue glow of
the heart monitor.

"I was just over at Annie's house," she said.

"Did you have fun?"

"Yeah, yeah. That we did."

"You want another pill?"

"It's too soon. I'll get sick to my stomach," she said, and all of a
sudden she sounded perfectly cogent. "I think I need a Xanax."

I struggled to my feet, knees cracking, and filled a glass of water
from the pitcher. She rolled to one side and I held the glass to her lips.
She swallowed the Xanax and then drank another sip of water, dutifully, because I'd been nagging her about her dehydration. "The will
to live," she said, as she rolled onto her back. "I'm so glad to be rid of
it. You must say that in your book. That's the greatest thing about the
drug. It frees you from the compulsion to keep going on, marching
on and on." She dragged one hand along her chest. "I'd be perfectly
happy to pull this out, and end it all right now," she added, and I
realized that she was pointing to the oxygen tube that cut across her
cheeks, like some kind of harness that tethered her to the earth.

"Don't," I said, still standing over her, holding onto the glass of
water, uselessly, in case she should need it.

"Once, in Burma, I saw a bunch of military police beating someone. I could smell the blood, and then blood speckled all over the
dirt, and I knew I should run and stop them from killing the man.
I knew absolutely down to my core that it was the right thing to do.

But I didn't. Because of the stupid fear of death. It perverted me. Made me so small and mean. But now that's gone. I feel brave."

"You are brave," I said, and I leaned over her a little further, to study the fleshless cheeks that had shrunk away, making the sides of her face appear to be powdered with violet-colored makeup, the tacky plumage of death.

She opened her mouth, revealing, in the dim seasick light, the teeth of a beautiful woman. "Put that in your book," she said sleepily.

She died two days later.

And I became the owner of the Litminov place, lord of this crumbling mansion and the weed-choked pond, the sodden meadow that squishes under my feet and sixteen acres of forest, all the land you can see up to the ridge. Sue Fontaine left it all to me. "You'll make good use of it," she had whispered. And I knew what she meant to say: Turn the house into your base of operations. Keep boxes of flyers in the living room. Send out pamphlets. Get a web site. Tell everyone. Without the drug, you have to die by plunging forwards, into the horrible future where you will not exist. But with Mem, it's entirely different: you can die by going backwards into your mother's lap, and then into the whoosh, whoosh, whoosh of her womb, and out the other side. Death can be a place you already know, an oblivion as familiar as the TV room in the house where you grew up. It does not have to hurt. Everyone has a right to it, she believed.

Myself, I'm not sure. I used to agree with her, but after what happened, after the strange story that materialized about Litminov during this winter, I never felt sure again.

• • • • •

After Sue died in December, I took two things away from the hospital: the deed to this house and an antique Milk of Magnesia bottle made of midnight-blue glass. She had kept her stockpile of pills in that bottle. Now it contained only three.

I drove up here, to this crumbling mansion, with that bottle on the seat beside me. At the gate out front, I leaned out of the window of the car and punched a code into the security box. Then, because the hinge had broken, I had to climb out of the car, my shoes slipping on wet leaves, and throw my shoulder against the gate to push it open. For a moment, before I returned to the Saab, I stood with one hand on the weathered wood of the gate, surveying the trees that cast a gloom over the gravel drive and the pearl-handled sky. "Mine," I thought. The word sounded hollow, meaningless. Two days before, I'd touched the hand of a dead woman. I wasn't back in the ordinary stream of life yet, or not enough so that it made sense to me that a piece of paper gave me dominion over trees and meadows and a house.

I drove up the path, but had to stop the car again because a branch had fallen across the road. It was slippery as a fish, cold, and wanted to twist out of my grasp. I wrestled with it, hearing myself say, "Huh, huh, huh" with the effort. Then, finally, I was at the door, unlocking it with a silver key, and the smell of mold and forgotten things came at me as I walked in. In the living room, Andrei Litminov stared down at me from his painting, his bald head like a pale orb—he was mine, too, I supposed.

I turned the heat up, and then, still wearing my coat, I climbed under a blanket in one of the upstairs bedrooms. While Sue was dying, my mind had been chiseled onto one sharp point: what did she need next? Now all of my responsibilities had dropped away. Time hung on me like the wool coat, trapping my arms, stifling. I shook a pill out of the bottle and put it in my mouth. Within minutes, the awful feeling of being stuck in a particular moment melted away; a painful crick in my back loosened; and then all the sensations of my body grew distant.

Soon, I was a twenty-seven year-old student perched next to the window in Low Library, with my elbow resting on a pile of books. Out the window, the snow gathered in the nooks of the casement windows across the way, giving the campus a feeling of being somewhere else, England or Germany.

Now he—this young Win Duncan—shifted his gaze to the book in his lap, and his eye caught the word "amanuensis" on the yellowed page, and this word evoked a pulse of bliss; then there was the smell of wet wool, which he'd always loved; and the girl in the green sweater just behind his back, inching along a bookshelf toward him, pretending to search for title. It was obvious that she had a crush on him; he could feel her admiration warming the back of his neck. The snow falling in ribbons through the gray sky seemed to him to be *nineteenth century snow,* a rare and particularly beautiful kind he had never before seen. And all these pleasures heaped together, into one almost unbearable pile.

Ordinary memories "wear out" when you try to run them over and over again through your mind—they seem to tatter and fray the more you hold them up to the light of consciousness. But when you're on Mem, with a little practice you can learn to run through a memory over and over again, to instant-replay it, and the memory never seems to wear out. I reran it again. And again. One undistinguished moment when I had been truly happy. I stayed in that moment for hours, the word "amanuensis" ringing in my mind's ear; the girl caught in mid-step; a few snowflakes stopped in mid-air just outside the window, defying gravity. I could study not only the lost world that surrounded that younger Win Duncan (the dust that had settled, just so, on the scrollwork of the radiator), but also the fine grain of his elation.

In the past few years, I had invented a story about why I'd been hap-py back then. I believed there were logical reasons for it, and I could give you a list of those reasons. But now as I soaked in the happiness of this young Win Duncan, scrutinized it moment by moment, I saw there was no reason for it at all. His good mood just was. Its motives were inexplicable. It had simply decided to move into his chest; it lived in him, singing its inane and gorgeous message over and over.

He'd just won the Whitman prize. But his happiness had nothing to do with that. He, the young Win Duncan, felt happy one moment because the snow had brought with it the hush of a Quaker meeting hall that shushed the campus around him. And then the next mo-ment he enjoyed the prickly tickle of his wool socks on the top of his feet. The young Win Duncan was happy in the most stupid, reflexive way—he was thrilled simply to exist.

And then the drug wore off, and the young man's joy drained away, and I woke up alone in the house, my stomach twanging with hunger, arm tingling because it had fallen asleep underneath me. A winter's dusk was painting the walls gray, and the grayness sunk into my skin. I didn't want to be here at all, and I had to struggle against the urge to stuff another pill into my mouth. I sat up groggily, made myself shuffle downstairs to heat up some soup.

My restraint lasted only a few hours. By the next night, I'd eaten the other two pills. I'd even filled the Milk of Magnesia bottle with water and then drunk that, hoping for any last crumbs. There weren't any. After the Mem was gone, I moped around the house like an invalid.

I had to get more. Immediately. A plan, vivid as a fever dream, took shape in my mind. Tomorrow, I would withdraw every dollar from my bank account and drive to Banerjee's lab. I would offer him every-thing I had for more pills. He'd quibble a little, complain about the amount I could afford to pay, and then he'd hand me a stash. Or so I hoped. I couldn't live without Mem. That wasn't an option.

That afternoon, I pulled on my boots, shrugged on Dad's old coat and hiked down to the snowy driveway to fetch the mail, throwing my shoulder into the gate to open it. I found the mailbox stuffed with junk letters addressed to the Litminovs and Occupant and Residents.

But there was also one real letter, and it came from Bernie. Right there, up to my ankles in snow, my fingers red from the cold, the junk mail stuffed in my coat pocket, I tore through Bernie's envelope and opened up the note inside. It was a bright day, the sun falling through the branches like a spotlight and bouncing off the snow; the white paper shown in my hands, so that I had to squint to read it.

> Win, I've been trying to contact you for days now. I let the phone ring and ring, but no one picked up. Is there no answering machine in that House of Usher where you hide out? I'm worried about you. Please call me as soon as you get this, and let me know you're OK. Enclosed is an article that should interest you very much.

• • • • •

He'd included a printout of an article from a Euroupean news service. "Body Discovered Near Berezhany, Ukraine." The story had run in August—many months before. It told of a crashed car in a ravine. The driver's body had been mangled, and then rotted for days, before locals found it. Some item found inside the car—the article didn't say what—led investigators to believe that the dead man might be an American, Philip Litminov.

I read the article over and over, and then stood for a long time, shifting my weight back and forth in my own snowy footprints, watching my breath come out of my mouth like the ghost of a sigh. A bird blew by, like a broken leaf. I turned and trudged through the gate, not bothering to close it, and through the stippled shadows up to the house. Inside, Andrei Litminov gazed down at me from his frame, his lips curled into something between a smile and a smirk, those painted eyes seeming to watch me. I rifled through a pile of papers, until I found a yellowed newspaper clipping—the obituary of Andrei and Olga. They'd died near a village called Urman. Then I threw a world atlas across a table, and compared Berezhany—the region where the man presumed to be Phil Litminov had died—with the village where the boy and his parents had crashed so many years ago. It was the same place. I stood frozen with my finger on the map. So he'd gone back there. So that's what happened to him.

But for now, I did not let myself think about all that—the events that had led to Litminov's second, fatal crash. Instead, I found a phone, an old rotary model, and dialed slowly, cranking out each number. Bernie wasn't in his office or at home. I finally managed to get him on his cell.

"It's me," I told him, and gave him a mournful account of the last few weeks, of Sue's death and my lonely vigil here in the house.

"Don't you want to get out of that place?" he wanted to know.

"Naw," I said. "It suits me. So, Bernie, where'd you find that article about Litminov?"

"Oh, I'm subscribed to a lot of news databases. I just plugged Litminov's name in everywhere I could. And, Win, I just found a follow-up piece. They've tried to match the body found in the Ukraine to Phil Litminov's dental records back in the States, but the remains were too smashed-up to make any positive identification. So it might not be him after all."

Now, I glanced upward and found myself meeting the painted gaze of Andrei Litminov, those hard black eyes under a Caesar-fringe of graying hair. His sly grin that reminded me so much of *my* Litminov.

"Win, are you still there?" Bernie said.

"Yeah, I'm here."

"Look," he said, "nothing's certain. Litminov could be alive."

"No. He's gone."

"You can't be sure of that," Bernie insisted. "There's room to hope."

"Hope?" I said. This didn't sound like the Bernie I knew. "You sound strange," I told him. "Much more jovial than usual."

"I do?"

"Yeah. What's going on?"

"Actually, I *am* feeling optimistic. Because of Sarah."

It took me a moment to remember that name: the postdoc at Yale, with whom he'd been trading so many long e-mail messages.

"So it's going well?"

"Amazing," he said, and poured out a lengthy account of the courtship. They were traveling back and forth to see each other every weekend now. I could tell by the way his words gushed out just how smitten he was.

"Why didn't you say anything before about all this?" I asked him.

"I was afraid you might make fun of me," he said simply. "You'd tease me about meeting someone on the internet. Or about being so infatuated."

"Christ. Am I really such a bastard as that?"

He sighed. "You were kind of a bastard last year."

"I know. I'm sorry," I said. "I really am."

"That's OK. You're over it now," he said.

"You sure?" I asked him.

"Yeah. You're starting to sound like your old self again."

"My old self," I repeated. People always seemed to use that phrase around me. And what did they mean by the 'old self?' The version of Win Duncan they liked. And how was I to become him again?

• • • • •

That night I packed the fireplace with newspapers and wood I'd scavenged from the porch out back, and then stretched out before the flames, propped up on a pile of blankets. I'd draped a *New York Times* across my lap, but I couldn't seem to concentrate on it. I kept closing my eyes and trying to imagine Litminov. I found it nearly impossible to remember what his face had looked like—except the scar, the little puckered hook at the end of his mouth. That I could still see vividly.

He would have arrived in the Ukraine in July, I thought—that was when he'd disappeared. He would have explored the back streets, maybe bought himself a hooker; he might have eaten lavish meals without exactly tasting them, terrified and elated by what he was about to do next. One day, he would walk into an office and—paying cash—he would have rented the car; it would have surely been a black, bulbous thing made in Eastern Europe, shaped like a Homburg hat and equipped with strange knobs on the dashboard. Then he'd drive.

It might have taken him days to get to the right place, days of puttering along dusty roads, through farmland, one of his arms cocked out the window. The vial full of powder would have rolled around on the passenger seat; or maybe he kept the vial crammed into his shirt pocket, near his heart. The last time I talked to him, he'd told me that he'd confronted all of his darkest memories, except for one. Now he would do just that. He would find the exact spot where it happened, and he would dose himself on the drug there.

The road, when he finally found it, would not have looked familiar in the evening light, with long shadows of trees striping it. But he knew he had only to wait for nightfall for it to transform into the road he remembered. He would have pulled the car over onto a patch of dirt and waited.

I pictured him parked at the edge of a forest—the spires of pine trees poking high into the sky, the velvety shadows on the bark, the red carpet of pine needles, the dying light of the day. The car would sit stolidly beside the empty road, inscrutable to the farmer who sputtered by on his tractor. Litminov would sit crammed in behind the wheel, his fat legs wedged against the dash, breathing greedily, trying to calm himself, trying to think clearly. Was he really going to do this? His shirt would become sweaty and twisted on his chest; he would undo the top two buttons in an effort to feel more air. His skin would gleam in the fading light.

For twenty years, he had been terrified of this road. It had reared up in nightmares. The blackness of its asphalt had haunted him. It had taunted him. It had been bigger than he was, the only goddamn thing in the world that really scared the shit out of him. And now he would beat it. Clean it out of his brain. Exorcise himself of it.

Now, the light has drained away; the sky has turned the darkest blue, the color of an old Milk of Magnesia bottle, and the road has melted into the blackness of the forest. He has to feel along the dashboard to find the knob for the headlights. When he switches them on, a branch of a pine tree jumps into existence. Beyond that, he can see a piece of the road, black as a shadow, seeming to absorb the light. Yes, it does look familiar now. This is the bastard that has him by the balls, this goddamn stretch of road.

Now, he is measuring powder out of the vial, tapping it onto the palm of one hand. His hand trembles. He stares at the pile, eyeballing it. Then he licks. Rasp, rasp, rasp on his palm. The powder burns his throat. He wipes his mouth with the back of his hand. He begins shivering. He rests his head against the back of the seat, with his eyes closed. He waits like that for ten minutes. Or maybe twenty. He comforts himself with the thought that it will all be over soon. He'll pull the car out onto the road, and it will turn into two roads: one in the early twenty-first century; and simultaneously, it will also be the terrible road of 1988. He will be driving along one road, and at the same time, he will be riding in the back seat behind his father. The truck will come, out of the fog of twenty years' time. Its headlights will blind him. The inside of the car will shine. There will be the little sound his mother makes—a gasp, as if already she is deflating. He will notice, just before it happens, the stubble on the back of his father's neck, the blue nubs of razor-cut hairs.

And then the impact itself. He cannot begin to imagine it. Will he black out? All he knows is that it will be over very quickly. And then he will come to himself again, and he will be driving a car on an empty road in the present, and he will have survived. He will have passed through that memory like a door, and come out the other side. He will be free as he never has been before. Nothing will scare him. Nothing will have him by the balls.

Or that's how I told the story to myself. That's how I imagined Litminov's end. I had to imagine it. Because no one will ever know exactly what happened.

I'd forced myself to see it all—I ran and re-ran his death in my mind—because I had to make it real for myself. And for another reason. I needed to kill my appetite for the drug. I needed to teach myself not to want it. And, indeed, as I stared into the fireplace now, watching a wisp of smoke curl into an S and then a question mark, I could feel my desire for Mem ebbing. I had to go on and live.

· · · · ·

The next morning, I woke up to a shrieking and chirping and brr-rr-ringing, a whole cacophony of bells. The Litminov place was outfitted with rotary phones that squatted like frogs everywhere. I'd grown used to their silence. But now, they were going off, shrieking upstairs and downstairs, and I ran for the nearest one—a black model that hunched on top of a 1981 Catskills Region phone book.

"Win," Melinda said, "what happened? I've been waiting for an hour."

"Waiting where?" I said, feeling my forehead wrinkle with confusion.

"The bus station."

"You're up here?"

"Of course I am. You wanted me to come. That's what we agreed last week."

"Oh shit," I heard myself say.

"Did you change your mind?"

"No," I spat out. "No, no. I'm glad you're here. But I forgot. How could I have forgotten?"

"It's OK," she said, soothingly now, over the crackle of cell phone. "No big deal."

"There's something wrong with me, Melinda." I was surprised how my voice sounded—as if I might cry.

"Sssh, shh, it's OK, Honey. Just get in your car and come get me." And then she kept right on talking, but the cell phone turned her into nothing but a murmur.

"What?" I said.

"Gabble, gabble," she said.

I jumped in my car—wearing sweatpants, a bathrobe, boots, and an old wool coat—and hurried off to get her.

Melinda believes I'm a good man, something of a saint even. During the weeks when I took care of Sue, I would stumble back to Melinda's apartment in Brooklyn, fall asleep beside her without bothering to crawl under the covers, and then hurry out the door to the hospital again. I think Melinda fell in love with the man with the burning eyes and the stubble, the man who hovered over a deathbed.

Now, I spotted her on the sidewalk in the little town square. She waved at me with a wool-mittened hand. And now she was loading a lumpy bag of groceries into the back of the car, and then bustling into the passenger seat. Her little huff of satisfaction. Her smell of cinnamon. Her cold chin against my cheek and then her warm tongue against mine.

"Thank god you're here," I said, as we spun away. "I've been having a hard time." I told her about Litminov, explaining what had happened haltingly, for I was not clear anymore what I had invented and what was true.

"You shouldn't blame yourself," she said. She had misinterpreted the anguish she heard in my voice; she had thought I wanted to save Litminov, when in truth I only wanted to save myself. I didn't bother to set her straight.

"You're such a good man," she went on, passionately defending me to myself. "What you did for Sue was incredible. You gave her everything you had. You can't help everyone."

I nodded, and let her keep talking, alone with my thoughts.

At the house, we had sex, and we ate thick pieces of bread smeared with cheese and drank burning cups of coffee, and she laughed at the mess I'd made of things here, with her gone. And I began to feel restored to myself.

That night, we sat out on a broken-down sofa on the back porch of the house, bundled up against the cold, a blanket across our laps. She touched the lobe of my ear with a finger. "And what about the drug?" she said. "You're not going to do any more of it, are you?"

"No, I'm not." Then, suddenly inspired, I threw off the blanket, jumped up, headed into the house. I came back out onto the porch carrying the Milk of Magnesia bottle. I opened the porch door, and hurled it out into the field. The bottle was empty, of course, because I'd already taken every last pill inside it, the gesture was purely symbolic. Still, when I'd felt the bottle leave my hands, as I'd watch it arc upwards and then disappear into the dark, I felt something release inside me. Some hook no longer seemed to hold me.

Melinda stood behind me, a wool hat perched uncertainly on her head. She was laughing. "Did you hear that? I think it hit the wheelbarrow." She punched me lightly on the shoulder. And I pretended to punch back. And then we performed an impromptu boxing match around the broken pots and dead plants, laughing and jabbing at the air.

• • • • •

In the past few months, she has come up to visit every other weekend or so, lugging bags of winter vegetables and books. We cut up piles of squash and potatoes and make a beef stew, and we eat out on the sofa on the porch. It's cold out there, and a pane of glass has broken so the damp has gotten in, but when we turn off all the lights we can pick out the stars scattered above the tree line.

"I see why you don't want to leave here," she said once, dreamily, her spoon poised before her mouth. "So beautiful." She doesn't mind the stink of mildew and the floorboards that are about to give way and the freezer that leaves a puddle on the kitchen floor. Maybe in ten years she'll become the kind of woman who does mind such things, but for now, all she sees are the stars.

When she's here, I feel smoothed out, uncomplicated, able to move from having sex to exploring the forest to reading pages of her dissertation, flowing from one thing to the next without thinking too hard.

But mostly this winter, I've been alone, and sometimes I've gotten pretty weird, rattling around this place with no one to talk to.

One day in early February, I woke up and thought I heard my brother Bruce running down the hall, slippers slapping on the pine floor. For maybe ten seconds, I believed that I was a ten-year-old boy in Greensboro, North Carolina, and that soon my mother would poke her head through the door and twitter, "Honey, you're late."

I reached out of the covers to turn off a Mickey Mouse alarm clock that wasn't there. I waved my hand, feeling for the familiar round metal bells. Instead, my fingers brushed against nothing. Air.

I sat up. I saw my own boots, size 12, poised side by side on the braided rug.

Oh no, I thought, as it all came back to me, all thirty years with their sad load of deaths and failures. My mother had been burned and put in a box the size of a phone book. I'd fucked up my marriage. My best friend Bernie lived hundreds of miles away. And now I was marooned here, in this future I didn't understand yet. I had a strong urge to call Sue then; she was the only one who would have understood—like me, a refusenik against the present moment, a time traveler, a connoisseur of lost hope.

I slid out of bed and took a few steps toward the phone that sat on the bureau, and rested my handed on it, trying to read the cryptic messages written on its rotary dial: "MNO," it said, and "WXYZ." I half-thought that I could call Sue even though she was dead—maybe if I had the right number, I could reach the Sue of two years ago, the Sue I'd known this summer. I picked up the receiver. I began to dial

Melinda's number, because she was the one I called, now, in moments of despair. Halfway through, I stopped, put the receiver down again. I was fond of her, Melinda, but I didn't want to talk to her right now. I wished, terribly, for Sue or Litminov, or even one of the Dartmouth men who used to wander through this house during the drug bashes—anyone who knew what it was like to be dosed on Mem, anyone who could understand how much I missed the drug.

I padded downstairs and found the pile of books that I'd stacked on the dining room table and sorted through them until I came upon my broken-spined copy of De Quincey's *Confessions of an English Opium Eater*, bristling with yellow Post-its. I peeled off one of the yellow notes that I'd written two or three years ago.

"Francois Magendie," it read, and then "1821." I'd underlined the date three times. That was the year that Magendie published the first book ever to systematically catalogue the effects of chemicals on the body and brain, founding the science of pharmacology. It was also the year that De Quincey published his confessions in the *London Magazine*. Back when I was working at Mercy College, when I was trying to write the book that would get me tenure, I kept returning to that date, trying to understand its magic. 1821. That year, a man in Paris and another man in London grasped the same startling truth: our moods, our thoughts, our sense of the divine, our precious selves, depend on nothing but the play of molecules in the brain.

And now, I flipped the pages of De Quincey's book with such force that several Post-its fell out, scattering on the floor around me. I could see him, De Quincey, a tiny man with a simian face, dirty lace dripping from his wrist as he held his quill poised over paper. He'd been hired to write a scientific article about opium, but he ended up pouring out his life story. Now, I understood why. He was lonely. He'd spent years living mostly in hallucinations and dreams that no one, not even his fellow opium eaters, could exactly understand. And so he set out to bring readers into his addiction with him, to take them through his soaring hallucinations and his nightmares about a cancerous crocodile.

I opened the book, and read, and I could almost hear him whispering the words behind me. "There is no such thing as forgetting possible to the mind," he said to me in his English accent, words slurred by laudanum. "The inscription remains forever." Yes, after taking Mem I'm sure that's true, that every thought and feeling I've ever had has been burned into my mind and stays. The tragedy is that I can't get at it, this warehouse of my former selves, this land that should be mine—I can't get there without drugs.

On an impulse, I pulled out one of the Chippendale chairs, sat at the table, and opened up a file in my laptop. I deleted everything that I'd already written about Mem, my theories and speculations, cultural observations, opinions, predictions, presumptions. Enough with theories. What I really wanted was to get the whole damn weird year down on paper. I needed to tell someone what I'd been through. And since Sue and Litminov were gone, I decided to tell you, dear stranger, invisible friend, drug buddy.

My fingers rested on the keys. The laptop hummed. "Where to begin? I remembered that first call from Litminov, how his voice had unspooled from the phone receiver and curled around me, holding me in its net. His voice. You couldn't resist it. He always seemed to be speaking to you as if for the last time, as if he were about to wink out, vanish, poof away into thin air. And now he had. I would start, then, with Litminov's voice. I began typing, and kept on until the window darkened and I had to turn on the dusty chandelier overhead. For three months, I wrote furiously, barely stopping to come up for air, sandwiches, Guinness, showers, etc., such was my determination to get the story down. And now it is down, and I'm reading through it, making the last few changes before I send it in to my agent in New York.

At the moment, I'm sitting in the dining room of the Litminov house on a May morning, a blanket draped over my shoulders, the laptop purring to itself. There's a mug on the table that gives off a smell of cold coffee. I'm watching out the window as swallows flutter down into the muddy field and then rise up again. It's so bright outside, so spangled and blue, that I have to squint. The birds plunge into the grass, and teem among the fallen barley and wheat stalks, and then, as if on agreement, they rise up again. They're as choreographed as a cloud of dust. They're all of one mind. They have habits, yes. But they have no memory. Today, for the first time in years, that seems like a good thing to me. I am here in the present moment—blanket scratching the back of my neck, smell of shaving cream lingering on my hands, sunlight sliding over the walnut table top—and I like it well enough. I think I might just go on.

· · · · ·

A few weeks ago, my father drove up here with a woman he referred to only as Wendy. He had decided that I needed help disposing of the Litminov house, and Wendy was his solution. When I heard the tires crunching on the driveway, I laced up my boots and then consulted the mirror over the mantle, trying to smooth down my hair, which had grown into a man-of-the-mountain mess over the winter. By the time I opened the front door and stepped out into the brisk air, both of them had forgotten about me. Wendy—a tiny woman with an outsized poof of hair—was arguing on her cell phone. My father had produced a tape measure from somewhere and fastened one end of it to the corner of the house. He was walking backwards, spinning out a silver ribbon from his hands.

Finally, Wendy folded up her phone, and shook my hand, introduced herself. "So," she said, "I hear you're looking at a huge tax bill."

I blinked, taken aback by her directness, and then I decided I liked her for it. This was a woman who could make my problems go away. I nodded. "The estate tax on this place is going to be huge. Tens of thousands of dollars. So, yes, it's pretty much impossible for me to hang on to this place."

"He's screwed," my father called, from around the corner of the house. "He's got to sell."

Wendy nodded to me. "No problem," she said. She smiled her rigor mortis smile.

I caught my own reflection in the back window of the SUV. I had draped a blanket around my shoulders like hermit's robe; my beard had grown out; and I wore the alarmed expression of a man who is not used to dealing with real estate agents.

"Well, let's have the tour," Dad boomed, reappearing near the box-woods, reeling in the silver tape with a satisfied air. He likes to measure things, my father.

Wendy was the first to step inside the house. She coughed and put her hand over her nose, as if she were entering a crypt. "Oh," she said. "Oh."

"It's a bit musty," I said.

"Awful," Dad said. "Can you believe he's been living here?"

Wendy twirled slowly in the center of the living room, taking in Andrei Litminov's black eyes, and the dwarfish chintz chairs and the water stains all over the ceiling.

"Well," she said, "it doesn't matter. They're going to tear down the house anyway."

"Who?" I said, alarmed.

"Whoever buys the property." She began strutting away from us in her high heels. Dad and I trailed behind her as she hurried through the dining room. "What I want to see is the acreage," she said breathlessly, pushing through the kitchen doors. In her mind, I suppose, the house had already been demolished, and so she rushed through it as if it were nothing but a memory. "Ah," she said, when she spotted the glass doors behind that led to the back patio, and then she was pushing through them, out onto a stone platform surrounded by marble balustrades—everything was covered in a layer of leaves and muck. She stepped past the puddles, and then stood with her arms crossed and surveyed the land that stretched out below us: the pond to the left, swelling its banks and leaking out into the fields; a barn whose roof had imploded; a long stretch of muddy meadow; and then the trees, pricked with bright green buds.

"The property includes the lake?" she asked.

"Yes." I struggled against the urge to correct her. Pond, you idiot.

Her smile curled up her cheeks. "Well then, you've got something here. A developer could come in and put up town houses. Depending on the zoning. Or divide it up and sell it as lots." She cocked her head, craned her neck, tried to look me straight in the eyes, though I was so much taller. "We can turn this around very quickly," she said.

About a half-hour later, my father and I stood together on the front drive, under an elm with gray, elephantine bark. Wendy had disappeared into the back of her SUV, searching for some form she needed me to sign.

Dad wore his coat now and he rubbed his hands to keep them warm. He cast a worried glance at the SUV, and the one piece of Wendy that we could see—a high-heeled foot waving from the open door. "The fellow who used to own this place, what was his name?" he began.

"Litminov," I supplied.

"Litminov. There isn't going to be any trouble with the family, is there?"

"No, they're all gone." I drew the blanket tighter around my shoulders.

"Good. That will make it simple."

"It's not simple, Dad. I don't know whether I can sell it. This house is all that's left of them. I have some obligation, don't I?"

Dad wouldn't look at me. He was staring at the polished black SUV and my broken-down Saab beside it, the muffler tied on with a tangle of wire. Finally, he said, "You sell this place and you're set for years. You won't have to get some teaching job in East Asshole, Louisiana. She thinks you'll clear at least $400,000, after taxes."

I kicked at some gravel, and then ran the toe of my boot through the dirt. I found myself trying to imagine what was hidden under-

neath—a whole system of roots, some rocks, maybe that collie I'd
seen in photographs all over the house, wrapped in an old towel that
was turning to shreds. "I know, Dad," I finally said. "But I don't feel
good about it. Litminov wouldn't want some developer bulldozing
the house where he grew up."

My father reached out, put one hand on my blanket, found my
shoulder through the wool, and squeezed.

· · · · ·

Yesterday, I began packing his things. I have bought two-dozen storage boxes, the kind that seal tight, and I am sorting through the treasures that Litminov might want to have saved: letters from camp, a
silver serving tray, tags from a dog collar.

I wander from room to room with a box under arm, pulling open
drawers, pushing past the pencil stubs and old keys in search of whatever carries some whiff of memory. This morning, I found myself in
the room where I last saw Litminov, that basement bedroom where I
spied on him as he lay next to Sue Fontaine.

I set the box down on the carpet and glanced around. There was not
much here worth saving. But just to be sure, I got down on my knees
and lifted up the bedspread. Underneath the bed, I found a lot of
dust and a lump that I thought at first might be a bunched-up t-shirt.
I grabbed it and slid it along the floor. It turned out to be a fur hat
with earflaps snapped up onto its crown and a royal-blue silk lining
inside. I recognized it instantly as Litminov's hat, the one he'd been
wearing when he exploded through the front door of this very house
more than a year ago. It gave off a particular aroma that reminded me
of my own childhood: back in Greensboro, my friend and I used to
shoot at cans with his Dad's rifle; afterwards, the rifle smelled the way
Litminov's hat smelled now, of gunpowder and smoke and boyhood
joys.

Then—with my fingers deep in that fur, and the odor of Litminov
wafting up—I knew I would not sell the house after all. I could not let
bulldozers plow it under. Over the last few months here, I'd become a
curator in a museum of the Litminovs. I had been sent here to watch
over their stopped lives. I could not sell them out. More than that, I
suddenly had a vision of how comfortingly small my life would be if
I burrowed into this house for the next few decades; the house would
be like the drug, a refuge from the onslaught of the future, an island
of timelessness.

I stared at the midnight-blue silk, and stroked the fur with one
finger—it was so soft it felt like nothing. A whole plan was taking

shape in my mind. I would keep the house; somehow I would find the millions of dollars required to protect it from rot, water, mold, tax collectors. I would turn it into a monument to the Litminovs and to Sue Fontaine. I'd restore the dock that she had loved, the one she used to lie on during summers in the 1980s. I'd raise the barn back up from its knees. I would keep them alive, all of them, by protecting the pink paper napkins stuffed into the back of the utensil drawer and the piles of towels bearing strange map-like stains. I would save these people from the worst and cruelest kind of death, which is being forgotten.

And then the urge passed. I tossed the hat into the box, went upstairs to brew another pot off coffee. As I filled the kettle—an ancient copper affair, nicked and scarred and wizened—I knew I had to get out of here.

I sat down. I took out a yellow legal pad, I made a list: rent a Dumpster, call Goodwill, get more 30-gallon trash bags. And then, pen still poised over the paper, I squinted out at the meadow, and then I tore off the top sheet and began another list.

> —Write to Dr. Banerjee and see whether he would be willing to tell me more about Mem, its chemical structure, etc. Do NOT meet with him, as temptation to buy drugs might be too great.
>
> —Search out botanical drawings and other info about rhododendron varieties that grow in Himalayas.
>
> —Find historical texts about the use of these plants in folk medicine. Might need to hire translator.
>
> —Rent studio apartment in Manhattan or Brooklyn.
>
> —Buy microscope (?), amass small ethnobotany library; make contact with others who can help.

On this yellow pad of paper, I was struggling to build a future. The money from the house would buy me several years in which I could do whatever I wanted, and this is what I thought maybe I could want: to understand Mem, its secret chemical swirls, and how it had lived inside me. I didn't expect to get answers; I was, after all, an amateur. But I hoped that the questions would flare up inside of me, and I would be gripped with the kind of passionate curiosity that for me is a synonym for happiness. That's what I desired—to be consumed by a question, any question. Indeed, maybe I'd end up pursuing a line of investigation that had nothing to do with Mem; maybe some other enthusiasm would flame up in me. But I was sure now—and I don't know why, but I was sure—I would become passionate about something. I would rediscover that happiness that has flickered on and off, throughout my life. Good moments lay ahead, I told myself, piles of them.

There is, of course, no drug that will allow us to see what will happen to us; no way to fly, Mem-like, into our future selves. The best you can do is jot down a list on a piece of paper, a set of directions that you will follow into the future that you want. I rubbed my hand against my just-shaved cheek, feeling the smooth skin, which was also the absence of a beard, the memory of what had been there in the tips of my fingers. My hand smelled of Litminov's hat. I resisted the urge to sink into thoughts of him. I had to learn to go forward now. I closed my eyes and tried to jump into the body of Win-43, a man two years my senior. And for a split-second, it worked. I was inside him.

Win-43 pored over an index in a thick, leather-bound tome. He took a sip of coffee in a paper cup, then made a note to himself. A little shiver of pleasure went through him as he wrote; he felt himself about to grasp some concept that had about it the mathematical beauty of a seed pod splitting into four precise sections, a shimmering insight into the design of things. For a moment, I tasted, along with him, that happiness. It had come to him without cause or reason and without a resume. He had simply learned the art of enjoying himself; that happiness he thought he had owned as young man had visited him again, this time more complicated, striated with regrets and qualifications.

I opened my eyes to the water-stained wall and the picture of the Litminov's collie hanging crooked on its nail. The present moment surprised me with its tawdriness, its sense of already being over and gone. I knew then that I would leave it; I was already setting off to find something better.

About the Author

Pagan Kennedy is the author of seven previous books in a variety of genres, including novels and non-fiction narratives. Her most recently published book, a biography titled *Black Livingstone: A True Tale of Adventure in the 19th-Century Congo*, made the *New York Times* Notable list of 2002 and won a Massachusetts Book Award Honor. A novel, *Spinsters*, was short-listed for the Orange Prize. She also has been the recepient of a Barnes and Noble Discover Award and a National Endowment for the Arts Fellowship in Fiction. As a journalist for the *New York Times Magazine* and *Boston Globe Magazine*, she has ridden in a car powered by vegetable oil, eaten sloppy Joes with the world's strongest woman, and toured a room that houses 3,000 human brains.

ABOUT THE TYPE

This book was set in Garamond, a typeface based on the types of the sixteenth-century printer, publisher, and type designer Claude Garamond, whose sixteenth-century types were modeled on those of Venetian printers from the end of the previous century. The italics are based on types by Robert Granjon, a contemporary of Garamond's. The Garamond typeface and its variations have been a standard among book designers and printers for four centuries.

Composed by JTC Imagineering, Santa Maria,CA
Designed by John Taylor-Convery